The River Runs Free

by Ruth Nimmo

The River Runs Free

by Ruth Nimmo

Faithful Life Publishers
North Fort Myers, FL
FLPublishers.com

The River Runs Free

Copyright © 2009 Ruth Nimmo

ISBN: 978-0-9824931-6-8

Ruth Nimmo
2424 N. Dittmer Rd.
Oklahoma City, OK 73127

E-Mail: rnimmo@cox.net

Faithful Life Publishers
3335 Galaxy Way
North Fort Myers, FL   33903

www.FLPublishers.com
editor@FLPublishers.com

Printed in the United States of America
18   17   16   15   14   13   12   11   10   09   1 2 3 4 5

Dedication

To my wonderful husband who supported me throughout the writing of *The River Runs Free* and gave me the encouragement I needed. He is admired for his faithfulness to the Lord and his Godly character which has been an inspiration to me and our children, grandchildren and all who know him. He has always been faithful to witness for the Lord and as a result, multitudes have come to the saving knowledge of Christ.

I also want to dedicate this book to my brother, Dale Hedges, my one living sibling who has always been an inspiration to me and means more to me than I could ever tell him.

Also, special thanks to all my family for their generous support and assistance. Thanks to my son-in-law, Douglas Dobbs, for his marvellous talent in creating the illustrations. Thanks to Mrs. Irene Kidd and Jason Henson for their assistance with my song. Finally, thanks to my publisher, Jim Wendorf, for all his advice and encouragement.

— Mrs. Ruth Nimmo

The River Runs Free

Ruth Nimmo

Chapter 1
The River Runs Free
1945

Tom Marshall stood looking down at his father's grave with head bowed and hands clasped behind him, as he recalled his father's last words to him. "Son, remember the land's the only thing you can count on to never change. Cherish it, Son. Let it become a part of you, and you become a part of it. It'll always be there. I'm countin' on you."

Tom reached into his vest pocket and pulled out a piece of worn, dingy paper that bore record that the Land (as the late Colbert Marshall always called it) now belonged to Thomas Colbert Marshall, *TC* to his friends. This (along with a sizable amount of money left in savings, plus an insurance policy) would take care of rebuilding and restocking the ranch—but it wouldn't take care of the emptiness in his heart, the loneliness, and the bitterness. Where could he go? What should he do?

Tom was a tall, handsome young man with thick brown hair. He was not as rugged looking as his father had been. Wind and sun had toughened his father's skin and had given him a harder appearance, but perhaps time also had a lot to do with that.

Tom's dad had purchased a small piece of land in 1908. He had cleared it and built a home, a barn large enough for a winter's hay, a tool shed, several outhouses, a salt house for pork, a silo, a chicken house, and a woodshed. He had started a small herd of fine cattle, gradually adding to both the land and the herd. He had known many hard times—everything from cattle rustling, sickness, the death of his loving wife, the Depression, Anthrax (which took his entire herd), the hard times of rebuilding, and finally to a horrible fire that destroyed the entire ranch and took his own life.

Tom stood there wondering and questioning in his heart, *What could have driven Dad to work so hard? And for what? What could have empowered him to keep on going after so much hardship and heartache?*

Tom remembered when his dad almost did give up after his mom died. His mom and dad had been so close—so happy together. They were both hard workers, but they seemed to enjoy life to the fullest. When the work day was over, they strolled around the beautiful gardens together or sat in the lawn swing and sang together. Tom never recalled hearing his dad sing by himself, but he sounded pretty good with Mom. She sang all the time and had such a beautiful voice. She made home a very happy place to be.

Then Tom's mom came down with cancer. She lived only eight months before God took her home. At that point, Tom's dad lost almost all will to live. He didn't work for several weeks and no one could get him to eat. A lot of folks thought he would die, too. Then one day (no one ever knew just why) he got busy, bought more cattle, purchased more land, and began to make things happen. He poured himself into his work and really began to make the ranch thrive again. He was a perfectionist about everything he did, driving himself to exhaustion every day.

Tom remembered those words again, *The land's the only thing you can count on to never change. Cherish it, Son. Let it become a part of you and you become a part of it. It'll always be there. I'm countin' on you.*

Tom fell to the ground sobbing. "Dad. Oh, Dad! I can't! You can't expect me to. I can't do this without you. I don't even want to. You worked so hard, and for what! No! No! I can't!" But his father's words echoed again in his mind, and yes, in his heart. Son, I'm countin' on you.

Tom got up and slowly walked up the hill and out to the road where he had left his old pickup. He laid his arm on the truck, put his head on his arm, and almost gave in to sobbing again. He felt so alone and so defeated—like a little boy who was lost and couldn't find his way home.

Tom got into his truck and drove back to Marshall Ranch, or what used to be a ranch. It wasn't much of anything anymore, just black, scorched earth as far as the eye could see. The buildings were gone, the cattle was gone, and the beauty was gone. But before the fire, Tom thought Marshall Ranch was the most beautiful place in the world. The beautiful mountains—the rolling meadows—the mighty raging river that broadened as it made its bend around the ranch, churning and rushing, wild and free. It was a view that always brought an unexplainable excitement and, sometimes, a lump to his throat that even he didn't understand.

The river was a special place. There was a spot by a huge old oak tree where Tom spent many hours through the years. It was his favorite place to go when he had serious thinking to do. And when he was a boy, all his free time was spent there with a fishing pole in one hand and scratching the ear of his faithful old dog, Rascal, with the other. Tom had given Rascal that name as a puppy because he was always stealing shoes and chewing them up or hiding them somewhere. Yes, that puppy was definitely a rascal. As he got older though, Rascal became a loyal companion and a hard worker on the ranch. He could do the work of ten men on a round-up, but it was on one of those round-ups that took his life. Something spooked the cattle and poor Rascal was trampled. That was a hard, sad day for Tom.

Every memory seemed to bring heartache. Everything Tom had loved was gone. There was nothing but ugliness surrounding him. He leaned over and picked up a handful of ashes and let them sift through his fingers. Bitterness, loneliness, and anger overwhelmed him. Could he stay here in this horrible God-forsaken place? Had God really forsaken the ranch and him? It certainly seemed that way to him right now. The Land! Oh, why had his father asked him to stay? Why had he counted on him to be a part of this dreadful, killer land? There was nothing left, nothing to love, nothing to enjoy—only ugliness, cruel memories, and heartache. Oh, the river was still there—the fierce, raging, rushing river crashing against the rocks and the shore. Today it seemed especially wild and out of control—but the beauty was gone, just angry waters tearing their way through all this ugliness.

Tom wanted to yell out at someone, or kick something. But who, or what? What could have caused this terrible disaster? What could have started that horrible fire? There had been no storm, no lightning. Was it an act of God? Or was it an act of some malicious, perhaps envious scoundrel of a human being? Would anyone ever know? Maybe it would be better if no one ever did know. God knew. "Vengeance is mine, I will repay, thus saith the Lord." But Tom was not in any frame of mind to trust God for anything right now. In spite of his training, his only thoughts toward God were anger.

What could he do? As Tom looked around, an almost overwhelming urge came over him to jump into his pickup and drive as far and as fast as he could, away from this horrible scene. But in his heart he knew he couldn't do that, so he tried to pull himself together to decide what he should do. First, he needed to find a room for the night. He had very little money in his wallet and at this hour the bank was closed. He should have thought about that earlier, but his thinking was clouded with heartache and anger.

The Woodleys had been kind enough to invite Tom to stay with them until after the funeral, but now he must get on with his life. Anyway, the Woodleys were taking the train to Oregon for a few weeks to visit Mr. Woodley's brother and his wife, who had moved there to work in the shipyards. Their son was in the Navy and they wanted to feel that they were helping him and, in some way, doing their part for their country. So they put all their effort toward helping build battleships. Tom was not quite sure what they were doing now that the war had ended, but they were still living there.

Tom certainly knew about those ships. He had spent many months on just such a ship serving his country in the United States Navy. He wondered many times if Mr. Woodley's brother and his wife had labored with loving hearts and hands on his ship. Tom was very proud to have been a part of defending his country, but at the same time he was very glad to have it behind him.

Tom gave one last look around and (almost as if he were in a trance) got back into the pickup and slowly drove toward town. The sun had begun to go down, giving the sky the appearance of an enormous fire. It would have been beautiful to most people, but to Tom it brought back horrible memories. He drove, passing cars, houses, stores, and people, not even conscious of his surroundings. His thoughts were racing from one thing to another, trying to put his future into some perspective—but it was hopeless. Maybe after a good night's sleep he could think more clearly—but first, where would he find that good night's sleep?

Up ahead was a familiar sign—Josie's Diner. Perhaps if he had some food in his stomach, his brain would function better. Everyone loved Josie—and her cooking was fabulous. He had eaten there many times with his dad. There were always folks there he knew. Everyone liked him and they all thought the world of his dad. His dad had been a good neighbor to everyone, always willing to help anyone who had a need. Tom, however, was not wanting conversation tonight. He just hoped for a quick sandwich and perhaps a suggestion of a good room to rent for the night. But that was not to be.

Upon entering, Tom saw many familiar faces and they began to surround him, offering their condolences. Tom knew they meant well and he loved them all, but he just wanted to be alone. He saw Bill and Jenny Jeffers, the Tomkins, Jim and Reba Davis, and the Laynes. Two of his buddies were also there, Jack Edwards and Billy Johnson. They didn't come over to talk with him though. Perhaps they didn't know what to say, or maybe they just wanted to wait until there weren't so many people around.

The Laynes came to him first to tell him how much they thought of his father and how sorry they were about the tragedy. Tom had dated their daughter, Cassandra, several times before he went into the Navy. He and most of her friends called her Cassie. Once when he was home on furlough, he sat with her at church. After the service, they went out for ice cream. He thought she was really something special—the most beautiful girl around. She was small with shoulder length blonde hair—or platinum hair, some would say. She carried her chin high, which gave her an independent air, and she had the clearest, bluest eyes Tom had ever seen. Anytime she was near, she captured his attention and caused his heart to race. He even found himself stumbling over words when he talked with her. He had never had trouble before talking with anyone in his life. He tried to envision what married life with her would be like, but the subject had never come up. When he got out of the service, she was away at college. Then he got caught up with work on the ranch and he never saw her again.

"TC, are you okay?" Mr. Layne asked. "We didn't get a chance to speak with you at the funeral. Cassie tried to get over to talk to you at the cemetery, but there were too many people around you, so she decided to wait. Come see us, TC. Don't make yourself so scarce."

"I will, Mr. Layne. I have to get some organization in my life first. I'm just not exactly sure what I'm gonna do yet."

"If we can be of help to you, let us know," Mrs. Layne said with a sympathetic smile.

Tom forced a smile and replied, "Thanks, I will."

Others followed with their well wishes. Although it wasn't what Tom wanted, he had to admit it was good to know people cared and to see their love. It was also good to know that he had friends he could turn to. Many offered a place for him to stay, but he felt the need to be alone and to show some responsibility. He always admired his father's ability to be strong and make wise decisions in times of crisis. Tom wanted to be like his father in that respect. Perhaps he was afraid that if he depended on friends now, it would become a way of life.

As he seated himself at a table, Josie appeared with a dinner in hand before Tom had even ordered. "Hi, TC. This is the best we have today. Want ya to know we love ya and are here for ya."

"Thanks, Josie. I can't tell you how much that means to me."

Josie went back to the kitchen and Tom ate while friends continued to come around one by one with either offers of help or a loving pat on the back. He was even glad that they were coming around. His whole attitude and frame of mind had changed.

Jack and Billy slowly walked over to TC's table. "Hey, TC! Sorry about your dad. Billy and I sure want to do something for you, but we just don't know what."

"Well, I don't know myself, Jack, but I sure appreciate your friendship. I guess at this point, I just have to shake off the self pity and get goin'."

"A little help along the way won't hurt," Jack said with a pat on the back. "Do you have a place to stay? You know you can always hang out at our place."

TC smiled at Billy in appreciation. "I know that, Billy. You and your family have always been great, but I need to do this on my own. I'll stay in touch. Who knows, I may take you up on that offer down the road. Right now, I'm just lookin' to rent a room close by until I decide what direction to go."

TC knew that it would really be an inconvenience for him to stay with either Billy or Jack. They both had small homes. Jack's family had seven children and Billy's folks were struggling to make ends meet. They didn't need an additional burden right now. They said their goodbyes and left TC feeling uplifted and more determined to go forward.

Finally, when Tom had almost finished his dinner, Josie came out to see how he was doing. She sat down at his table and laid her hand on his arm. She was such a kind, jolly soul. It was almost impossible to be depressed around her.

"TC, I overheard you say you need a room. We have extra rooms at our house, and Joe and I would love to have you there." Knowing in her heart that he would shun her offer if she didn't let him pay, she added, "I will check around and find out what others are getting for room and board. Will you come, TC? You could go on over right now. Joe is at home. I'll call him and let him know you are coming."

Josie was a short plump woman in her late 60's. She had a round pleasant face, framed with graying hair that had once been reddish brown. She always wore it in a bun on the back of her head. She had probably been quite a beauty when she was young. Her skin was smooth with very few wrinkles. Her black eyes sparkled and snapped as she talked, and her smile could melt any heart. All the children loved her. They knew that a big hug for Josie meant a homemade cookie for them, so they all flocked to her. Joe and Josie never had any children of their own. That was certainly unfortunate too, but it could not have been for lack of want. Josie loved on every child that came around. She would have been a great mom. Josie and her husband were generous, kind, and easy to love. They were, at the same time, too quick to give advice on any given subject. Tom was very adamant about standing on his own two feet and making his own decisions. But right now, he sure did feel alone, and what with Josie's cooking—well, the temptation was just too great. And besides, he surely didn't want to hurt her feelings. He smiled, and reached out for her hand.

"Sure Josie, I would love to rent from you. You and Joe are the kindest people I know. I expect many folks have taken advantage of your generosity. I surely don't want that to happen here."

Tears welled up in Josie's eyes. She just smiled, squeezed Tom's hand without reply, and returned to the kitchen.

Tom breathed a sigh of relief. That was one decision that came easier than he had expected. He knew, at least, where he would lay his head tonight. Sleep, on the other hand, would not come so easily. He rose from the table and walked over toward the cash register. As he leaned around the corner he called out, "Hey, Josie, where's my ticket?"

Josie came at once. "Now, TC, this one's on me and don't you give me any trouble about it. It's the least I can do."

"Thanks a lot, Josie. You're the greatest." He donned his hat and slowly walked out the door. The world didn't look quite as bleak as it had before he stopped in at Josie's. Friends, food, and a destination sure make a big difference in one's outlook on life.

Tom drove out to Joe and Josie's place. Joe and Josie Hoffman were well known and loved by everyone in town and many other communities for miles around. They had a farm just east of town. It was a small farm with a small frame home on it. Behind the house was a large barn, a machine shed, and a big silo for grain storage. Joe had farmed the ground and raised a few cattle before his accident two years ago. He had not been able to work or do much of anything since. He was helping a neighbor plow a field, when his tractor wheel went into an old well and turned over. When they found him, he was pinned under the tractor. They thought at first he wouldn't live; but with everyone's prayers, good doctoring, and Josie's good care and love (not to mention her good cooking), he had pulled through. He walked with a cane now, but seemed to manage life pretty well. His jovial spirit sure hadn't hurt him any, either. In fact, it may have been one of the greatest contributors to his quick recovery. The Bible says, "A merry heart doeth good like a medicine." Well, Joe certainly had a merry heart. Nothing seemed to dampen his spirits.

When Tom pulled into the Hoffman's lane, he saw Joe pull the curtain back and look out the window. Then the kitchen door opened and he beckoned for Tom to come in. His big smile almost made Tom feel like he was coming home. When he walked up the steps, Joe gave him a big hug.

"Son, I was hoping Josie would get you over here. You shore are a welcome sight. I'm real sorry about your pa. I know he's brightnin' up heaven some. He shore was a great man. We loved him, TC."

"Thanks, Joe. I sure appreciate you opening your home to me. You and Josie are terrific. Dad thought the world of you folks, too. Yes,

I think you're right about Dad brightening up heaven. He and Mom are probably singin' up a storm right now and havin' a grand old time."

"Come on in, TC," Joe said. "Have a cup of coffee and some a' these cookies Josie made."

"I'll have that coffee, but no cookies for me. I just finished a big, scrumptious meal at the diner. There's no room for even a crumb. Boy, Josie can cook!"

"Yeah, she feeds everybody but me," Joe said with a chuckle.

Tom laughed and retorted, "You sure don't look like you're wastin' away."

Joe patted his stomach and said, "Well, ya' know I'm watchin' my weight. I'm gettin' it out here where I can keep a good eye on it." They both had a good laugh and sat down to some steaming coffee.

Soon after Josie came home, Tom said his goodnights and went to the room that Josie had designated to be his room. It was all anyone could ask for. It was clean, comfortable, and cheerful. There were even fresh flowers on the little table. Tom wondered if somehow Josie had known before he did, that he was coming to stay here. But of course not! That would be impossible. Perhaps she just kept things that way all the time. But even with all its beauty and comfort, Tom could not sleep. He heard every cricket, every frog, every leaf rustle in the breeze. He tossed and turned as terrible memories clouded his mind. The sky had begun to get light when he finally dozed off. Too soon, he was awakened by Edgar, Josie's old rooster, as he perched on a fence post out by the barn and gave his morning wake-up call.

Tom could smell the coffee brewing as he got dressed. When he entered the kitchen, Josie was busily working on a breakfast fit for a king.

"Josie," Tom called. "You aren't preparing that breakfast for me, are you? I can come down to the diner to get my meals and pay for them just like anyone else. I don't want you putting yourself out for me."

Joe stood up and pointed a finger toward Tom. "Now listen here, young man! Don't you come off thinkin' you're getting any special treatment. We'll treat you just like we do all our boarders and meals come with the package. Understand?"

"All your boarders?" Tom put his hands on his hips and arched his eyebrows in question. "I didn't know you had any other boarders."

Joe was all grins. "Well, we don't yet, but if'n we get any more, you won't get any special treatment. Until that time, you'll just have to live by the rules."

Tom smiled and said, "You just may be one tough old landlord to put up with. But seriously, Josie, from now on, I'll come to the diner for breakfast. You two keep your normal schedule."

Joe chuckled, "Now listen here! I meant what I said about those rules. Besides, if'n she fixes breakfast for you, maybe she'll let me have a little bite or two."

"I'm gonna let you have this pan on your backside if you don't quit tryin' to make folks think I'm so mean to you, you old spoiled baby," Josie growled.

Tom laughed and shook his head. "I think what you two need is a referee."

They all sat down to breakfast and Joe prayed. "Thank you, Lord for all your provisions. Now give us all comfort and strength, especially TC. We love You, Lord, and know You will provide. You ain't never failed us yet. Amen." Tom leaned back in his chair and smiled a contented smile, feeling more like a loved son than a boarder. It was good to have a home and family. One thing was for sure—the Lord had never failed him.

Chapter 2

A New Beginning

As soon as Tom finished breakfast, he said his goodbyes to the Hoffmans and drove into town. If he was going to actually rebuild the ranch, he needed to get things rolling. He had never been one to procrastinate when there was something to do. Tom's first stop was the bank. He wanted to double check his finances and talk with the banker. He felt the need for some outside wisdom. He wasn't too confident of his own judgment right now.

He laid out his plans to Mr. Boyd, the Vice President of the First National Bank. If anyone could give him some sound advice and point him in the right direction, it was Jack Boyd.

Mr. Boyd listened intently. He sat frowning and staring at Tom for what seemed like an hour. Finally, he cleared his throat, scratched his head, and began to drum his fingers on his desk. "Tom, I can see you sure are Colbert's son. He would have worked just exactly the same way. You're going to be alright. Just don't go too fast. There's nobody pushing you. Keep it slow and enjoy the ride. We're all pulling for you, so don't be too full of pride to accept a little help along the way. You know the Good Book says that *it's more blessed to give than it is to receive,* so let some other folks receive a blessing by giving you a helping hand."

"Thank you, sir. I appreciate you taking the time to listen. I just wanted to make sure I'm not making any mistakes." He rose and picked his hat up from the table giving it a couple thumps.

"Well, Tom, there's nothing wrong with making a mistake now and then as long as you learn something from it. I don't think there are any perfect folks in this world and I don't suppose the good Lord is going to change that circumstance beginning with you. Good luck to you, TC. Come in anytime. I'd be glad to hear how you're doing."

"Thank you, sir. You'll probably be seeing a lot of me. I hope I won't wear out my welcome." Tom smiled and tipped his hat as he walked out the door.

Tom began putting his plans into action. He headed to the post office where there were "Work wanted" notes posted all over the north wall. He studied them and took down the names of the ones most fitting to his needs. The first one that looked interesting was a young man whose ad stated that he was strong and quick, and would do any kind of work to earn money for his education. That was impressive to Tom. He was sure he would need just such a person, and soon.

Tom followed the directions on the note, and soon found the home of the young man who called himself Jed Coulter. Tom seemed to have a new spring in his step and renewed energy as his plan unfolded. Maybe it was because of his course of action, maybe it was Josie's delectable meals, or maybe it was Joe's prayer. At any rate, Tom had become enthusiastic about his venture, and the bitterness he had felt yesterday had faded to some degree.

Tom knocked on the door and a little elderly lady appeared. She wiped her forehead with her white apron and looked Tom up and down, then simply frowned and waited for him to state his business.

"Would Mr. Coulter be here?" Tom asked.

"There ain't no Mr. Coulter," she replied, "lessen you mean Jed. He's out back choppin' down an old dead tree. You want me to fetch 'em?"

"No, ma'am. I'll just go around and see him, if that's alright?" She just nodded her head and closed the door.

Tom found Jed swinging an axe, giving it all he had. Jed wore a short sleeved shirt and very faded jeans that had been patched to the limit. Sweat dripped from his face and his muscles were plenty of evidence that work was not new to him.

"Hello there," Tom called. "Would you be the young man looking for work?"

Jed turned quickly and displayed a big smile. "You bet I am." He sprang over the fence and offered Tom his hand. "I'm Jed Coulter, Sir. Who might you be?"

"I'm Tom Marshall. I'm going to be needing a lot of help. Some of it will be hard work and long hours. If you are looking for work, you can start right now."

"I'm your man! Where to? First I have to tell my ma and Miss Billie. They would worry if I just took off."

"That's fine, Jed. I'll wait for you in the truck." Tom watched him as he bounded into the house. "Man?" Tom grinned. He was just a boy. But he looked strong and eager. He just might be perfect for the job. It was not Tom's plan to hire men in this fashion, but he had a feeling about this one.

Tom climbed into the truck and began to look around. The little house in front of him that had once been white was now faded, peeling, and in much need of paint and repair. The porch had some missing boards and the screen on the door was pulled loose from one side. The grass was mowed, but that was the extent of the lawn care. Maybe he would be able to teach Jed how to do some trimming and special manicuring around this place. It could certainly stand some TLC.

Tom wondered what had happened to Jed's father. The lady who came to the door had said there was no Mr. Coulter. Perhaps he would ask Jed after they became better acquainted.

He saw several chickens scratching for a tasty morsel. They were free to go in any direction they chose. There were fences, but there were holes large enough for a horse to go through and the gate was lying on the ground. A large yellow cat sunned itself on the porch swing. There were flowers haphazardly scattered around that appeared to be there by accident, rather than intention.

Jed came bounding from the house. He noticed Tom looking around and felt a little embarrassed. "Not much to look at, is it?"

"Any place should look good that's called home," Tom said.

"Well, this has been home for 18 years. It's the only home I've ever had. I aim to build a new one for Ma and Miss Billie after I get out of school and get a good job. They are both deservin' and I'm gonna do it," Jed said.

"That's a very admirable goal, Jed. I hope you'll be able to fulfill that dream—and I believe you will."

"Well, where do we go from here?" Jed asked.

He handed Jed some papers. "The first job I have for you is to locate these men and tell them, if they're still looking for work, to meet me in front of the Town Hall at 2 this afternoon. Tell them to be prompt if they're serious about a job. I'll give them all the details in person. Then give them my name and tell them I'll be waiting for them in the little park at the picnic table.

Jed looked over the papers and nodded his head.

"This'll be a snap. I know most all these places. I'll be back in no time."

Tom pulled up in front of the general store. Jed started to jump out, but Tom reached out and grabbed his arm. "Wait! Take the truck. I have some business here in town, and you can make better time if you drive."

Jed gave a big grin. "Hey, I'm likin' this job already." He quickly changed sides of the truck, and sped off on his first assignment.

Tom already liked Jed and felt pretty certain that he would be permanent around the ranch, at least until school started. Now if he could just find about five more men who would be compatible and who would work. That would be sufficient for now. He remembered how difficult it had been for his father to find good ranch hands. He wasn't actually looking for ranch hands right now though. He was looking for a clean-up crew and men who could build a house and a bunk house. He would add more men and more buildings later as the need arose.

Next, he would start looking for good cattle. His father had always been partial to Herefords, but he wanted to do some inquiring about Charlets. He knew his father would probably not approve; but he had heard some good reports about this breed, and he wanted to learn more about them. Black Angus also appealed to him. It was easy to envision them roaming the hillside. He wasn't going to make any hasty decisions though. He wanted to seek some wise counsel on this matter.

Tom went into Bailey's General Store and Farm Supply and began to look around. They had nearly everything there a person could want—from groceries to building supplies to clothing. Tom gave Mr. Miller a list of the groceries he would be needing, and then he began to look for camping equipment. This would be necessary until his buildings were finished. He needed two tents, a small camping stove, pans, dishes, dinnerware, kerosene, and matches. His selections took nearly an hour. Finally, he came to the building supplies. He had made quite a list of the things he would be needing, including tools. He hoped that some of the men he would hire would have some tools of their own. He would hold off on tools until after he interviewed his prospects.

After completing his shopping, he headed toward the diner. His timing was perfect. Jed was driving up in the pickup. Spotting Tom, he stuck his head out the window and yelled, "I got 'em. They'll be here at 2 o'clock just like you wanted. Every single one is comin'."

"Hey, that's a lot better than I expected. You must be quite a sales-man," Tom said.

"Na," Jed shook his head. "I just told 'em you were a swell boss, that we had gotten along great ever since I started working for you. They didn't need to know that was just a couple hours ago." He grinned and jumped out of the truck.

"Come on, Jed," Tom said. "I want you to meet Josie. She's my landlady and a long time friend, and the greatest cook you'll ever meet. We might as well eat some lunch while we're here."

"Wow"! Jed exclaimed, "I'm all for that." Jed was enthusiastic about everything. TC liked that. A great attitude was half the battle in any situation.

Tom and Jed sat down at a small table. A blonde waitress appeared promptly at their side. This was a new face to TC. "What will it be for you today?" she asked.

"Is Josie around?" TC asked.

"Oh, you won't see Josie on the floor this time of day. She's busy in the kitchen cooking. It won't let up until about 3 o'clock. We're always busy at lunch time. I think everyone in town eats here.

"Have you worked here very long?" TC inquired. "I don't recall seeing you before."

"About a month," she replied. "I moved here with my parents from Damson Creek. Name's Shirley Brennan."

"Pretty name, pretty girl!" Jed interjected. Tom noticed that Jed hadn't taken his eyes off the little waitress. He also had to admit that she was attractive and seemed very pleasant. Tom just hoped that maybe Josie would show up before they had to leave.

Tom and Jed looked over the menu. "I think I'll have some of Josie's stew and biscuits and some blackberry cobbler. And I think I'll have a glass of milk with that." He handed Shirley the menu and looked at Jed.

"Just make mine the same. That sounds good to me." He was still watching Shirley rather intently.

Shirley took the menus and headed toward the kitchen. Tom grinned and looked at Jed. "Well, well! Looks like we'll be coming to Josie's on a regular basis, huh?"

Jed's face turned a little red. He grinned, but made no comment.

After paying for their lunches, Tom instructed Jed to go over to the General Store and start loading up the supplies while he headed toward the Town Hall to wait for his prospective hands. When he got there, he saw one man leaning against the building. Tom didn't think he was one of the men he would be interviewing as it was only 1:30; but when he sat down at the little table in the park area, the man, dressed in levis, plaid shirt, and boots, headed in his direction. Tom watched him as he approached. He had a long slow stride. He wasn't quick and energetic like Jed, but as Tom was making a mental impression of him, he perceived him to be a slow, steady, hard worker. Tom was already impressed with the fact that he was prompt. He had always been a stickler for being on time.

"You wouldn't be Tom Marshall, would you?" he asked.

"Sure am,"

"I'm Brad Perry," said the tall lanky cowboy. "Your boy said you are looking for workers, so here I am."

TC talked with him and learned he had done everything from working a cattle drive and cooking (which he was quick to interject he didn't care to do again) to baby sitting his ten-year-old nephew on a train trip to Oregon (which he also didn't care to do again.) He was a likable, quiet sort of guy who looked TC in the eye as he answered his questions. TC liked that about a man. He was generally a pretty good judge of character, and he decided Brad looked like a good man. TC told him he would give him a try and gave him directions to the ranch with instructions to be there at 8 the next morning.

At 2pm sharp, two men pulled up in a truck. They both got out and walked over to the table where TC was sitting. A second truck drove up and one man got out from the passenger's side and the driver of the truck drove away. He interviewed these three, but chose only one. One of the men was too cocky. TC thought he would be a trouble maker. The other didn't look like a worker. Tom thought he would turn out to be lazy, and he sure didn't need any of that. Davey Burkett, the young man he chose, had blonde curly hair (enough for three heads) and a harmonica in his pocket. He had a big smile on his face most of the time. *Good trait*, TC thought. He wanted a cheerful bunch, if possible.

Tom had almost completed his conversation with his last group when three men came walking down the street. Tom was a little surprised to learn they were all coming to apply for work. He was expecting only two more. They explained that they had been watching from up the street for him to finish his interview with the previous prospect. His plan had been to hire two more men today, if possible; but he was impressed with all three, so he recruited them to make a crew of six.

Two of the men in this last group were cousins. Kent Wills invited his cousin, Calvin, to come along with him, because he knew he was also looking for work. The other man was Jack Archer. He was several years older than the others. He was a heavy set man with a hearty laugh. He was rugged looking and had extremely large arms. He had previously been a blacksmith, so Tom was sure he could swing a hammer. Jack mentioned there wasn't enough work blacksmithing anymore to make a living.

Tom gathered up all his papers that contained the information he had written about his new crew. He then headed toward the General Store where Jed was loading the supplies that Tom had ordered. Brad Perry and Jack Archer were the only men who had tools, so Tom gave Mr. Miller a new list of the tools he needed. He then paid him, and he and Jed headed to the ranch.

Chapter 3

Press Toward the Mark

Tom stopped by the diner to tell Josie that he wouldn't be staying at the house tonight. He couldn't leave all the supplies at the ranch with no one to look after them, and he wasn't quite ready yet to leave Jed out there by himself. He might be capable, but he was still just a boy—even if he did call himself a man.

"Jed, do you need to call your mother while we're here to let her know you'll be staying at the ranch?" TC asked.

"No," Jed replied. "I told her I might not be home tonight."

Josie heard Tom's voice and came in from the kitchen. "Well, look who's here! How's everything going, TC?"

"Well, I hired my crew and bought my supplies. We're heading out to the ranch now to unload. I wanted to let you know I wouldn't be staying at the house tonight. Jed and I are gonna camp at the ranch. Oh, Josie, I want you to meet him. Jed, this is Josie Hoffman. Josie, this is Jed Coulter. He was my first man, and the best of the lot."

Jed beamed and gave Josie a big smile. She reached her hand out to shake hands. "Welcome, Jed. Glad to know you. If Tom likes you, I love you already. It's a little early for dinner I suppose, but how about a piece of pie?"

"Nice to meet you ma'am. You'll have to ask Tom about the pie though."

"We better get on over to the ranch, Josie," Tom said. "We've got a lot to do before dark. We'll take a rain check though."

"You'll take more than that, my boy," Josie said with a stern voice. "I'll pack you some food to see you through the night."

Josie didn't wait for a reply. She hurried off to the kitchen and began to collect enough food for ten men. "That'll hold you over till tomorrow. When will you be back to the house?"

"Thanks Josie. You're a peach." Tom gave her a big hug. "I'll probably be back Friday. Tomorrow will be a pretty full day getting the men lined out and organized. We have a lot of clean-up to do before we can start building. Then Friday I have to come into town and contact the power company and phone company to get service out there again. I'll stop in then to let you know what my plans are. Say, we met your new waitress when we were here today. She did a good job, Josie." Tom mentioned her for Jed's benefit. He noticed Jed looking around and knew he was looking for her.

"Oh, you mean Shirley. Yeah, she's a honey. She's a hard worker and as sweet as they come. I'll probably lose her this fall though. She has her heart set on going to college. I wouldn't want to discourage that, but I'll never be able to replace her."

Tom and Jed began to gather up the food that Josie had prepared for them and started toward the door.

"You boys be careful now, you hear?"

"We'll be careful, Josie. Thanks for everything," Tom replied.

The drive to the ranch took about an hour but seemed only minutes to Jed. He talked non stop until they reached it. "Wow! Are we here already?" Jed exclaimed. "So this is your ranch?"

"This is it." Tom looked around, and the enthusiastic feeling he once had suddenly left him. The memory of the fire and his father's death caused the anger he felt to come rushing back to him as he viewed the charred earth around him. Again he wanted to flee the horror, but a phrase that his father had used so often came back to him—*Press toward the mark. Yes, he must press toward the mark at any cost.*

Tom knew that was a phrase from the Bible, but he didn't know where. He decided to look it up tomorrow. His father had read the Bible every morning, but Tom had never been very faithful to follow that practice. He vowed he would do that from now on. It would be a good example to set for those who would be working for him, and tomorrow would be a good time to start. If ever he needed to know what the Good Lord had to say, it was now.

There was a small New Testament in the glove box of his truck; at least, he supposed it was still there. He hadn't opened it for some time. He had a Bible at Josie's, which also hadn't been used for longer than he cared to admit. Tom felt good about his decision to make Bible reading a part of his daily routine.

Jed was excited. "What a place! How much is yours? Boy, with a good rain to wash it down good, it'll green up in no time. With a little work, this will be one magnificent place."

Tom knew that was true. Jed's excitement helped put things in a new perspective. Maybe everything would look brighter tomorrow. They unloaded the tents and put them up. Then they unloaded all the supplies. The building materials would be delivered tomorrow morning.

By the time they had finished, the sun was beginning to set. The sky was resplendent, a brilliant orange fading to pink and then to purple.

Tom lit the little stove so they could warm their food for dinner. There wasn't much conversation during their meal. They both just sat, watching the sunset. Finally, the silence was broken. Tom was the first to speak. "In answer to your question awhile ago, Jed, all the land as far as you can see west of here is part of the ranch—5,000 acres in all."

"Whoa, Mr. Marshall! Whatcha aimin' to do with all that land?"

"Well, I plan to fill it with the most beautiful cattle you've ever seen. Yes, Jed, I'm going to do it. I'm going to press toward the mark."

"Well, I'm guessin' that's quite a mark you got for yourself, Mr. Marshall. But I'm bettin' you can do it. I believe you could do just about anything you set your mind to."

Tom grinned and put his arm around Jed. "You're sure what I needed to give me the confidence to get the job done. And, by the way, call me TC."

Tom stretched and looked around. "Might not be a bad idea to build a little campfire. We sure don't need it for heat, but it might deter any wolves that came nosing around."

"Well, I'm all for anything that'll keep any kind of critters away," Jed was quick to reply. He jumped up and began gathering anything that looked like it would burn. Nearly everything around had already burned in the fire.

"We may have to drive over past the canyon tomorrow and cut some wood for campfires," Tom said, "but tonight we can break up some of those crates. If they don't last through the night, we'll just have to keep our guns handy."

Jed dropped the wood and turned toward Tom. "Glad I didn't bring Bosco. That's my dog. Bravery just ain't one of his greatest attributes. He's a smart dog, as smart as they come, and he's sure smart enough not to tangle with a pack of wolves."

Tom smiled and said, "Well, maybe the wolves will be smart enough not to tangle with us. I think we'd better get some shut-eye, Jed. We have a big day ahead of us."

Sleep came easily for both. Except for crickets and an old owl, everything was quiet throughout the night. The wolves were wise enough to stay away. When the sun came up, it was all that Tom needed to nudge him into the new day. He pulled the tent flap open, stretched, and took several deep breaths. The smell of burnt timber still hung in the air; but this was indeed a gorgeous day, and it gave Tom new hope. The mountains seemed higher and the sky seemed bluer than ever before. Yes, this was definitely a grand day.

Only moments later Jed popped out of his tent, just as chipper as he had been the day before. "Hey, why didn't you call me? You don't want me to get a bad reputation for being lazy, do you?" he spouted.

"Well, I don't think a 6 o'clock rise is going to hurt your reputation too much," Tom teased.

The new day went pretty much according to plan. Tom started by pulling out his New Testament as he had intended. He began looking for the verse, press toward the mark. He knew he needed to become more familiar with the Bible. He didn't have a clue where to start looking. It might even be in the Old Testament, but he didn't think so. Well, he would have to look for that when he got his complete Bible from Josie's. He would just read a few chapters for now from Galatians. That's where it had opened. He could see Jed watching him out of the corner of his eye. It somehow gave him a good feeling to know that he was showing Jed the importance of putting God's Word in your life. When he was finished, he put the New Testament by his bunk.

The new crew all proved to be good workers. Jack Archer was probably the best, much to Tom's surprise. Tom thought that because of his size and age he would get tired quickly, but Jack had more endurance than any man on the crew. Brad Perry worked just as Tom had expected, slow and steady. He kept pretty much to himself and didn't stop for a break, unless Tom demanded it. Kent and Calvin Wills, the cousins, were cut-ups. They worked hard, but they teased and joked all day. They did everything from throwing dirt clods at each other to having water fights. Tom didn't mind any of their nonsense though. It seemed to make the day go by quicker and made it more enjoyable for everyone. Besides, they did their fair share of the work. Davey Burkett was a good worker and good natured. He seemed to like everything and everybody. He wasn't as strong as the others, but he worked hard and gave it all he had. Every break, he pulled out his harmonica and put his heart into his music. He could play almost any request they gave him, and they sure were giving him a variety.

Yes, Tom was pleased with his crew. They were quite a collection of personalities, but they complemented each other well. Tom was also pleased with all they had accomplished today. In fact, they had exceeded his goal for the day. They would be able to get started building forms for the footings on the storage building tomorrow.

Tom realized he couldn't be there to supervise all the time—he needed a foreman. Of the men he had, Tom thought Jack would be the best choice—he was older, the best worker, and probably the most authoritative. He would approach him about this idea tomorrow.

The week flew by. The building was almost complete, but Tom still had no foreman. When he discussed this with Jack, Jack had quickly told him he didn't think he was cut out for the job. Even when Tom had told him there would be a raise in pay, he declined by saying, "Tom, I'll work hard for you. I can take orders, but I can't give 'em. You need to find someone that's cut out for the job, and I know it's not me."

That left Tom faced with the task of finding a new man. He would have to go into town tomorrow and try to find someone. He really needed several more men. This might be a good time to check the work wanted posts again. If he was going to start building a herd anytime soon (and he certainly was anxious to do that) he would need to begin repairing fences. The grass was pretty green beyond the canyon, but the fences were in bad shape. Once they were repaired, he could start look-ing for some good stock.

All the men had put in a full, hard day. At the first suggestion of getting some sleep, they were all ready. Davey was the last to unroll his bed roll and crawl in for the night. He sat by the campfire, still playing his harmonica, until Calvin finally yelled out, "Knock off that juice harp and go to bed."

Davey thumped it on his hand a couple times and reluctantly strolled toward his tent. "Some folks just don't appreciate a good bed-time lullaby," he said.

There was little stirring throughout the night. Jed was the first one awake, not counting the sun. He lit the stove and started the coffee. Tom was the next to pull himself out saying, "I'm gonna have to get myself a rooster. We'll all be sleeping til noon if I don't."

One by one they all came out, some groaning and others bright and chipper. Everyone soon learned not to even talk to Calvin until he had his first cup of coffee. His cousin, Kent, teased and tormented him about being a grump. He even made up a jingle.

Cal, Cal, the mean old grump
Might as well throw him in the dump.
He won't get off his lazy rump
Until he's had his coffee.

Kent tossed sticks and clods at Calvin until finally Calvin slung his coffee mug toward Kent, drenching him with coffee. Kent yelled and everyone roared with laughter.

Tom was finishing his Bible reading when all of a sudden he let out an exhilarating whoop. "I found it! I found it!" Everyone stopped talking and stared at Tom in astonishment. He looked up and realized that he had startled every one of them. He laughed and said, "Not to worry everyone, I just found the Bible verse I've been looking for. My Father used to say, *Press toward the mark.* I knew it came from the Bible, but I didn't know where. I just found it in the book of Philippians."

After breakfast was over, Tom lined everyone out for the day and told them of his plans of going to town and hiring some new men. "Oh, Jed, I want you to go with me. I need you to get the supplies while I take care of some other business."

"I'm your man," Jed said, as he jumped up off the ground where he had been drawing pictures in the dirt with a stick.

"Don't forget to hire a cook," Kent yelled. "Cookin' just ain't Jack's callin'."

"Well, my breakfast was a far cry better than that stuff you called beans the other night. I think you made them with stump water," Jack growled.

"Okay, okay," Tom said. "I get the picture. I'll look for a cook." He grinned and walked toward the truck giving a wave as he climbed in. Jed hopped in on the other side.

Tom turned to Jed, still grinning. "I thought we better go see how badly Shirley's been missin' you."

"Well she may not admit it to the world, but she didn't forget me," Jed teased.

"Okay, lover boy, we'll see," Tom chided.

Chapter 4

Davey's Song

Tom's first stop was the General Store. He gave Sam a list of the supplies he needed and told him that Jed would pick them up. He looked around for Mr. Miller, but didn't see him. He was most likely behind the store unloading some new shipment.

Their next stop was to go say hi to Josie. They found her sitting at a desk writing on some papers when they walked in the diner.

"Hey, how's my favorite gal?" Tom yelled.

Josie looked up and jumped from her desk with arms outstretched. "Tom, where have you been? We were about to send the sheriff out lookin' for you."

"I've been a busy man. My crew has been workin' me to death," Tom grinned.

"Well, I don't think it's supposed to work that way. Where's your control? You're supposed to hold the whip you know," she teased.

"Just joking. I've got a great crew except for this love struck puppy." Tom turned to Jed and chuckled when he saw his red face. Then with a wink he asked, "By the way, where's Shirley?"

Josie picked up on Tom's gist and joined in. "Well, Jed, you sure have good taste in girls. I couldn't have picked you out a better one myself. I heartily approve. Shirley won't be in til 11 o'clock. Her mother is in town and she's spending some time with her. She'll be serving lunch though. You boys will be having lunch here, won't you?"

"You can count on it. I've sure missed your cooking. Say, you wouldn't want to give up this diner and come be our cook, would you, Josie?" Tom teased.

They all laughed, but then Josie replied. "That's a mighty temptin' idea, but I guess I'll have to pass this time. However, I do know someone who would make you a great cook. Jake Fry's son cooks up a storm, and I was told he's looking for work. You knew he lost his wife last winter?"

"Yes, I heard about that," Tom said. "But isn't he having a drinkin' problem? I sure don't need to have that to deal with. My law is NO DRINKING on the ranch."

"Good law," Josie said, "but he has that licked. The last report I had, he's doing real good. He was always a hard worker and very dependable when Sally was alive. I don't suppose his character has changed any."

"I might just give him a call," Tom said. "Isn't his name Bart?"

Josie frowned and looked up toward the ceiling as if the answer was written up there. "You might be right, but I think his name is Johnny. I think Bart is his little brother."

"Oh yeah, that's right. Come on, Jed. We better get started. See you at noon, Josie."

Tom sent Jed over to the General Store to load up the supplies. Then he went to the Post Office to look for some of the "work wanted" notices that were posted on the wall. While he was in the post office, Bill Landers came in.

"Say, TC, how's that ranch of yours coming along. I hear you're buildin' and gettin' it back like your pa had it."

"Well, I'm just startin', but I'm headed in that direction. I have a long way to go."

"Wouldn't be interested in some cattle, would ya?"

"Well, I will be. I haven't actually started buying my cattle yet. We're still repairin' fences. I have two sections finished though. What've you got?"

"I really need to sell mine now. I hate to let 'em go, but I've got some bills need payin'. I've got 80 head of Angus and 30 head of Holstein.

"Well, if we can come to a meetin' of the minds on price, I'll take your Angus. I couldn't use the Holstein though. I don't have any use for milk cows. I'll ride out and look at 'em tomorrow."

Next Tom called Johnny Fry to talk to him about being the ranch cook. Johnny didn't live very far away so he came on over and met with

TC. After talking with him, he hired him on a trial basis, even though he felt a little uneasy about it. It seemed like Johnny had a chip on his shoulder. He was mad at God and everyone one else because of the death of his wife, but maybe this crew would be good for him. Maybe they would be able to help pull him out of his depression and give him a new outlook on life. He would give him a try. He knew full well about being helped through a hard time.

Tom took several of the "work wanted" posters and contacted them by phone. None of them impressed him very much, but he did arrange several interviews to be held at the ranch. He also put up his own "help wanted" poster. He hoped to get some good responses to it.

When TC and Jed had accomplished their missions, they met at the diner and had lunch. They sat and talked for awhile. TC told Jed about the Lander's herd and the probability of buying them. Jed got as excited about them as if they were his. Tom finished his coffee and whacked Jed on the arm with his hat and said, "Hey Bud, we've got to get movin'. I have to stop at the Hoffman farm on the way back to the ranch to pick up a few things." The main thing he wanted was his Bible.

When they returned to the ranch, Calvin was giving Davey a rough time about his new song. Davey just tried to ignore him, but Calvin was not to be ignored for long.

"What's that mournful thing you're playin'? You're gonna make all of us start cryin'. Let's have some dancin' music," Calvin chided. "What do you call that anyway?"

Davey hit his harmonica on his knee a couple times and sat looking into the fire. "Well, I haven't named it yet. I can't name it until I come up with some words. That's the hard part. It's gotta be somethin' about the river though, cause the river is what gave me the song. When I watch the river, that's what comes out."

"You don't say?" said Calvin. "You mean you wrote that song yourself? I'll be doggoned! I didn't know you could do that."

Kent yelled out from the other side of the fire. "Some folks got it and some folks ain't. Cal, ol' boy, you ain't! You've been blessed with a tin ear." Then he threw himself back laughing.

"Oh, I don't know. Most people think I'm very talented, musically speakin'. I think you're just jealous 'cause you can't charm the gals with your voice like I can," Calvin retorted.

"Well, I heard you could charm snakes, but nobody ever told me 'bout you charmin' any gals. Guess you'll just have to show us," Kent replied.

Their feuding continued until everyone turned in for the night. But sleep was just an intermission. They started right back at it the next morning—and so it was, day after day.

The next few weeks passed quickly. The storage building and bunk house were soon finished. The fences were repaired. New faces around the ranch became a common thing as new men were being hired for all the added chores.

Tom hired a new foreman. Clay Hampton was a nice looking man with light brown hair, graying at the temples. He was 48 years old and had once been a foreman on another ranch. They decided to move to Missouri to be closer to his wife's family. He was a likeable man, despite a stern face. Tom believed he would be able to handle this bunch with no problems. He seemed to be forceful, yet he had a pleasing way about him.

Johnny, the new cook, had a hard time adjusting to his new station. Calvin started calling him "Cookie" and soon he became Cookie to everyone. He griped about it and refused to answer. Johnny proved to be a great cook, and good cooking can be the best asset there is to keeping a happy crew. However, Johnny had some very bad days. There were times when he would sulk and not talk to anyone. All of the men were aware of the rough time Johnny was having. They teased him a lot, trying to bring him out of it. They would say he was serving rotten food, or yell for a knife to slice the coffee; but, in the end, they let him know they were glad he was there and that they thought his food was great. It took several months for him to come around and warm up to them. Johnny eventually recognized that they had caring hearts. It wasn't long until they saw a grin on his face when they gave him a rough time. He finally learned to be a good sport. It certainly hadn't started out that way though. In the beginning, he had growled and griped and threatened to throw hot pans at the ornery teasers. Once he even threatened to put poison in the stew, but Johnny eventually grew to love the crew and to feel like they were family.

Tom noticed that nearly all of the men had picked up Davey's song. They were either whistling it or humming it. Even Tom had it going over and over in his head. He had to agree with Calvin, though—it was sort of mournful, but he liked it. He hoped that one day Davey would put some words to it.

One night, Rusty, one of the new men, had been into town. Something must have happened while he was there, because when he came back to camp, he was mad at the world. Calvin made some teasing remark, and Rusty shoved him back into the tent. Calvin and the tent crashed to the ground. He jumped up ready to tear into Rusty when Johnny stepped between them.

"Let it be, Cal," said Johnny. "He's got a lump he can't swallow, and you just happened to get in the way. Let him cool down."

That wasn't quite the end of Rusty's tantrum though. Davey was playing his song (as was his daily routine) and Rusty grabbed the harmonica and threw it in the fire. Davey made a lunge for it, but Rusty kicked it further into the fire. Davey grabbed a large stick and cracked Rusty on the shoulder. It would have turned into a nasty fight, but several of the men pulled them apart and stopped the scuffle.

Johnny dug the harmonica out of the fire, but it was no longer playable. Davey shoved his hands into his pockets and stomped down to the river. That was a turning point in Davey's life. To Davey, the harmonica was much more than just an instrument to play music. It belonged to his brother who had been killed in the war. His brother had given it to him the last time he went away. His instructions had been, "Learn to play this, little brother, and when I get home, we'll play a duet. Think of me every time you play it, and I'll be thinking of you."

Rusty bought another harmonica for Davey the next time he went to town. It was a nice one, probably better than the original, but Davey never put it to his lips. He never sang or whistled, and he no longer joked with the other men. Every evening after he ate, he headed down to the river and just sat gazing at the water. Rusty made several attempts to make amends. Davey told him that he forgave him, but he remained sullen, and the song was gone. Everyone was afraid Davey would never sing or play again.

Chapter 5

Love Comes Calling

Tom continued to read his Bible every morning, with one exception. One morning something woke him early out of a deep sleep. He stretched and went outside to see what the noise was. Just as he reached the gate, a rider jumped on his horse and rode off as fast as he could get his horse to travel. Tom was sure he had been up to no good, but what, he didn't know. He immediately rang the large bell by the porch, which was the call for everyone to come at once. The men knew if it wasn't time to eat, there was trouble.

Tom told them of his strange wake up and the rider who blazed out of the camp. Everyone tried to think what possibly could have brought a thief into the camp. They could find nothing missing, nor could they see any damage. It was puzzling. Maybe he was scared off before he had the chance to find what he was looking for. Tom realized he had been lax in locking the gates at night; but after this, he would be more careful.

The following morning when Tom awoke, he was quick to thank the Lord for the safety of all his men and that, to his knowledge, nothing had been taken. When he began his Bible reading he noticed that several of the other men were also reading. He later learned that they had each purchased Bibles the last time they went to town. Tom hoped that one day they would all be able to have Bible study and prayer together before they started their day. Maybe that would be a reality sooner than he had anticipated.

Tom decided to go to church the following Sunday. There were a lot of reasons he felt he should go. First of all, it was a commandment of God. Secondly, he felt it necessary to be a good example to his men. Thirdly, Josie had been asking him to. And finally (but by all means, not the least of importance), he wanted to see if Cassie was still attending with her family. He had longed to see her again, but for some reason he always postponed the actual meeting. This week he was determined to go.

When Sunday rolled around, Tom dressed in his suit, which the men had not seen before. They all whistled and cheered and teased about who she might be that had lured him to church. He hoped they couldn't detect the extra loud thumping of his heart or the fact that his hands were wet with perspiration—or they would really give him a hard time.

"It wouldn't hurt any of you scoundrels to be in church," Tom said.

When he drove up to the church, he looked around for familiar faces. Bill and Jenny Jeffers parked right beside him. They were elated to see him there. After hugs and small talk, he walked to the church with them. They invited him to sit with them, but he had already promised the Hoffmans so he made his apologies and started looking for Josie and Joe. They were already seated. They were always one of the first couples to arrive.

As Tom walked down the aisle to their pew, he let his eyes roam over the congregation. There she was! Cassie was sitting on the opposite side of the church—seated beside her was a young man about her age. Well, why should he think she wouldn't be seeing someone. He certainly hadn't been giving her any of his time. Nonetheless, he still felt somewhat betrayed and very disappointed.

The sermon meant more to him than sermons had in the past. Perhaps it was because he was spending time in his Bible, or maybe it was because he now knew that the Bible was personalized, and that God was talking to him. For whatever reason, he was enthralled by the message and took every word to heart. One of the verses that kept going over and over in his head was "Whatsoever ye sow, that shall ye also reap." He knew first hand just how true that verse really was. It seemed to hold true in any kind of situation.

After the service ended, Tom and Cassie both walked toward the center aisle from opposite directions and met. Tom reached his hand out to her and she greeted him with a big smile. She seemed genuinely glad to see him. She fired questions at him faster than he could give her answers. Finally he said, "Wait, tell me about you. How have you been, and what have you been doing?" She filled him in briefly on her latest adventures, and they both started laughing—they realized they were trying to cram a year into five minutes.

"Why don't you come over for dinner. We can catch up on everything. Mom and Dad would love to see you. Please, TC, say you'll come," she pleaded.

Cassie was always so cheerful and energetic. She hadn't changed at all. She still made his heart race and was still just as lovely as ever. How could he turn down this invitation that he wanted so badly? Yet what about the man she was sitting with? Well, she asked him so he wasn't going to pass up this opportunity to be with her. *All's fair in love and war,* they say, he thought.

Tom had a wonderful time. The Laynes made him feel so welcome. He and Cassie talked for hours about what she had been doing and about the ranch and the progress of the building. He told her about the home he was building and asked her advice on many things that needed a woman's input. She was more than happy to give her opinions.

She told him that she had been working in a doctor's office for the past year and had sent an application to a doctor's office in Tulsa, where she had gone to college. She hoped to work there and go back to school part-time and work toward a medical degree. She was still unsure of her plans for the future, but she thought she might want to become a doctor.

Tom secretly did not want her to go back to school. He did not want her to become a doctor. And he definitely did not want her to move to Tulsa. He felt so strongly about it that it was hard for him to control his tongue and simply listen to her proposed plans. All the while he was thinking, What can I say to change her mind? He decided it would be best not to say anything now. He would talk to God about it. God could change her mind.

Tom glanced down at his watch and realized that it was long past the time he had intended to leave. He wanted to get to the Hoffman's in time to visit with them and fill them in on everything that was happening at the ranch. They had been so kind to him and he wanted them to know how much he appreciated everything they had done. After all, they were just like family. They had loved him and given him some very good advice along the way. They would be very disappointed if he didn't spend some time with them.

But Tom knew he couldn't leave without making a date to see her again. He felt in his heart that he was being given another chance and he must not blow this opportunity. When he started out the door he said, "Cassie, could I see you again, perhaps Friday?"

She smiled and said, "Oh, TC, I would love that, but I'm spending Friday afternoon with Nancy Deemer. We should be back by five or six though."

"Well, how about if I came by about seven and we go have dinner somewhere?"

"That's great," she said. "I'll see you Friday."

Tom felt good about the evening. He whistled all the way to the Hoffman's. He really wished he had someone to confide in about Cassie. He wanted someone to give him some advice or maybe just listen. Sometimes it helped just to talk a situation out. He surely didn't want to make any mistakes and say the wrong thing to her and ruin his chances. He knew her well enough to know that she was strong and determined. It would be hard to deter her if she had her mind set, but somehow he must try.

"Oh, Lord, can I talk to you about this? Do you care about something like this? You said you even know how many hairs I have on my head, so isn't this at least that important? I know it is to me. Help me, Lord. I want this girl to be my wife. Can you help me?" Those words were even a shock to him. "My wife?" Tom repeated. Then he grinned and confessed to the Lord, "Yes, Lord, I do. I want this girl to be my wife."

When Tom returned to the ranch, he started toward the bunkhouse, but something caught his eye by the river. It was late, so he hadn't expected anyone to be down there. He decided he better have a look, so he headed in that direction. As he neared the river, he could see someone sitting on a large rock. Who would be down here this late? As he approached, he could hear the humming of a song. It was Davey's song. All the men whistled it or hummed it, so he still wasn't sure who it was.

"Davey! Is that you?" It was! He was humming his song again. That was great news.

"Hi TC. What are you doing down here so late? I thought you would be sawing logs by now."

"Just got home. I saw you down here and came to see who was river-watching. It sure is good to hear you humming that song."

"I've been working on some words for it. I can't just leave it hanging, now can I?"

"I should say not," Tom said as he gave Davey a pat on the back. "Well, let's hear it."

"Well, it's not finished but it starts this way. My heart is like a river. Can't be bound, it must be free. I haven't got any more yet, but I will," Davey promised.

"That's great! Keep it up. I want to hear the finished work."

"Thanks, TC. You will." Davey stood and they walked back to the bunkhouse together.

Tom spent the following Friday evening with Cassie, and the following Sunday afternoon, and the next Friday evening. This continued for several weeks. One Sunday afternoon, Tom invited Cassie to go horseback riding with him. He really wanted her to see the ranch, to see what he had done with it, and to love it like he did. Maybe she would be able to visualize herself living there. He hoped so.

They rode for miles. The hills were especially beautiful. To Tom's way of thinking, this was the most scenic place on earth. In his heart, it was a little piece of heaven. In the distance, they could see the cattle grazing on the hillside. The river was beautiful as it flowed around the ranch. The rushing water over the rocks sounded almost like music. This was the perfect setting. Wild flowers were everywhere. The sky couldn't have been more beautiful. Maybe I should propose to her today. But Tom almost choked just thinking about trying to get those words out. No, he had to do some planning on what to say. This was something he couldn't rush into. He must do it right. But surely she would fall in love with his land. She could not help loving all this beauty as he did.

They stopped and walked down close to the river to let the horses get a drink. Then they climbed on a large rock and sat looking at the river.

"It seems so lonesome out here," Cassie said.

"Lonesome!" Tom was in shock at the very idea. "It's not lonesome. I never feel lonesome on the ranch."

"Goodness! I didn't mean to upset you. I just meant it's so quiet and there's no one around for miles. Don't you miss people?"

Tom turned and looked into her eyes. "I miss you," he said. "I want you here all the time, Cassie." In his mind he was thinking, Oh you fool, you blew it! You opened your mouth and stuck your foot in. But he started something, so now he must finish.

"Cassie, I want more than anything in the world, for you to marry me. I know you don't feel about this place like I do, but you would in time. You couldn't live here long and not love it. Oh, Cassie, please say you will marry me. I love you, Cassie, and I'll do anything to make you happy."

"I don't know what to say, TC. I think I love you, too. But I have so many plans that are important to me. I don't think I can make that decision right now. I need to think about it, and pray about it, and talk it over with my parents. This isn't easy for me. I'm terribly honored. You're so sweet, and you have a beautiful, breathtaking place, but I'm not sure I'm the one to fill this role. Please, TC, let me think about it for awhile."

"I won't rush you, Cassie. I'll give you all the time you need. But I want you to know that the Lord and I have already been talking about this, and I'm sure you're supposed to be here. You might as well give in." He grinned as he gave her his hand to help her down from the rock. She smiled back in return, but gave no answer. He drew her close and brushed his lips against hers. "I love you, Cassie, and I always will."

They walked back to the horses and he held her horse as she mounted. They rode back to the corral in silence, both pondering the prospect of her becoming *Mrs. Marshall*. Tom took her home, and nothing more was said about it that afternoon.

Cassie spent the next two weeks in Tulsa. She had gone there to interview for the position at the Beacon Medical Tower. Tom's heart ached. Was this her answer? Well, he wouldn't give up. He would keep praying and keep hoping. This was where real faith came in.

Chapter 6

Cherokee

It was Monday morning and Clay, the new foreman, had just finished giving the crew their work assignments for the day, when a large truck pulling a horse trailer drove through the gate. The driver got out and yelled out to Clay.

"Are you Mr. Marshall?"

"No," Clay said. "Mr. Marshall spent the weekend at the Hoffman's and isn't back from town yet. He should be back most any time though. He said he'd be back this morning. What can we do for you?"

"My boss told Mr. Marshall about his wild horses. They are the finest you'll ever see. He sent six of them over for Mr. Marshall to look at. If he likes the looks of them, he has 44 more that he'll sell him for the price he quoted him in town the other day. I'll just wait here in the truck til he gets back."

"No need for that," Clay said. "Go on over to the cook shack. Cookie will give you a cup of coffee. You can sit in there and wait for Mr. Marshall. He'd use the whip on us if we left you out here in the truck. What's your name?"

"My name's Ben, Ben Cory. I'll take you up on that coffee. It'll be good to get in out of the sun for a little bit."

Clay walked over to look at the horses. "Well, you're right. Those are mighty fine looking animals. But you say they're wild? I'm not sure who around here could tame 'em and train 'em."

"Oh, that's all taken care of. Cherokee, who works for Mr. Jordan will come work for Mr. Marshall until they're trained. He's the best horse trainer in the country. I can't say he's too sociable with people though. He's an Indian. He feels like his people got a pretty raw deal. I think he's probably right, but he goes around with a chip on his shoulder all the time. He hardly ever talks, and won't answer any questions about himself—but like I said, as a horse trainer, he's the best."

Clay frowned and said, "Oh boy, that's all we need around here! Another grump!"

All the men seemed edgy and out of sorts since Rusty made his horrendous exhibition. It certainly was not the same without Davey's music. It seemed the enjoyable spirit they once had could not be recaptured. No one knew quite what to say. But there was plenty of work to keep everyone busy, so there wasn't much time for arguments or play.

Ben was talking with Cookie and swallowing his last sip of coffee when Tom walked in. He came over and shook hands with Ben and introduced himself.

"Just looked over your horses. You can tell Mr. Jordan it's a deal. If the rest of the horses look as good as these, I'll take 'em. And tell him his man can start working as soon as the horses are delivered."

"Cherokee will be here in the morning, and the rest of the horses can be delivered on Friday. Mr. Jordan said you and he would get together later to settle up." Ben started toward the door and then called back, "Oh, where do you want me to unload these horses?"

"I'll have Clay take you to the pasture we just fenced in for them. They should like it there. Plenty of water, lotsa shade and lotsa grass. It's a horse's heaven," Tom said with a big smile. They walked out together and headed toward the truck.

Cherokee arrived the next morning right on schedule. Everyone was a little surprised to see him drive up in a car though. They all expected to see him on horseback. He got out of his car and walked over to the group of men that were working on a gate that had a broken hinge. Ben had described him well. He had a frown on his face and just stood there without a word. Calvin saw him first and stuck his hand out to shake hands with him.

"I'm looking for Marshall," Cherokee said.

"Oh, TC! I'll see if I can find him." He headed toward the storage building. The other men introduced themselves and quickly learned that Cherokee wasn't interested in knowing anything about anybody, so they all went back to their gate repair.

TC came out shortly and had no more success than the others in conversation with Cherokee. He pointed him toward the horses, told him where the cook shack was, and told him to make himself at home. Cherokee grunted and headed toward the horses.

Tom shook his head and shrugged. "Nice guy," he spouted sarcastically.

Cherokee worked very hard the next few weeks and proved to be as skilled in his trade as Ben had predicted. He could train a horse quicker than anyone Tom had ever seen. It was almost as if he and the horses had a special understanding between them. But no matter how much anyone tried, no one could break through the barrier that separated them from Cherokee's world.

Cherokee was about halfway through training the wild horses when he got his belongings together one Friday evening, got in the car, and headed for home just as he had done every weekend. However, the following Monday Cherokee didn't return. Tom figured he just couldn't handle working there at the ranch anymore.

Tom waited a couple days and then gave Mr. Jordan a call to see if he knew why Cherokee hadn't returned. But Jordan hadn't heard from Cherokee since the day he sent him to the Marshall ranch.

One morning after everyone had gotten well into their work, Tom decided to drive over to Cherokee's place to check on him. When he got there, Cherokee came to the door but barely opened it. Tom said, "Cherokee, could we talk?"

"Can't work for you anymore, "Cherokee said.

"Did someone say or do something to offend you?" Tom quizzed. "You know we still need you. Was I not paying you enough?"

"No one offended me. You paid enough. I can't come." That was Cherokee's only reply.

"You surely must have a reason. Don't you think I deserve to know why you won't work for me anymore?" Tom implored.

"My wife, she is very sick. She is dying. I must stay with her," Cherokee said in a low voice, probably so that his wife wouldn't hear.

"Why don't you take her to a hospital? Maybe with good care she could get well. They have a cure for almost anything today," Tom said.

Cherokee could see the genuine concern in Tom's voice. He stepped out on the porch and closed the door so he could talk with Tom.

"My people don't have hospitals where I can take her, and I don't have any money to take her to yours. Besides your people wouldn't want to treat her." Cherokee's voice broke with his answer.

"Cherokee, give us a chance. We're not all as inhuman as you think. Let me help you. I'll get an ambulance for you, and we can take her to the hospital right away. Please, Cherokee," Tom said. "Let's give it a try."

After some persuasion, Cherokee agreed. Not that his views on Tom's people had changed, but he didn't want to lose his wife.

Tom contacted the best doctor he knew and made all the arrangements for Rheanna, Cherokee's wife, to be admitted to the hospital. During the next few weeks, Tom kept Cherokee on the payroll and continued to visit him and his wife at the hospital. Most all of the men at the ranch stopped in from time to time to let Cherokee know they cared. Tom and some of the others told Cherokee they were praying for his wife.

Cherokee was right about his wife's condition. The doctor said she was definitely in critical condition. She was in a coma when she arrived at the hospital. It was soon discovered that she had a tumor at the base of her skull. At first Cherokee was reluctant to let the doctors remove it, but he soon relented when they told him it was her only hope.

The surgery went well, but Rheanna's condition was very serious. The doctors weren't sure she would pull through. Days turned into weeks, and still there was little change. She remained in a coma and Cherokee became very discouraged. All of the hours spent at the hospital, not eating right, worrying, and not getting enough sleep had taken a toll on him. He was looking in poor health himself. Tom and the others were concerned about him. Cherokee worked only part time, just enough to make ends meet. The rest of the time he was at the hospital beside Rheanna.

One evening about 6 o'clock, Tom came in from putting fresh hay in the barn. He was tired and decided to call it a day. The phone rang. When he answered, the voice on the other end was one of a very excited Cherokee.

"TC, your prayers to your God have worked. Rheanna is awake. She is smiling, and the doctor says she will be okay. I thank you, my friend. I will be forever grateful to you."

"Don't be grateful to me, Cherokee. Let your gratitude go to God. Rheanna was in His hands."

Rheanna stayed in the hospital for another week before the doctor would release her, and only then if she had someone to look after her. Tom hired a nurse for her for the first few days. Her mother was also on hand. She watched everything the nurse did so that she could continue the care after the nurse had gone.

After two weeks, Cherokee returned to the ranch. He was most definitely a changed man. It was the first time any of the men had seen a smile on his face. He went to Tom inquiring what he might do for all Tom had done for Rheanna.

"Cherokee, just remember," Tom said, "there are good white men, there are good Indians. There are bad white men, there are bad Indians. There is one God who loves us all. Don't go around with a chip on your shoulder blaming all people for what a few bad people do. Let us be your friends. That's all I ask."

"Your God is good," Cherokee said. "I wish I knew your God."

Tom talked with Cherokee for nearly an hour explaining the Scriptures to him and telling him how God's Son had died for him. Tom and Cherokee finished by praying together and Cherokee invited Jesus into his heart. The men all watched from a distance and were all elated that Cherokee left knowing Tom's God.

In the days to come, Cherokee always joined the men in the cook shack and shared their jokes and discussions. It wasn't easy for him at first because he had always been a loner, but it didn't take him long to accept their friendship. It took a little longer to relate to their joking and teasing. But he had learned they meant well, so he just smiled and shook his head.

Chapter 7

Dream House Completed

Heavy rains came which brought construction to a halt. This gave Tom a chance to work on the house plans and make some changes Cassie had suggested. He wanted so much for her to love this house. Maybe if she loved the house, she could learn to love the land. There were times that he was certain that she loved him, but he knew she had reservations about the land—or maybe it was just her love for the city that drew her away.

Tom spent hours on the plans, adding storage space, taking out a hallway, rearranging the kitchen. Cassie's suggestions were good, he had to admit. They were definitely an improvement. He could hardly wait for Cassie to get back from Tulsa to see them on paper.

The weather continued to be uncooperative with the building plans. It rained for nearly a week. Tom called daily to see if Cassie had returned from Tulsa. Then one day Mrs. Layne said that Cassie wouldn't be coming home for awhile. She had taken a position at a doctor's office in Tulsa. Tom's heart sank. Was this her way of telling him that she wouldn't marry him? How could he win her heart with so much distance between them?

The next few weeks were difficult. No work was done on the house. Tom lost all enthusiasm about his dream house. He directed his efforts toward the cattle. Some of the herd had gotten lost. Tom and five of the men rode up in the hills in hopes of finding the strays. There was the dread of cattle rustlers. That would mean more trouble, people getting hurt, or possibly some even getting killed. He remembered that happening when his father was alive. Two men were killed and one man was shot in the leg and was never able to work again.

Tom and the other men rode for three days before spotting the strays down in a ravine. One of the steers was injured. There was no way to get the animal up the steep hill to shelter. Tom knew the hungry, prowling wolves would not pass up this opportunity for an easy meal, so as unpleasant as the task was, he had to shoot the steer. Then they drove the other strays back to the herd.

They were all hot and exhausted and very glad their work was completed. Autumn was drawing near, but the days were still very warm. The summer had been unusually hot. Everyone was anxious for cooler weather to come. Autumn days were always beautiful in Missouri, with the changing colors of the trees on the hillsides.

It was about 5:30 when they rode in. Tom dismounted and dropped down by a giant old oak. The others rode on up to the bunkhouse. It wasn't time for the dinner bell, so Tom thought he'd grab a quick nap. He had very little sleep this past week. As he sat there pondering his life and chewing on a piece of straw, he thought to himself, Who even gives a rip about this place? Who cares if there are 5,000 head of cattle or five? He knew his father would have cared, but he's gone. The work was just routine, almost drudgery. The joy was gone. The words *Press toward the mark ran through his mind.* "What is my mark?" Tom muttered. He pulled himself to his feet and gave the tree a hard kick. He groaned in pain. "Go ahead and break your fool toe! That won't bring her back."

It had been three weeks since Cassie left, and not a phone call nor letter had come. The ache in Tom's heart had not subsided. The work on the dream house had resumed, but he had no enthusiasm about its completion.

As Tom headed toward the cook shack, he heard a ruckus behind the tool shed. Josh, one of the newest hands, and Cal were in a fight. Josh Fuller was a big man with a hot temper. Tom had hired him only a month before and had reservations at the time about bringing him on the ranch. He sized him up to be trouble at the time, but Josh had come just at a time when another hand was badly needed. He looked like he could handle hard work, so Tom decided to go against his better judgment and give him a chance.

Cal had apparently been tormenting him, as he did everyone. Josh, however, was not amused. He had warned him to get lost, but Cal continued his teasing. Josh lost his temper and the fight began. When Tom arrived on the scene, Cal had been beaten almost to unconsciousness. Josh was holding his hair and pounding his head on the ground. Tom ordered Josh to stop, but his orders were ignored. Tom and two other men pulled Josh off Cal. He told him to meet him at the bunkhouse where he would receive his pay, gather his things, and be on his way.

They took Cal to the bunkhouse where they treated his cuts. He was in pretty bad shape. His eye was swollen and his nose was bleeding, perhaps broken. He was tough though. There was nothing wrong that wouldn't mend.

Tom was leaving the bunkhouse to go to the cook shack and talk with Cookie when he heard a car drive in. It was Cherokee. He hadn't seen him for quite awhile. He had thought about him a lot though, wishing for time to check on him and his wife and to see how they were getting along. Cherokee got out of the car and pulled a basket out of the back. With a huge smile on his face, he brought a bushel of apples for Tom and everyone at the ranch.

"Hey Cherokee. Good to see you. How've you been?" Tom greeted him with a big grin.

"Good. I have big news. Thanks to you, I'm going to be a father."

"Cherokee! Congratulations! That's great news. I'm so happy for you. How's Rheanna? And what do you mean by Thanks to me? How do you figure that?" Tom asked.

"If it weren't for you, I wouldn't even have a wife. Now, because of you, she's well and happy and going to have a baby." Cherokee was beaming.

"Her being well and happy had nothing to do with me, but I'm thankful that she is. And I'm sure happy about your baby. Hey, those apples are beauties. Thanks, Cherokee. Come on down to the cook shack and eat with us," Tom said.

"Sounds good, but Rheanna has dinner cooking and is expecting me home. Maybe I'll eat with you next time. I better go now. I just wanted you to know about the baby."

Tom started to go to the cook shack, but he looked over in the direction of the house and decided to look it over first. A lot had taken place on the house while Tom was gone. It was really starting to take shape. Probably another month and it would be finished. Tom scrutinized every inch. He was very pleased with the results. The carpenters were real craftsmen and had done a superb job. It was a beautiful place—if only he could share it with Cassie. His heart ached. He didn't feel like joining in the joking and conversation with the men tonight. He just wanted to be alone. He didn't feel like putting a smile on his face and he didn't want anyone to know how he really felt. He greeted Cookie and presented him with the apples that Cherokee had given him. Then he told Cookie not to expect him for dinner. He was going to get cleaned up and hit the sack. He was too tired to eat.

"You're not going to eat with us?" Cookie asked with a frown.

"Not tonight, Cookie. I'm just too tired. Besides, I have to get up early in the morning. I've decided to ride into town tomorrow and spend the day and night with Joe and Josie." Tom said. He knew he needed a caring ear on which to pour out his heart.

"Could I bring you a tray? You need to eat," Cookie pleaded.

"I won't go hungry, I promise. I held out on you and kept a couple apples. I'll see you when I get back. Thanks for the offer though," Tom said as he turned and walked out the door.

Cookie stopped him. "Wait, Tom. I didn't get a chance to tell you about your visitor."

"Visitor?" Tom said. "Who would that be?"

"Your little girlfriend rode in on her horse this morning. When she discovered you were gone, she looked through the house and then went back home."

"Cassie? She did?" Tom exclaimed. "I'll get cleaned up and drive over there."

"Well now! I don't know what happened to I'm too tired to eat and I'm going to hit the sack, but you sure lit up like a Christmas tree all of a sudden." Then he chuckled.

Tom just grinned, tipped his hat, and backed out the door.

While he was showering and getting dressed, he was wondering what Cassie would have to tell him. It might not necessarily be what he wanted to hear. He couldn't help being excited, though, just at the prospect of seeing her again.

Thoughts raced through his mind as he drove to her house. Would she be home? He hadn't even called before he left the ranch. Doe she want to see me as much as I want to see her? Will this be his last time to ever see her? Was it wrong to ask God to turn her heart toward me, and let her be my wife? Is that selfish? How could that be wrong? She's a good woman. God said He wants to give us the desires of our heart. Anyway, Tom couldn't help what was in his heart, and he couldn't hide it from God, so he was going to keep on asking.

The distance from the ranch to Cassie's home seemed longer than it had ever been before. When he reached her place, he jumped out of the truck and ran to the door. If she saw him and thought he was over anxious, well, he was. He rang the door bell and Cassie opened the door. She gave a squeal and threw her arms around his neck.

"Oh, TC, I'm so glad you came. I tried so hard not to contact you for one month. I thought I needed that much time to know the right answer. I also thought if I worked for a doctor, it would help me decide if that is what I wanted to do. But I couldn't stick it out for the whole month. I know now, that if you still want me, I want to be where you are. Even if it is away from civilization." She laughed and said, "I'm kidding about your ranch being away from civilization. I do love the city, but I love your ranch too. And the house is gorgeous. It's so big. I didn't realize that it would be so large when I saw the house plans. It's magnificent! But I'd be happy to live with you in your old tent that you told me about."

"Well, okay. I guess we could do that. We could use the big house for a bunk house for the hands." They both laughed and she threw her arms around his neck again. He gave her a swing around the room and suddenly Tom's world looked bright and beautiful again.

Tom thought this was probably the happiest moment in his entire life. He looked up and said, "Thank you Lord. Thank you Lord. Thank you Lord."

Tom had dinner with Cassie and her parents. They spent all evening making plans and sharing their past month's activities. They finally decided May would be the month for the wedding. Tom thought it should be sooner, but Cassie and her mother felt they needed that much time to make all the necessary plans.

Tom commented, "Plans? What plans? We know we're getting married, so let's go get the license and get married."

They all laughed at him. Even Cassie's dad joined in the laughter. He knew from past experience what a wedding entailed. Tom was a good sport about their teasing and soon gave in to their plan to have time for preparations.

The time passed more quickly than he had anticipated. There was much to be done on the ranch. The house was finally finished. Cassie spent much of her time decorating and putting on the finishing touches. Tom had decided he would not stay in the house until after the wedding. He wanted them to start out there together. Then it wouldn't be a house. It would be a home.

He spent a lot of time in the early fall planting perennials. The outside was beginning to look as beautiful as the inside. Jed helped him some, but then he had to return to college. Tom had to admit, he really missed him. Jed and Shirley dated frequently throughout the summer and then attended the same college. Before they left, he took her out to meet his mother. They hit it off immediately.

Picking the best man and the groomsmen were not easy decisions for Tom. He had sort of drifted away from those he once considered his best friends. Now he guessed his ranch hands were his best friends. They were the best bunch of men he had ever seen. Of course, it took some culling out to come up with this compatible group. He made the decision that Jed would be his best man. And, yes he was a man. He had proven that a number of times. He smiled when he thought back at his first impression of him. He sure seemed like a boy then, but he had matured a lot this past year. Davey would probably be his next choice. From there, it was a toss-up. They were all special. Maybe he would have everyone put their name in a pot and he would draw names. He had to decide soon. Cassie would not let him rest until he did.

Tom went through the house once again. Yes, it was a dream house, and it was finally complete.

Chapter 8

Queen for the Castle

The big day finally arrived. May 10, 1947, would be a date to remember forever. Tom was so nervous, he couldn't tie his tie. You would have thought every man at the ranch was getting married. They were all nervous. There was so much excitement. It was the first time some of the them had ever put on a suit.

Jed was Tom's best man. Brad, Kent, Calvin, and Jack were the groomsmen. Davey sang two songs he had written especially for this occasion.

The flower girl was Cassie's four-year-old cousin. She stole everyone's heart. She was a little doll. She sprinkled petals as she walked down the aisle, but if anyone smiled at her, she would walk over to them and present them with a petal. A couple of times, she got embarrassed at people's laughter. She stopped and put her arm over her eyes. After a moment she proceeded down the aisle with her head down. She was so precious.

Tom asked Joe and Josie to sit in the honored spot for his parents. It was very evident that Josie was touched with this special gesture. At one point, she cried just like a mother would. Tom had grown to really love them, and vice versa.

As Tom faced the people in the church, anxiously awaiting Cassie's appearance, his eyes roamed over the crowd. It looked as if everyone in the entire town was present. Cherokee and Rheanna were sitting in the third row. He was so happy they had come.

Then a hush fell on the crowd. The wedding march began. The crowd stood to their feet. Tom's heart pounded and he got a lump in his throat. Cassie appeared in the doorway. She looked like an angel, or maybe a queen. No one had ever looked more beautiful than she did in her long, white, chantilly gown with a long flowing train. But Cassie always looked beautiful, even in jeans and a flannel shirt.

As Cassie's father lifted her hand to him, Davey sang his beautiful song, "Two Hearts Become One." His voice rang out with a strength and clarity that seemed to captivate everyone.

Everything was going smoothly until Brad, with no advance warning, crashed to the floor. A couple of the men in the congregation ran up and carried him out. Brad had locked his knees and fainted. He got teased unmercifully about it when they all got back to the ranch. He apologized over and over to Cassie, but she just laughed and told him a great show always needs something to spice it up and make it more memorable.

Tom was overcome by the number of the gifts they received. He said, "I'm already getting the greatest gift, so why should they give me more?" Cassie squeezed his arm and smiled.

"Haven't you ever been to a wedding before, TC?" she asked.

"Well, no, I don't guess I have. I suppose it's a good thing I haven't, because I wouldn't have taken them a gift."

Tom and Cassie had a fabulous honeymoon. They spent ten glorious days in England. It had always been Cassie's dream to visit this grand old country, but never did she think it would become a reality. They took in all the sights, toured some old castles, and spent hours and hours sharing their hearts with each other. Cassie was so thankful. She knew the importance of a couple being able to impart their ideas, hopes, dreams, and innermost feelings—to be able to pray together—and to share even their fears.

Tom used the money he had set aside for a large herd he planned on buying from a rancher in Wyoming for the honeymoon. He didn't share that fact with Cassie though. There would be another herd at another time, if it were to be.

When they returned home, they were overwhelmed by the welcome they received. The ranch hands got together a little band from town to play for them as they drove through the gates. They had a huge banner across the gate saying "WELCOME HOME MR. & MRS. MARSHALL." They climbed on the roof of the new house and attached streamers everywhere, then filled the inside of the house with fresh flowers and fruit. When they saw them coming down the lane, they started the record player softly playing Always, then dashed out the back door.

Tom picked his new bride up and carried her over the threshold. When they entered their home and saw all that the men had done, they just stood in the doorway with their mouths open.

"Oh, TC! They are such dears. How thoughtful! They must have put in hours doing this. Oh, how beautiful!" Then she burst into tears.

Tom laughed at Cassie. Then he just walked around the house shaking his head.

"What a bunch of swell characters they are. I sure never would have expected this."

Shortly, they heard a knock at the door. It was Cookie carrying a silver tray with a matching silver cover. He grinned as he set it on the table. "Dinner is served, My Lady. If the Queen requires anything else, just ring." Then he bowed and went out the door.

They were stunned. Then they turned to each other and roared with laughter.

"Silver!" Tom exclaimed. "Now where do you suppose they got that?"

The dinner was delicious. Johnny was a gourmet cook. He could have been a chef in the finest restaurant in New York City; but no one could have loved him or appreciated him more than they did here at the ranch, and he certainly had needed that.

After the dinner, Tom turned to Cassie and said, "You are, you know. You are the queen of this castle, and the queen of my heart."

"Oh, TC, you are better than any Prince Charming that any girl has ever dreamed of."

Chapter 9

The City Beckons

Ranch life was certainly a new experience for Cassie. There was a lot to do taking care of her new home and her new husband. She wanted to be involved in everything he did, but there was so much to learn. Everyone on the ranch was very kind to her, but she still felt like an outsider at times.

Jed was out of school for the summer, so he came back to work at the ranch. Cassie really liked him. It was difficult to choose a favorite, for they were all special in different ways. No one would be surprised to hear in the near future that Jed and Shirley got engaged. She seemed to be all he talked about these days. Cassie hadn't met Shirley yet, but she must be something special. Tom had Jed working on the yard and flower beds all afternoon. He said it was something he had been planning to do for two years. That puzzled Cassie. Maybe he would explain it when he came in that evening.

When Tom came in later that afternoon, he handed Cassie a list. "Do you suppose you could get these things together for me. I have to go on a round-up to brand all the new calves. I probably won't be home for a couple days. I'll need to take these things with me."

Cassie collected everything Tom had on his list and had it all ready for him when he came in. She had hoped they would go riding together that afternoon, but certainly not to brand calves. She didn't want any part of branding little baby animals. That seemed so barbarian. She guessed she would have to busy herself around the house.

After Tom left, Cassie realized she had nothing left to do. She thought about all the exciting things there was to do in the city and a feeling of remorse came over her. Then she stood to her feet and exclaimed, "I will not sit here and feel sorry for myself. I'll go into town and visit with my mom and dad. They always lift my spirits."

Cassie had not seen her parents for a couple of weeks. She loved chatting with her mom and she missed her dad so much. She hurriedly got ready, gathered only the essentials and threw them in a suitcase. Then she jumped in the car and was on her way. She couldn't believe she was doing this. She used to plan everything she did in intricate detail, making lists and leaving nothing to chance. But here she was, no schedule or plan of any kind, with probably not half the things she needed to take with her, flying down the road in sheer delirium. This was definitely a new Cassie. Her mother would be delighted, but her father would be exasperated. He, too, was very meticulous in his planning, always having everything in order, all details itemized.

It was so good to see her parents again. Her dad had to leave shortly after she arrived, but she and her mom talked for hours. Her mother filled her in on all the latest happenings in town. Then she mentioned that she was going to Denver next week. Her face lit up as she said, "Cassie! I'd love to have you go with me. Do you think you could? We would have such fun."

"Oh, Mom, I'd love to go," she shrieked. Then her face fell. "I don't think I really can. I don't know how TC would feel about it. It's almost as if he's jealous of the city. He doesn't like me to talk about it or share all the things I love about it. I'll have to let you know later."

" Well, Cassie, I understand. He almost lost you to the city, you know."

"Not really, Mom. I think I knew from the beginning that I would choose TC."

"Yes, but he didn't know that. When he would call here while you were gone, there was a fear in his voice. It was very evident that he was afraid you might not return. Try to be understanding," her mother said. " Maybe it wouldn't be wise for you to go this time. There will be many other times, you know. Just give him time to feel secure in your love, Cassie."

"You're terrific, Mom. I wonder if TC knows just how fortunate he is to have a mother-in-law like you." Cassie sat staring at her mother in admiration.

"Of course he does," she said, laughing. "Why do you think he married you? It was to get me for a mother-in-law."

Cassie jumped up and gave her mom a squeeze. "Yep, I bet you're right. Let's go fix dinner. I'm starving."

They had a good visit. Cassie fired questions at her mom about everyone in town. Then when her dad came in, Cassie talked non-stop to him about everything that was going on at the ranch.

Cassie returned home the next morning. She felt she had made a wise decision, but she couldn't help longing to go. There was a special excitement in city life that could not be found at the ranch. The ranch was beautiful and peaceful, but so lonely. She loved all the ranch hands. It was like having a bunch of new brothers. But there were times she felt almost as if she were imprisoned. This was not something she could discuss with anyone though. She felt disloyal to TC even thinking this way.

But the simple truth was she did feel this way and didn't know what to do about it. Would this longing for the city ever go away? There was not even a remote chance TC would ever leave his precious land for city life. Cassie smiled as she said aloud, "Oh Cassie, are you as jealous of his land as he is of the city?"

When Tom returned, she told him about visiting with her mother. She also told him of her mother's invitation, hoping he would say, "Oh Cassie, you should go." But he didn't. He just sat there frowning. He finally said,"Cassie, if you want friends to visit with, you ought to go over and meet Rheanna, Cherokee's wife. I told you about them. She'll be having her baby soon. You would love her. It might be good for both of you."

"I will, TC. I would like very much to meet her," Cassie said. "In fact, I think I'll go first thing in the morning. Do you think I should call first? Oh, of course I should. What's the matter with me? I can't just pop in."

Tom squeezed her hand and smiled. As he stood to his feet, he said, "Well, I'm sure glad I got you straightened out on that question." Then he walked out the door.

After Tom had gone, Cassie leaned back on the sofa and twisted a piece of her hair in her fingers while she thought about the advice her mother gave her. Just give him time to feel secure in your love, she had said. That's what I've got to do. She couldn't let Tom know how much she longed for city life. He had undergone so much hurt the past two years. She was determined she would never add one iota of unhappiness for him.

Cassie woke up the next morning exuberant about the prospect of visiting with Rheanna. She finished her chores as quickly as possible and packed some things she wanted to take to her. She had baked some banana bread and cookies and she packed a jar of jam her mother had given her. She would wait to get a gift for the baby until its arrival. Maybe she could give Rheanna a baby shower. She was electrified as she thought about that possibility. Her mother had given many showers. She could give her some pointers.

When Cassie called Rheanna, she said she would be delighted to have her come. Rheanna had such a soft, sweet voice. Cassie decided if she were anything at all like she sounded on the phone, she would love her.

When Cassie arrived, she was pleasantly surprised at the loveliness of the little home. It was so well cared for. The yard was beautiful with flowers in bloom in strategic locations all around the house. She could see part of a vegetable garden behind the house where plants were beginning to break through the ground. Even the well at the side of the house was adorable. It was bricked with a roof over it that matched the roof on the house. Cassie wasn't sure what she had expected, but it wasn't anything as lovely as this. The dwelling was a white frame house with tan shutters that looked like it came directly from a storybook.

Cassie started to knock on the door, but Rheanna opened the door before she could.

"Oh, Cassie! I'm so happy you came. Please come in. I've been so eager to meet you." She had on a blue checked gingham dress with lace on the bodice and a full skirt. Her hair was shiny jet black, very long and straight. Cassie saw her at the wedding, but didn't remember her being this pretty. TC had said she was soon to have a baby, but it was barely evident, perhaps because of the dress she was wearing.

Rheanna motioned for Cassie to go into the living room. There were two large overstuffed chairs, a small rocker, a rather worn sofa, and several tables of various shapes and sizes. The floors were hardwood with braided rugs throughout the room. Everything was neat and clean. Although there was nothing elaborate about this home, Rheanna definitely had a knack for decorating. The tables were covered with crocheted doilies, and there were knick-knacks and handiwork everywhere.

"Rheanna, your home is beautiful. Did you make all of these lovely doilies? You must be a very talented lady."

"Thank you. I did make them, but that doesn't take talent. They're very simple patterns" .

"I think you are too modest. They certainly don't look simple to me. I admire anyone who can crochet and sew. I've tried my hand at sewing, but I never did attempt crocheting. That's something I must learn to do."

Rheanna smiled. "Maybe I could teach you. I would love to do that."

"Oh, would you? I would be forever grateful."

Rheanna immediately began telling her what she needed to buy to begin her new craft. She said she would also teach her to knit. Cassie made a list of everything she needed and hoped to get started on it very soon. Cassie was so excited about the prospect of being able to decorate her new home with things she made herself. She could hardly wait to start on a project.

They talked about many things: recipes, flowers, their childhood, and families. Rheanna was a most interesting lady. Cassie was so glad she had gotten to know her. She felt they would become good friends.

During their conversation, Cassie learned that Rheanna had just one month to wait before her baby was due. That would mean that the baby would arrive in July. She showed Cassie the room she had prepared for the nursery. It was adorable. She had wallpapered the walls with hobbyhorse paper and had a little rocking horse sitting in the corner of the room. It had belonged to Cherokee when he was a little boy. Rheanna didn't really say so, but it was pretty evident that both she and Cherokee were hoping for a little boy.

Rheanna fixed a simple, but delicious lunch. It was nearly 2 o'clock before Cassie left. Before she went home, she drove into town to buy the things she needed for her new hobby. She could hardly wait to get started. It would be a feeling of accomplishment to beautify her home with things she had made instead of with things purchased in a store.

As she was driving home, she wondered what it would be like if she and TC were to have a baby, but she quickly concluded that she was not ready for that yet. She really wanted to wait a couple more years to start their family.

That evening, as she was cooking dinner, she got to thinking about her new hobby and tried to decide what to crochet first. She got the pattern book out of her sack and began to search for her first creation. Perhaps she could make something for Rheanna's baby.

All of a sudden she realized that something was burning. "Oh, my dinner!" she exclaimed. "Oh no! It's ruined." She had wanted this dinner to be special. It was a recipe Rheanna had given her. What could she do now? There was no salvaging any of it. Just about that time there was a knock on the door. "Wouldn't you know it. Why did anyone have to come now with this horrible smell and all the smoke in the house." She was so upset, at the point of tears.

Cassie opened the door to see Kent, all smiles, holding a little puppy. "Thought you would like to see my little cutie. Isn't he a honey? He's going to be my tough protector and helper with the cattle," he said as he looked at the chubby little ball of fur in his arms. He then looked up at Cassie and realized something was wrong. "Are you okay, Cassie?" he said. "Can I help? Do you want me to call TC?"

"Oh, no! Don't call TC. I don't want him in here yet." Then she burst into tears.

Kent set the puppy down and put his arm around her, trying to console her without a clue what the problem was. "What is it, Cassie?" he asked. "What can I do?"

"Oh, Kent. I burned my dinner, and TC will be coming home soon."

Kent had to laugh. "Is that all."

"Is that all?" She stormed. "Is that all?" Then she started sobbing again and ran into the bedroom and shut the door.

Well, this was a new experience for Kent and he had no idea how to fix it. He walked over to the cook shack where Johnny was busy with something that smelled like heaven. He relayed what had happened and asked him what he could do. Johnny laughed too, but he told him he had a solution.

Cassie went back to the kitchen and was in the process of cleaning up the charred remains of what she had hoped would be a delicious dinner, when she heard another knock on the door.

"Now who!" she said in a disgusted tone. She jerked the door open to see Johnny holding a large basket.

"Your dinner, Ms. Cassie. Kent told me of your dilemma. I hope this will help."

She smiled and said, "Cookie, you're an angel of mercy. How sweet and how very thoughtful." Then, realizing the humor of her previous actions, she began to laugh. Johnny joined in with her, and they laughed together.

"I'll bet Kent thinks I'm a number one dope. I'll probably never live this down."

Johnny came into the kitchen and helped her get everything on the table. He said, "If it will make you feel any better, you might like to know that I burn something at least twice a week."

Cassie grinned and said, "Do you cry about it?" Then they laughed again.

"Well, I might if I was a new bride." Again they laughed and he left her with her new dinner.

When Tom sat down to dinner, he complimented her on her good stew and told her it was better than Cookie's stew. She just smiled in acknowledgment, but thought to herself that for now this would be her and Cookie's secret.

The next afternoon, she walked over to the tool shed where Kent was working. "I apologize for the lack of enthusiasm I displayed over your precious little puppy. Could I see him? You did say it was a little male, didn't you? Oh, and I wanted to invite you over for dinner some time. We'll have scorched roast, charred potatoes, smoked corn, and yams seasoned with soot. I'm an expert with that menu." She grinned as she waited for his reply.

"Yummm, I can hardly wait," he said. Then he motioned for her to follow him. "Cowboy is in the shed. Come take a look." The little puppy was sleeping in a pile of straw, whimpering as if he was having a bad dream. Cassie knelt beside him and patted him gently.

"Ah, poor baby. Did they leave you all by yourself?" He opened one little eye and then snuggled down in the straw to finish his nap.

Kent said, "Now don't you baby him. He's got to learn to be a tough, hard worker."

Calvin stuck his head in the door and said, "Ha, that's rich. He slept with you last night and you talked baby talk to him all night."

Kent gave Calvin a shove out the door and slammed the door. "One of these days, I'm going to have one less cousin."

Cassie smiled as she walked toward the door. "He's an adorable puppy, Kent. Accept my apology about last night?"

"No apology is necessary. I'm just glad to see you're back to your old spunky self."

She waved and then headed toward the cook shack to thank Johnny and tell him what a lifesaver he was, and how delicious his stew was.

Chapter 10

Horror At Rocky Canyon

It was a beautiful morning. The sun was just coming up and the eastern sky was ablaze. The smell of bacon and freshly brewed coffee came wafting into the bunkhouse. One by one the men began to stretch and yawn. With the aroma of breakfast calling, it didn't take them long to gather at the cook shack.

There was a new excitement in the air. Today was the day the new herd would arrive. Nine hundred head of beautiful black Angus would soon be roaming the hills and grazing on the picturesque pastures. This was a dream come true for TC. He had worked toward this day for months. The men had put in countless hours mending old fences and putting in new fencing. Now it had finally arrived. He could remember when the whole thing had been a nightmare; but the more he worked, and the more he accomplished, the more he grew to love the land, just as his father had.

The herd was being shipped in by rail. Ten hands would meet the train to drive the herd in. Some of the men would be riding the newly trained stallions that represented Cherokee's hard work. Although Cherokee's work was complete, he was going to be on hand to watch the great event. Everyone was jubilant. It was long past the expected time for the arrival of the herd at the ranch. There was much to be done, but no one wanted to venture too far away and miss seeing the new herd enter the gate. Evidently the train was late.

A blue pickup pulled in the gate. The men didn't recognize it and thought it was probably someone who wanted to look over the new herd. TC came out of the cook shack with a cup of coffee in his hand. He also saw the truck drive in and walked on out to see who it was.

"Hi ya, Ben," he said. "What brings you out our way? We sure do like the horses I bought from you. They all turned out to be good ones."

"Well, I'm not here to see the horses, and I'm not here to be the bearer of good news today. Little Dustin Tomkins is missing. You know Jim and Reba, don't you? Their little nine-year-old son has been missing since yesterday afternoon. We have the whole town searching for him. I doubt he would have come this far, but could you have your men look around your place, just in case? There are a lot of things around here that would draw a young lad. I sure hope he stays away from the river, but you know how boys love the water. I really don't think anyone has kidnapped him. We've never had anything like that happen around here, and there haven't been any strangers in town. His mom said he was out riding his bicycle, and he just never came home."

Tom pushed his hat back and frowned. "We sure will look for him, Ben. There are a lot of dangerous places around here. I just hope he didn't come out this far."

Tom rang the immense dinner bell to call everyone in. All the men came running, knowing that sound meant something was urgent, since it wasn't time to eat. Each man was given a designated area to search. Tom took Randy, Jered, and two of the new men and rode up Banner Creek. Kent and Cal rode to what they recently named Crooked Oak Pass. Davey, Clay, and Cherokee rode down to Rocky Canyon. Brad and Johnny took Billy Joe (who was also a new man) and they rode up the river. None of these places would be safe for a boy, but any one of them would be intriguing and could entice one to explore. When Cassie heard the news, she immediately went into town to be with Reba. They had been good friends for a long time.

Tom instructed everyone that if they found the boy they were to fire two shots. When the two shots were heard, everyone should return to the corral.

When the men rode in with the new herd, there was no one to greet them. Dale, Dennis, Pokey, and Gene rode in first. Carl, Jake, Bo, Caleb, Mark, and Big John rode in behind the herd. They were puzzled by the absence of the men, because when they left, the whole place was buzzing with excitement about the new herd. Since no one was around, they drove the herd on out to pasture through the east gate.

"This is one lucky bunch of cattle," Dale said. "Look at that green grass. That is, if you call getting fattened up for the kill lucky."

Two men stayed with the herd. The rest went back to the bunkhouse. They were all trying to figure out where everyone was and what was going on, when they heard two gunshots. They all ran outside to check it out. Shortly, some of the men came riding in. They explained about the disappearance of little Dustin. They weren't sure who fired the shots, nor from what direction they came.

Dustin was riding his bicycle and had gone farther away from home than he intended. He saw a trail that looked fascinating. He was just going to ride a short distance down the trail and then turn around and go home. However, the trail was winding and had several turn-offs. He made a wrong turn and became quite lost. He rode for hours looking for his way back home. Night came and he couldn't see where he was going, so he leaned his bike against a tree and curled up on the ground. He was tired, but far too scared to sleep. He dozed a little, but for the most part, he spent a long sleepless night, shivering and crying, listening to every little movement in the night.

When the sun came up, the sky was ablaze. He ventured out again, trying to remember his way home. He wound up at Rocky Canyon. It was a gorgeous place, but very dangerous. He laid his bike down and walked to the edge to get a closer look at the canyon—while unknowingly, he was being watched by a cougar. When he heard the terrifying howls and shrieks of the cougar behind him, he tried to run. The loose rocks under his feet rolled and he started slipping over the edge. He fell down and landed on a larger rock beneath him. (Fortunately, it was there to catch his fall.) Dustin was screaming and yelling at the cougar. He tried throwing rocks at the hungry animal, but that didn't deter him. The wall was too steep and the rock too small for him to move, which is the only thing that saved him from the cougar.

Dustin stayed perched on that rock, crying and trembling for over an hour when he heard men's voices and horses coming in his direction. He was so scared, he could barely get his voice to make a sound. When he did, he wasn't loud enough for the men to hear. Finally, he just screamed as loud as he could. They heard him, found him, but now what? They couldn't get down to him.

Finally, Davey said, "I'm going to tie this rope around my waist. You let me down slowly. When I give you the word, pull us up."

Davey eased himself slowly over the jagged rocks. He hoped the rope would hold him. It was a good rope, but it was being sawed through by the rough edges of the rocks.

Finally, he reached Dustin. When he was sure he had a tight hold on him, he yelled for Clay and Cherokee to pull them up. When they got close to the top, Clay reached down and pulled Dustin to safety. Just as Dustin was lifted up, the rope snapped and Davey crashed to the rocks below. He didn't fall to the bottom, but he fell much further than Dustin had. His body lay lifeless on the rocks. Cherokee went back to the ranch for a longer rope and more help, while Clay stayed to watch over Davey and Dustin. When Cherokee returned, he insisted on being the one to go down after Davey.

"Cherokee, do you know what you're doing? That's very risky. You have a wife to think about, you know, and she's going to have a baby," Clay said.

"I know what I'm doing. I've been climbing these hills since I was a boy. Besides, you have a wife, too."

Cherokee attached the rope to himself and quickly rappelled down the rocks. Clay had to admit, he could not have done it so quickly nor as well.

"Hold the rope tight while I lift Davey." Cherokee gently lifted Davey over his shoulder. "Okay," he yelled. "But go easy. He's still breathing, but he's in bad shape."

Davey was unconscious in the hospital for three weeks. One morning he opened his eyes, in a weak voice he called for Rusty. They brought Rusty to the hospital as quickly as possible. Rusty leaned over his bed and said, "Hey, Davey boy. You did a great job. Dustin is okay. He'll grow up to be a fine man because of you. We miss you at the ranch. Hurry up and get well."

Davey gave a faint grin and said, "My song is in the drawer in the bunkhouse. Sing it for me, will you? I finished it yesterday." He had no idea that he had been in the hospital for three weeks. "I was going to sing it for you, but I...." and his eyes closed.

The nurse looked at Rusty and shook her head. "No! No! Not Davey! It should have been me," Rusty yelled. He sat down in the chair next to the bed with his arms on his knees and his head on his arms and cried like a baby. He stayed there until they made him leave. He took Davey's death harder than anyone. He went back to the bunkhouse and searched for Davey's song. He found it written on a paper sack in his drawer. Rusty grinned and said, "That's my Davey."

Rusty sang Davey's song at his funeral. It was very hard for him, but it was beautiful. There wasn't a dry eye in the room. A few weeks later, Rusty had someone write the music on paper and then had the song engraved on Davey's tombstone. He gave a copy of the song to every hand on the ranch and, of course, to Tom and Cassie.

Chapter 11

Little Gray Eagle

It was a beautiful October afternoon. Cassie was walking down by the river, watching the wild geese fly south for the winter. Tom was going to be in late tonight. He told her when he left that morning not to expect him before 8 o'clock. They found some cattle down by the old stone bridge, which meant that somewhere a fence was down. Tom took Curly Frazier with him to repair the fence. Curly was Jed's classmate. He came with Jed in the spring to work at the ranch. He decided that school was not for him, so he stayed on to work until December. Then he was going to Illinois to be with his family. Cassie wasn't sure if he would be coming back to the ranch or not. He was the type that always did things on the spur of the moment. He never had a plan or reason for anything. It was amazing that he even knew what he was going to do in December.

The wind picked up. Cassie's hair was blowing in her face, so she pulled it back into a pony tail and then sat down on the big rock. The days were still very warm, so the breeze felt wonderful on her face. The sun was beginning to set and the reflection on the water was breathtaking. As she sat gazing at the beauty, she felt like she was in another world. She couldn't help being thankful that Tom was going to be late tonight. What if she had missed this dazzling sight! Was it this gorgeous every night? She and TC would have to bring a picnic down here occasionally and watch the sunset together. There was so much beauty in the world and very few people saw it or appreciated it. Well, she was going to make it a point to see more of the beautiful things around her.

As she watched the river, she began to think about Davey and his song. Poor, sweet, Davey! His life had been cut so short. "Well, I guess *poor* certainly doesn't apply to him now. I'll bet he's up there singing with the angels. *My Heart is Like a River, can't be bound, it must be free.* Now he is really free. And now he can even sing with his brother. Maybe they can play their harmonicas together. Oh, I hope Davey's brother knew the Lord, the way Davey did," Cassie said aloud. Then she began to hum Davey's song. The song didn't apply to her. Her heart wasn't free. She was happy about that, too.

Cassie still loved the city, but it didn't compare to this beautiful, wonderful ranch. I'm beginning to sound like TC, she thought. That brought a smile to her face. TC tried to appear tough and hard, but that was only on the surface. He was sweet, gentle, and very thoughtful. She couldn't begin to explain to him how very much she loved him. I hope he is secure in my love now, she thought. The sun was gone for the day, but she couldn't bring herself to leave this beautiful spot. She listened to the sound of the water as it splashed on the rocks. Yes, she loved this place. The city no longer had a hold on her. She was content in this peaceful, wonderful place. Could the Garden of Eden have been any more beautiful?

"Well now, look who's down here serenading the fish. My, how pretty you look, little Cassie, sitting here in the moonlight," said a voice behind her.

"Oh, Curly," Cassie gasped. "You startled me. Where's TC?"

"He'll be along in a little while. He sent me on ahead with some instructions for the men. I saw you sitting down here and thought you'd like to know what's going on."

"Thanks, Curly, now you'd better take the instructions on to the men." Cassie said curtly.

"Trying to get rid of me so quickly? Curly said, grinning. "Don't you like compliments? I thought all women liked to hear how pretty they are?"

"I do like compliments from my husband, but not from strange men," she snapped.

"Am I so strange, Cassie? Maybe you wouldn't think I was so strange if you got to know me better," Curly said as he walked closer.

"I refuse to pursue this conversation any further," she said, as she stood and brushed her clothes off. "I think you had better leave."

"Does this mean I'm fired?" he inquired.

Cassie stopped and turned toward him with a deep frown on her face. "We'll take that up with TC," she said. "Or maybe it would be better if you just decided that you wanted to see how lovely Illinois is in October. Don't make trouble, Curly!" Then she ran up to the porch, leaving him to contemplate his choices.

Cassie was filled with anger. Why did he have to spoil such a perfect evening? Should I tell TC about Curly's conversation? She felt she had handled it very well, so there was probably no point in upsetting TC. I'll just wait and see if Curly leaves, she thought as she entered the house.

She started toward the refrigerator to prepare a little snack for TC and herself. All of a sudden, she felt very dizzy. The next thing she remembered, she was lying on the sofa with a cold, wet cloth on her head. TC was kneeling beside her, patting her hands, and calling her name. What on earth had come over her? She had never fainted in her life. TC was very concerned.

"Cassie, I want you to make an appointment with Dr. Grayson the first thing in the morning. Promise me that you will."

"I'm fine, TC, really."

"Okay, I'll call him myself," he growled.

"Oh, TC, I don't think it's necessary, but I'll call him if it will make you happy," she snapped.

TC bent down and kissed her on the forehead, then went into the kitchen to finish the snack that Cassie had started. The next morning, before he went out the door, he reminded her again. She promised him that as soon as the doctor's office was open, she would call for an appointment.

The receptionist at the doctor's office said they had a cancellation that afternoon, and she could come in at 2 o'clock. Cassie thought that would work out great. Then she could stop in and see how Rheanna was and show her how her sweater was coming along. Her crocheting still was not as neat as Rheanna's, but she was improving, and she loved every minute of it. This was her third creation. She had started with a very simple doily, then a scarf. She had graduated to a sweater, which was much more difficult. She had some problems with it at first, but now it was coming along pretty well. Cassie tried to stop in and check on Rheanna at least twice a week. It was only three weeks until her baby was due. Cassie was almost as anxious for the arrival of their baby as Rheanna was. Their visits were the highlight of Cassie's week.

That evening as she was waiting for TC to come in, she was pondering what the doctor had said to her. She had not been at all prepared to hear his words.

"Cassie, my dear, you're going to have a baby. You have some problems, though, and you must take it very easy. I want you to get a lot of rest. I will have the nurse write down some instructions for you to follow. You pay attention, Cassie, if you want to carry this baby."

"Pregnant? That can't be! We were going to wait a couple years before we started our family," she said.

"I hope you are not unhappy about having this baby, Cassie. Your state of mind has a lot to do with having a safe, full term pregnancy. Evidently, God thought this was the perfect time for you to start your family. Let Him plan your life, Cassie. He always knows best."

She smiled at the doctor, but inside she wanted to cry. She wasn't ready to be a mother. She didn't want to tell anyone about the baby, not even TC. This isn't the way a new prospective mother is supposed to feel. She felt guilty that she couldn't find some joy in her heart about the baby. Cassie was so upset, she didn't even stop in to see Rheanna. When that fact occurred to her she thought, At least our babies can be playmates. Maybe this will be easier after I talk with Rheanna.

After dinner TC said, "Okay, out with it. What did Dr. Grayson have to say? You did go, didn't you?"

"Of course I did. The doctor said we're going to have a baby." Cassie didn't know what his reaction would be.

Tom jumped up from his chair and pulled her up to him. "Cassie, that's wonderful. We'll have to work on a name for him." He was laughing as he swung her around the dining room. She wished she could share his exuberance, but maybe it would come. She hoped she could hide her feelings from him for the present time.

The next morning Cassie decided to go talk with Rheanna. She probably should go tell her mother the news, but she wasn't ready for that. She drove about halfway to Rheanna's house when a strange feeling came over her, much like what had happened night before last. She stopped the car and got out to get some fresh air, but again she fainted. Fortunately, Mrs. Cory and her daughter-in-law, Corine, came by.

Mrs. Cory stayed with Cassie, while Corine went to call an ambulance. Cassie vaguely remembered being lifted into the ambulance. When she woke up, there were nurses around her.

"Your doctor will be here shortly," said one of the nurses, named Dorothy. "You'll be fine. Just rest until he comes." Just as she said that, Dr. Grayson walked into the room.

"Dr. Grayson, could I call TC?" Cassie asked.

"Not to worry, my dear. Mrs. Cory has already called him. I imagine he's on his way. Cassie, you're going to be fine, but you've lost the baby. I was afraid this might happen."

Cassie began to cry. She felt so guilty because she hadn't wanted this baby. Is that why God took it? she wondered. She was so sorry she felt that way. Poor TC! He was so happy about the baby. This would be difficult for him.

"Oh, I must call Rheanna! She's expecting me. She'll be wondering what happened. "

One of the nurses who was standing close by said, "If you have her number, I'll call her for you."

Dr. Grayson took Cassie's hand and smiled. "Now, Cassie, I'm going to give you something to help you rest. You quit worrying about everything now, you hear?"

"Okay, but can't I go home?"

"No. We need to keep you here at least until tomorrow. Then you can probably go home." He patted her hand and walked out the door.

The doctor met TC in the corridor and told him what happened. He also told him that she should not try to have another baby very soon. After hearing all the doctor had to say, he went in to see Cassie. Her eyes were red from crying, but her tears had stopped. She smiled at TC.

"I'm so sorry, TC," she said. "I know how happy you were about this baby, but we'll have another one."

Tom started to tell her what the doctor had said, but then thought better of it. She didn't need to know that news just now. Instead, he said, "You just recuperate for awhile, and then we'll talk about it."

The next few weeks passed slowly for Cassie. She temporarily lost interest in crocheting, and she didn't want to visit Rheanna for awhile. She knew that she needed to go over there soon though. Rheanna had come to see her the day after she got out of the hospital, but it wasn't easy for her. She had to come when Cherokee was home, because they had just one automobile. And, too, it was almost time for her baby to be born.

The first day of November brought a cold rain. Cassie decided this would be a good time to organize her pictures and put them into albums. She wished she had some pictures of TC when he was a little boy. All of his pictures had been destroyed in the fire. He didn't think they had many anyway. Her mother had given her a box full of pictures taken when she was a little girl. TC came in while she was pasting pictures and built a fire in the fireplace. He sat down with her and began looking through the pictures with her. They first looked at their wedding pictures. They had a good laugh when they came to the pictures of Brad, remembering how he had fainted during the ceremony. When they finished with the wedding pictures, Cassie said, "TC, I think we had the most beautiful wedding I've ever seen."

"Of course we did. That's because the bride was the most beautiful girl in the world."

"Oh yeah? Well, look at your beautiful bride here." She showed him a picture taken after she had fallen into some newly poured concrete when she was three years old. She was screaming as they hosed her down with the garden hose.

"That's my Cassie, always into some kind of mischief." She whacked him with a book and they both laughed.

They looked at another handful of pictures and then TC said, "Cassie, I think I'd better leave, or you won't get your project finished. We'll just stay here and look at pictures all day."

"Just one more, TC, Look at this. This is my baby picture. Do you think our baby would have looked like this?" Tears came to her eyes. "I wish we would have given our baby a name. Let's do that, TC."

"Well, how could we name our baby? We don't even know if it was a boy or a girl."

"We could pick out a name that would fit a boy or a girl. There are a lot of names like that."

"Okay, Cassie. But if we're going pick out a name, let's give it some serious thought and prayer."

"Let's each make a list, and then compare. If we have any duplicates, we'll choose from those. Okay?"

"Good idea. Tomorrow night we will have a naming ceremony."

Cassie immediately put the pictures away and started on her list. She started with Tommy–i, Billy–ie, Carol, Jacky–i, Micah, Sammy–i, Jerry–Gerri, Jimmy, Gene–Jean, Joe–Jo. Then she sat in a daze, thinking about whether or not she would know this baby in heaven, and know it as her child. She no longer could think of names, so she put her list away.

The next evening after dinner she asked Tom (thinking that he had forgotten), "Shall we have our naming ceremony now?"

"Just a minute. I'll go get my list," he said.

They exchanged lists. On his list was Tony, Barry, Bobby, Marian, Carman, Willie, Johnny, Chris, and Jackie. Tom was the first one to speak. "The only duplicates on our lists are not names that I would want to name our baby."

"Well, which one of your names do you like best?" asked Cassie.

"Actually, it's not one of my names. It's Micah. I never thought of that, but I really like that name. What do you think? And what do you think about Jo for a middle name, for Joe and Josie?"

"I like that name very much," she said. "Our baby's name is Micah Jo. TC, do you think I'll get to hold Micah someday?"

"I really don't know the answer to that, Cassie. Perhaps Micah will be grown when we get to heaven. Guess we'll have to wait and see."

"I have something for you, Cassie." He went into the other room and came back with a piece of paper rolled up with a ribbon on it, and in the other hand, a rose. He handed them both to her.

When Cassie unrolled the paper, tears came to her eyes. She threw her arms around Tom and said, "You are the best father in the world. I know Micah will love you." The paper was parchment that Tom had engraved at the print shop earlier today. They both signed it and printed the baby's name on the certificate.

On this day, November 2, 1947,
our precious baby is hereby given the name

Micah Jo Marshall

With everlasting love
from your Mommy and Daddy
Thomas Colbert Marshall
Cassandra Lynn Marshall

They signed the parchment, and Cassie gently put it in a box with their marriage certificate and some other treasured belongings. This would always be a special day they would remember forever.

The next morning, they woke to the sound of the telephone. Cassie looked at the clock. It was 5am.

"Who could be calling this early?" she asked. It was rather frightening to receive a call this early.

Tom answered the phone. "Hello....Well, good morning to you, Cherokee. What's up?....Is that right?...Well, congratulations!....That's wonderful. I'll tell Cassie. We'll be over there after we get up and about....Give Rheanna our love and congratulations....Bye." As soon as Tom hung up the phone, Cassie shrieked, "Rheanna had her baby?"

"Yes, and Cherokee is so excited, he could hardly talk. We need to eat right quick and go on over to the hospital."

"I'm so excited, I don't know if I can eat," Cassie said.

This was the most hurried breakfast they ever had. As they drove to the hospital, it was misting rain. Cassie thought the windshield wipers were in complete agreement with her. They seemed to be saying, "Hurry up, hurry up, hurry up, hurry up."

Rheanna was not completely awake when they walked into her room. She gave a faint smile and then dozed off.

Cherokee said, "Did you see the baby? We named him after you, Tom. His name is Thomas Leroy Love. His Indian name is Little Gray Eagle. That is a good name. He will be strong and mighty." When I looked out the window this morning, there was an eagle flying in the sky. It is very unusual for an eagle to be in the city. It is a sign that our baby will have the qualities of an eagle.

"Cherokee, I am so honored," Tom said. "I don't know what to say. We haven't seen the baby yet. We came directly to the room. Maybe we could go now while Rheanna is resting." Cassie bent and kissed Rheanna on the cheek before they left.

Cassie thought Little Gray Eagle was the most beautiful baby she had ever seen. He also had more hair than she had ever seen on a baby, and it was jet black. She could hardly wait to hold him; but, of course, she would have to wait until he went home.

"Cherokee, I know your Christian name is William Francis Love, but what is your Indian name?" Cassie asked.

"It is Running Deer. I was born on the back of a wagon as my mother and father traveled from Kentucky to Wyoming. My father saw a deer running across the trail. So I was called Running Deer."

"Oh, Cherokee, that's a great name. Deer have so many fine characteristics, and they are so beautiful."

They stayed with Cherokee until nearly noon and talked a little to Rheanna when she occasional opened her eyes. Then they headed back to the ranch.

"Oh, TC, didn't you just fall in love with Little Gray Eagle? What a precious little family," Cassie said.

Tom's only remark was, "Little Gray Eagle? Little Tom!"

Chapter 12

Roses For Cassie

The time passed so quickly. It seemed like only yesterday when little Gray Eagle was born. And now he was taking his first steps. He refused to try at first. Then Cassie put a toy in his hand and he took his first step. He felt secure if he held onto something.

"Rheanna, he gets more beautiful every day. His hair is so black, it's almost blue. I guess I'll have to start saying handsome, instead of beautiful, when he gets a little older. He was a chubby baby, full of smiles, with a deep dimple that went on display with every grin. His hair was a little unruly, but he was an all around, adorable baby.

TC walked in just in time to see him fall and start to cry. When he saw TC, his smiles surfaced again. He immediately started crawling toward him. He loved TC.

"Hi Buddy. How's my boy?" Little Gray Eagle reached his chubby little arms up to TC. "Let's go ride our horsey, Buddy," and out the door they went.

After they were gone, Cassie sighed and said, "TC sure wants a little boy, Rheanna."

"I'm sure it will happen. Just be patient, Cassie."

They went over to the window and watched as Uncle TC and Little Gray Eagle rode Lightning all around the corral. Little Gray Eagle laughed and shrieked with joy. He started to cry when he had to get down.

"Uncle TC has work to do, Buddy. You're going to have to go see Aunt Cassie. We'll ride again next time."

"Here, TC. I'll take him," Rheanna said. "We need to be going. I hadn't planned on staying this long."

Tom went out the door and headed toward the barn. Rheanna turned to Cassie and said, "Cassie, does it bother you to have Tommy come over? Please tell me the truth."

"Of course not, Rheanna! I love Tommy. He is a joy. Your visits always brighten my day. Don't be silly."

"Well, after losing your baby, I thought it might be hard on you to have him here."

"It would be horrible not to be able to see little Buddy." she adamantly responded.

"Okay, Cassie. I just wouldn't hurt you for anything."

"Well, don't give it another thought. Your friendship is so very important to me. You are the only woman I can talk with except my mother. What would I do without you?"

Rheanna smiled and said, "Guess you'll never know."

After they were gone, Cassie thought about Rheanna's question. There was a time when seeing little Gray Eagle did bother her, she had to admit. But she would never let Rheanna know that. But that had passed. She now looked forward to being with that precious little boy.

Cassie started back to the kitchen, when she heard one of the horses raising an awful ruckus outside. She looked out the window and saw him rearing up and making a terrible noise. She couldn't tell what the problem was from this distance. She ran out the door and yelled for TC, but neither he nor any of the men were anywhere around. As she approached the horse, she discovered the problem. There was an enormous rattlesnake coiled up ready to strike. I need a gun. No! I might hit the horse, or maybe the barn. Her aim was not that good. Anyway, there wasn't time to go after a gun. She grabbed a hoe and a brick. Those were the only things that were handy. As she approached, she said, "Oh, Lord, please don't let me miss." She threw the brick as hard as she could. Her aim was perfect. She hit the snake in the head and ran over and started chopping at the snake with the hoe. She was successful in killing the snake. The horse was still frightened and reared up, coming down on Cassie and knocking her to the ground. Her head hit a rock and knocked her unconscious.

Jack rode up and saw her there. He quickly rang the bell and then rushed to her. His first thought was that she had been bitten by the snake. Then he saw the ugly bump on her head. When he lifted her head, he discovered another large bump on the back of her head. She didn't appear to be breathing. Jack turned white with fear. He felt her pulse and gave a sigh of relief. He picked her up and carried her to the house. She was light, but his leg was still weak from his injury a few months back. By the time he got up to the house, he was limping. He laid Cassie on the bed and immediately went to the phone. Tom had gone into town to get a part for his plow. Jack called the general store in hopes that he would catch him.

Mr. Miller answered the phone and said he hadn't seen Tom today. Jack relayed what had happened and asked Mr. Miller to have Tom meet them at the hospital when he arrived. Then he rushed back to Cassie. He placed a cold cloth on her head. In a few minutes, she opened her eyes and started to sit up. She grabbed her head and moaned. Then she laid back on her pillow.

"Ms. Cassie, why in the world did you tangle with that snake?" Jack didn't know about the horse, for he was quite a distance away by the time Jack had arrived.

Cassie's head was spinning. It was hard for her to recollect what had happened. All she could say was, "We killed him."

"Well, you sure did. But who is this we? I didn't see anybody around here helpin' you. But from the looks of that snake, there could have been a whole army helpin' you. I thought you were trying to make snake soup."

"Well, the Lord helped me, Jack. I couldn't have done it alone."

"Come on, Ms. Cassie. I'll help you into the car. We have to get you to the hospital."

Cassie immediately protested. "I'll be all right. I don't need to go to the hospital."

"Oh, yes you do, little lady. In fact, TC is going to meet us there."

She wasn't happy about it, but reluctantly got into the car. Then she asked Jack, "Do you smell roses?"

"No Ma'am. I don't smell any roses." He turned to look in the back seat. "No flowers in here."

"I saw so many beautiful roses out in the corral," she said. "And I still smell them. They were yellow. Yellow roses are my favorite flowers."

"I'm thinkin' you had a mighty close call, little Cassie. You were almost pushing up daisies."

When they arrived, TC was already there. He ran and opened the car door for Cassie and helped her out of the car.

"Are you all right? What happened?"

"Well, I'll tell you, she's not all right, though she might tell you differently. Let's get her inside and we'll tell you the rest," Jack said.

After the hospital got all the information they required, and TC had all the facts that Jack could give him, Jack went to call the bunk-house. Someone should be there by now. If they had heard the bell, they would certainly be worried to find everyone gone when they returned. Cookie answered the phone. No one there had heard the bell. Evidently they were all too far away. Jack told them what had happened and then told them about the roses. "You know, it would be nice if we all pitched in and bought lots of yellow roses. She says that's her favorite flower."

The doctor examined Cassie and treated the wounds on her head. "You are one mighty lucky little lady," he said. "It's a miracle that you don't have a concussion. TC, you need to keep her from doing very much for a couple days. I'll give you something for pain. She is sure to have quite a headache from those two bumps."

TC drove Cassie home in the car, and Jack drove TC's truck. TC turned to Cassie and asked, "Do you feel like talking? What in the world were you doing out in the corral with that snake?"

Cassie poured the whole story out to him about the horse that was cornered by the rattlesnake. She could still see that poor scared horse rearing up in fear. "I had to do something, TC," she said.

"I can't believe you killed a rattlesnake." He shook his head and grinned. My little Cassie."

"Well, actually, it was me and the Lord. I certainly couldn't have done it by myself. I just picked up the tools. He did the rest."

When they arrived home, TC helped her into the house.

"Oh, TC," Cassie exclaimed. "I do smell roses. Look! Beautiful yellow roses! They're everywhere."

TC was as surprised as Cassie. He looked them over and found a card. "Hummm, I don't know if I like other men buying roses for my girl." He grinned and handed her the card.

"How sweet! I told Jack yellow roses were my favorite flowers, and look what they did. That was almost worth getting kicked in the head for."

"If you please, I prefer you never do that again," TC said.

Chapter 13

An Ill Wind Blowing

Tom rose early the next morning and went outside before Cassie got out of bed. He heard some kind of commotion out by the corral. Kent's dog, Cowboy, had a possum cornered and was going wild. All the men were gathered around to watch the action. In the meantime, Cassie woke up and looked out the window. She was enraged at what she saw. She quickly dressed and ran out the door.

"What are you men doing? Call that dog off at once! I can't believe my eyes! TC! Why are you allowing such cruelty?"

"Call him off, Kent," TC ordered. "He didn't hurt him, Cassie."

"Well, the poor little thing is scared to death. I thought you had more compassion than that," she said. When she turned, she gasped. "Curly! What are you doing here? I thought you went to Illinois."

"No, Ms. Cassie. I had a change of plans. I decided I would stick around for awhile." Then he gave her a grin and a wink.

"TC, I need to talk to you," she said.

"You don't need to worry, Ms. Cassie. I didn't tell TC about our little party. But I must tell you, I certainly did enjoy it."

"TC, he's lying!" she screamed.

"What's this all about, Curly?" Tom asked.

"Whatever the little lady says," he said. "I'm not one to cause trouble between a husband and a wife." Then, turning toward Cassie, he said, "But, Cassie, anytime you want to go down to the river with me again, just let me know. It was great fun."

"What are you saying? TC, he's lying! I was sitting down by the river when he came down there to tell me that you would be along shortly. He got out of line, in words only. I told him to leave. I told him he could either go back to Illinois, or we would talk to you about it. I thought he had left."

TC reached out and grabbed him by the shirt. With one hard jab, he knocked him through the fence. He picked Curly's hat up that had fallen to the ground and threw it at him. "Get your things together and be out of here in thirty minutes. If you have any pay coming, we'll send it to you. Don't ever show your face around here again."

Cassie started crying and ran into the house. It was at least an hour later before TC came in. He walked over to Cassie, put his arms around her, and said, "Cassie, don't worry. He's gone. I wish you would have told me. He would've been out of here that same night."

"If you remember, TC, we had another little distraction that night. We spent the night in the hospital," Cassie reminded him. "I wasn't thinking about Curly. And besides, I didn't want to bother you with it. I thought it was taken care of. I thought he was going to leave."

"Cassie, I do remember and I do understand that everything that happened that night might have caused you to forget the incident; but this business about you not wanting to bother me, I don't buy it. I think this was quite important enough to bother me about, as you put it. Don't you know that there is nothing more important to me than your well-being. I think you and I should discuss everything and not with-hold anything from each other."

"Okay, TC. From now on, we'll discuss everything and withhold nothing. Agree?"

"Agree. Oh, by the way, I'll be leaving early in the morning. I'm going into town to get supplies for the ranch. You can just sleep in if you want to. I'll be leaving before breakfast."

"Oh, TC, I want to go with you," she said.

"Sorry, Sugar, that won't work this time. I'm taking the truck, and Jed and Calvin are going with me to help load. There won't be any room. We'll have to plan a trip for the two of us another time."

"Fine." But in her heart, it was not fine. With everything that had happened recently, Cassie felt like she had to get away from the ranch for awhile. She just must get away. Yes, I will, she thought. As soon as TC leaves, I will pack and go to the city. But with whom could she go? She had lost contact with most of her friends. Going by herself would not be enjoyable.

"Amy! Amy Bishop!" she said aloud. She had heard that Amy was living in Tulsa. Perhaps she could visit Amy. They had been great friends in college. Amy had a knack for making everyone laugh. She would give her a call.

As soon as TC left the next morning, Cassie got up, showered, and dressed. She called Mrs. Bishop, who lived close to her mother, and asked her for Amy's phone number. Mrs. Bishop was as jolly and bubbly as Cassie had remembered her. Cassie always loved going to Amy's house, partly because of her mother. She was like a third friend, joining in their conversations and jaunts to the city or whatever they did. She was delighted to hear from Cassie. She thought Amy would love to have her visit, if she didn't have other plans. Just talking with Mrs. Bishop gave Cassie the assurance that she was doing the right thing. This was definitely what she needed.

The phone rang and Amy answered. "Hi Amy, this is Cassie. How are you?"   "Cassie!" she shrieked. "It's so good to hear from you? I'm fine. How about you?"   "Oh, I'm fine. I'm just calling to let you know that I'm coming to the city for a few days I was wondering if you had any time that we could do something together while I'm there."

"Have I! You bet I have. Where are you staying? Do you have relatives here?"

"No. I am going to make reservations somewhere. That was going to be my next question. Is there a nice hotel near you? Do you have any recommendations? You know the city better than I do."

"Oh, indeed I do," Amy exclaimed. "I know the perfect place. I'll make the reservations for you. When will you be arriving?"

"I'll be leaving here in about an hour," Cassie said. "I should be there around noon."

"That will be perfect. We can have lunch together. I have millions of things to tell you and show you. This will be fantastic. Oh, Cassie, I'm so excited. I've missed you so much. Do you have my address?"

"No. Let me get a pen. Just a minute. Okay, I'm ready. What is it?"

"It's 121 Sycamore Place, Tulsa, Oklahoma. Hurry, but be careful."

"Thanks, Amy. I'll see you soon. Bye." Cassie hurriedly packed and left a note for TC. It read:

Dearest TC,

I am going to the city for a few days. I hope you don't mind. I just felt that I needed to get away for awhile. You can enjoy Cookie's good cooking until I get back. I love you, and I'll see you soon.

Love, Cassie

P.S. Mizpah: The Lord watch between me and thee when we are absent one from another. Genesis 31:49

When TC returned, he saw Cassie's note. He frowned as he read it. He did mind. He didn't like Cassie being away. As he thought about it, perhaps he had been insensitive to her feelings lately. She had been through a lot. Maybe this trip to the city would cheer her up some. He would try to be happy about it. He did hope she would call when she arrived though, so he would know where she was staying and that she was all right. He wished she had talked with him about it before he left. Perhaps it was a spur of the moment idea. (The truth was, however, she was afraid he would try to talk her out of it.)

TC went about his day pretty much as usual. Hard work has a way of pushing things out of your mind. But when he came in the house that evening, it was strange not to have Cassie greet him. This was the first time they had been apart, and he didn't like it. The house seemed empty. There was an empty feeling in his heart. He hoped she wouldn't be gone long. He decided against eating at the cook shack. There were plenty of leftovers in the refrigerator. He warmed up some of those, read a little while, and decided to go to sleep early. He hoped Cassie would call before he went to bed.

He was almost asleep, when he heard a loud pounding on the door. He quickly opened the door to find Pokey, out of breath and very upset, trying to tell him something about the barn being on fire. "We got the horses out, but we couldn't save the barn. That's not all. You had better come," he said. TC ran out to the barn, which was still ablaze. There was a body lying on the ground about one hundred yards from the blaze.

"What happened?" TC yelled.

Kent spoke up first. "Curly came back and started the fire. Evidently, Cowboy attacked him and wouldn't let him get away. A burning beam fell on him and killed him. The fire was out of control before we got here."

TC put his hands over his face and turned away from the blaze. His thoughts were not on the loss of the barn, but on Curly. What happened in his life to cause him to turn out the way he did. Was there something he could have done to have changed this situation. Oh, if he had only taken time to get close to him and witness to him when they were mending fences. Perhaps then none of this would have happened. TC realized that he didn't know anything about Curly, except that he was a cocky young man, evidently filled with bitterness and vengeance. He must have had a great need in his life that had been overlooked. All these things were going around in his mind. "Oh, Lord, I'm sorry," he cried out.

"You're sorry?" Kent snapped. "He burned your barn, made a play for your wife, and you're sorry? I would say he got what he deserved."

"You don't understand, Kent. Maybe if I had given a little more thought to him and his needs before any of this happened, this could have been prevented. Maybe he just needed to know someone cared about him, and he sure needed to know that the Lord loved him. Did someone call the police to report this?"

"Yes. Jack called," Calvin said.

TC knelt down by Curly's body. I'm sure glad Cassie's not here to see this, he thought.

While he was outside talking with the men, Cassie tried to call. She assumed he had eaten at the cookshack and was still visiting with all the men. She had no idea of the tragic event that had taken place at the ranch in her absence.

TC went back in the house and dropped down in a chair. He must notify Curly's family. It seemed so cruel to give news like this by telephone. But on the other hand, it would take so long to drive to Illinois. Was it better to prolong the news or deliver it by phone? He decided there was really no choice. He must physically take the news to them. That was the only right thing to do. He would leave the first thing in the morning. He wished he had a way to let Cassie know, but he didn't know how to contact her.

TC told all of the men what his plans were. Several volunteered to go with him, but he chose Kent and Jed. He wanted to talk with Kent. He wanted to be sure he understood about Curly's death. Kent was right that Curly may have deserved what he got. He had placed himself in the situation that brought about his own death, but think what would happen if we all got what we deserve. Not one of us deserves heaven as our reward; but by God's grace and mercy, we can be forgiven and have a home there. It is not our place to judge what anyone deserves. TC was afraid that what he had said had caused Kent to feel some kind of guilt because of his dog's actions. The dog was doing only what he had been trained to do—protect the property from intruders. It was not even the dog's intention for Curly to get killed. And Jed, well, he just wanted to spend some time with him.

When Cassie arrived at Amy's, she asked where her hotel was located.

"Right here, silly. You don't think I would let you stay anywhere else, do you? We have too much to catch up on to waste time with a hotel."

Cassie started to object, but Amy put her hand over Cassie's mouth and said, "I won't discuss it any further."

They had a wonderful time. Cassie hadn't laughed this much in ages. She laughed so much, her side hurt. They spent hours catching up on each other's lives and planning the next few days: shopping, bowling, dinner theater, and talking. Amy also had someone she wanted Cassie to meet. That was part of Amy's exciting news. Amy was getting married next spring. They looked at wedding books, went to wedding shops, talked about Cassie's wedding, and Cassie told Amy all about TC. Amy had met TC, of course. She was in Cassie's wedding, but didn't get to know him very well. When it was time for Cassie to leave, it was hard to say goodbye. They both enjoyed the visit more than either one expected.

Cassie really missed TC though and was ready to return home. Besides, she was getting a little worried. Every time she called home, there was no answer. She even tried calling at 6:30 in the morning and still got no answer. Perhaps he had gone on a round-up or something. She would just be glad to get back home and make sure everything was all right.

TC made all the arrangements for Curly's body to be sent to a funeral home in Peoria, Illinois, where his parents lived. He left the following morning with Jed and Kent. They talked most of the way about what had happened. Tom expressed his regrets that he had not witnessed to Curly, thinking there was plenty of time. Kent brought up a very interesting and profound point. He said that if Curly would ever have eventually accepted the Lord, the Lord would have made a way to spare his life long enough for that to happen. God is in control, and nothing can happen unless He permits it. Tom seemed to feel better after thinking that over. He certainly agreed that God is in control.

When they arrived in Peoria at the Hollis residence, the three of them went to the door. Tom rang the doorbell. A woman answered the door. She was very short, and nearly as wide as she was tall.

"I'm Tom Marshall. This is Jed Coulter and Kent Wills. Are you Mrs. Hollis?"

"Yes, I am, Won't you come in," she replied.

"Is Mr. Hollis here? I'd like to speak with both of you."

Tom went in and stood next to a chair where she had invited him to sit. He waited for Mr. Hollis to enter the room. They shook hands. Tom immediately recognized him as one of the men who, at one time, worked for his father. "Mr. Hollis, how are you. I'm Tom Marshall. This is Jed Coulter and Kent Wills. You worked for my father, didn't you?" he asked.

"Yes I did. Your father fired me. Do you remember that?" he said in an angry voice.

"Well, no sir, I don't. My father never mentioned that to me. I'm sure there must have been a reason, but that's not why I'm here."

"Well, state your business," he growled. Mr. Hollis was a thin man, rather tall, but very bent over and walked with a limp. Tom thought he must have been injured at some time in his life.

"I'm very sorry to have to come here under these circumstances. I have some very bad news for you. Your son, Curly, was in an accident at the ranch and was killed. His body is being taken to the Crofton-Racherford Mortuary. You have my deepest sympathy. Is there anything I can do for you?"

"You can tell me how my son died," he snapped.

"Well, Sir, there was a fire in the barn, and one of the beams fell on him and killed him."

"I don't believe you. You killed him. You killed my boy to get even."

"Even for what, Mr. Hollis? What should I have against him. Is something I should know here?" Tom said as he scowled at Mr. Hollis.

Mrs. Hollis stepped between the two men and said, "Now hush, Roger. There's been enough said. This won't get Curly back. Just hush."

"He killed my boy. He's gonna pay."

Jed stepped in front of Tom and said, "Now look here! I think you need to know what really happened. TC was trying to spare you the fact that your son was mean and rotten, but you don't deserve to be spared the awful truth. The truth is, Curly started that fire intentionally, after TC had gone into his home for the evening and everyone was asleep. The barn burned to the ground. Don't you dare accuse TC of anything so despicable, or you will answer to me."

"Jed, don't," Tom said, pulling him back. "Let's go. We can't do anything here."

"Get out of here. Get off of my property. I wish you would've been on that ranch when your dad's place burned."

Tom started out the door, but when Mr. Hollis made that statement, he turned and glared at him. "How did you know about that fire. Did you have a hand in that? Did you kill my dad?"

Mrs. Hollis said, "You men leave! Roger, I told you to hush!"

Tom said, "We'll leave now, but I will have this investigated. You'll be hearing from me."

Kent drove on the trip back to the ranch. There was no conversation for the first fifty miles. Kent and Jed knew how very difficult this whole thing had been for TC. Finally Tom said, "I just knew there was more to that fire than happenstance. I'll get to the bottom of this." Not much else was said until they got back to the ranch. Then Tom saw Cassie's car.

"Cassie's home!" He jumped out of the car and ran toward the house. She heard him drive down the lane. When he ran upon the porch, she opened the door and threw her arms around him.

"Oh, Cassie, I'm so glad you are home. I've missed you so much."

"TC, I've missed you too. I was so worried about you. Jack told me about Curly. Was it awful breaking the news to his folks?"

"Yes, Cassie. It was one of the worst experiences I've ever had. I'll tell you all about it later. Right now, let me hear about your trip to the city." He kept her talking for some time. He wanted to prolong the subject of the Hollis family for awhile. Finally, he poured the whole story out to her. It was good to be able to share his heart with her. She cared more than anyone.

The following days and weeks were difficult ones. Tom went to the sheriff and told him everything he knew and what he suspected. He said he would pursue the matter to whatever extent was necessary in order to get the truth.

"It may take weeks or even months to get to the bottom of this, TC."

"Like I said, Sheriff Buckner, whatever it takes, I will do."

"You won't need to do anything for the time being, TC. We will look into it, and do all we can. We'll probably be back from time to time to ask you more about it. Just be patient. We'll be in touch."

Well, the sheriff was right. It did take months. But finally, the sheriff and two deputies came to the ranch. Tom was just riding in when they came through the gate. He invited them up to the house for some coffee.

"Thanks, TC. That sounds good."

When they walked in the house, Cassie was pushing a dresser down the hallway. "What are you doing, Cassie?" TC asked. "Oh, never mind that now. Would you come here for a moment? There's someone I want you to meet."

Cassie came over and greeted everyone with her usual smile, and offered her hand as Tom introduced Sheriff Buckner, Deputy Riggs, and Deputy Mauery. "I'm happy to meet you. Won't you come into the library and have a seat? I already know Deputy Mauery. We went to high school together. Do you remember that?" directing her question to him.

"Hey, Cassie! I sure do. I didn't recognize you at first. I guess I just wasn't expecting to see you here. You sure haven't changed any though. You were in my English class. You were the one that always made the rest of us look bad," he said, teasingly. "You always got your work done on time, and made straight As on everything you did."

"Could I get you gentlemen something to drink? We have tea, lemonade, or I could make some coffee."

Sheriff Buckner

TC said, "Coffee would be good. I already made the offer."

"I'll be back shortly," replied Cassie.

When she returned with the coffee, they were just finishing a conversation about the latest horses Tom had purchased. The sheriff cleared his throat and moved out to the edge of his chair.

"Well, TC, here's where we are. We have Mr. Hollis and his older son Kenneth in custody. You were right. He did start the fire when your dad's place burned and your dad was killed. He confessed to everything. Also, Kenneth made an attempt to burn your place once before, but you or someone woke up and saw him, so he ran away. Now, since there was no damage, we can't hold him unless you press charges. That's up to you. Mr. Hollis, on the other hand, he'll have to stand trial.

"What we found out is that Roger Hollis was stealing from your father and your father fired him. He's had financial difficulty ever since that time and he he's blamed your father for all his misfortune. He's drilled into his boys that your father was the cause of all his problems. Curly was always the cocky type, looking for an excuse to get into mischief. He came to your place on the pretense of looking for work, but the truth is, he came for trouble. He planned to kill your cattle off , a few at a time just for kicks, and then burn the whole place down like his father had done. Looks like it back-fired on him.

"To tell you the truth, I don't think Roger will hold up through a trial. He is in bad health. He's had a couple heart attacks and he has a very bad back condition . He fell off a horse a couple years ago, and the horse fell on him. He doesn't get around very well. We will continue to keep you posted as this progresses."

Tom put his elbows on his knees and his head in his hands and just sat there for a few minutes. Then he sat up and somberly said, "I'm not going to press charges against Kenneth, with one stipulation. I want him to come talk with me. I want to see if there is anything worth salvaging there. Maybe I can help him. Could you arrange that for me?"

"TC, I can't believe you. Most guys would be wanting to shoot him, or set him on fire, or something. Here you are, wanting to help him. Just be careful. He may be real trouble. Call me if you need anything, you hear?"

"Thanks Sheriff. I will, and thanks for all you've done. You've helped answer a lot of questions that I've had. I've wondered about the fire and that rider that rode in early one morning, and blazed out like the devil himself was after him. The pieces are starting to fall in place. That might also explain the dead steers we found."

After they left, Tom turned to Cassie. "Now, little lady, why are you moving furniture? I would do that for you, or any one of thirty men around here. What are you doing, anyway?"

"Well, I have some great news. I'm clearing out that bedroom to make a nursery. Oh, TC! We're going to have our baby. I have a good feeling about it. I think, this time, it will be okay."

Tom didn't show the excitement this time that he had before. His face was grim. He put his arms around her and his head against hers. He was remembering what the doctor had said.

Cassie leaned back, looking up at him, and asked, "TC, aren't you happy about it? I thought you would be."

"Yes, of course I am. It's just that it's so soon, and the doctor said we should wait."

"It's been eighteen months. That is a long wait. It'll be all right, I know it will."

"Well, no more moving furniture, and that's an order. Are you listening, Cassie? You must take care of yourself and be careful what you do."

"Okay, TC. I'll be careful, I promise."

Chapter 14

Dream Unfulfilled

Cassie was busy preparing dinner when Tom returned from town. She was very happy to see him come in. The past few weeks were very difficult for her. She had problems with her pregnancy and spent much of her time in bed. Her mother, who stayed with her most of the time because Tom was gone so much, left at noon today to take care of things at her own home. Cassie felt better than she had for some time. When Tom came in, she put her arms around him. "I'm glad you're home early. I hoped we could spend some time together tonight. It seems there's been something going on every evening this past week."

"Sounds good to me. I'd like nothing better than to sit by the fire with my wife and my little boy."

"Oh, TC, you mustn't say that. You know there's a very good possibility that we'll have a little daughter. Don't get your heart set on a son," she said as she turned to lift a pan from the stove.

"Well, I do have my heart set on a son. And I think you're wrong about there being a good possibility for us to have a daughter. After all, God knows the desires of our hearts and the Bible says that He wants to give us our desires. Well, I desire a son. I've even prayed for a son. I remember the times I spent with my father on this land, riding with him and working with him. I want that, Cassie, with my son. I want to teach him to work, ride, rope, fish—everything that my father taught me. Is that so wrong? You aren't praying against me are you, Cassie?" Tom stood frowning at her as he waited for her to answer.

"Well of course not, TC. But we can't tell God how to answer our prayers. Besides, don't you think that it might be a little bit selfish, and even presumptuous, to pray that way?"

"No, I don't! I want a son! God knows I want a son! So why on earth shouldn't I expect a son and pray for one? And why is that selfish?" Tom demanded.

"Well, did you ever consider that perhaps I might like to have a daughter? You are surrounded with men. I have no women. Maybe I would like to have a little girl. I could teach her to sew and cook. I could curl her hair and enjoy having another female around. I haven't asked God for a little girl, but I certainly wouldn't be disappointed if this baby was a girl."

Cassie bit her lip and turned toward the cabinet to busy herself with dinner in order to prevent Tom from seeing the tears well up in her eyes. He wouldn't have noticed though, because he stomped out of the kitchen and slammed the door. It was nearly four months before the new little arrival would make the grand appearance. Maybe Tom would have a change of heart before then.

Dinner that evening was not the enjoyable one Cassie had anticipated. It was, for the most part, consumed in silence. Cassie had hoped they could discuss decorating the nursery, but that certainly would be out of the question tonight.

The next few months continued to be difficult ones. It seemed there was one catastrophe after another on the ranch. One night during a storm, lightning struck the barn and killed Tom's favorite horse. Then Jack was riding down by Beaver Dam when some falling rocks startled him and his horse. He fell off and broke his leg. It was a bad break and the doctor didn't know how long he would be in a cast. Then, if that wasn't enough, Cal and Clay found three dead steers by the Cody Stream with no indication of what happened to them. Tom sent in samples of the water to have them tested, but the results were negative. There were no marks on the steers, so wolves were not responsible. Hopefully, they would solve this mystery before more steers died.

The time passed very slowly for Cassie. She began having trouble again. The doctor ordered complete bed rest; so once again, her mother came to be with her. The doctor also told her that this would be her last baby.

"Cassie, we're going to do everything we can to see you through this pregnancy. But after the baby is born you'll need to have a complete hysterectomy. You do want this baby to have a mother, don't you, Cassie?"

Cassie was broken hearted. What if this baby was a girl? How would TC take it, knowing she wouldn't be able to have his son?

During the next few weeks, Tom and Cassie conversed about many things, but the topic of the baby was avoided. Cassie decorated the nursery without even bringing up the subject to Tom. She used nursery rhymes in many pastel colors which would be fitting for girl or a boy. If the baby was a girl, she would add some frills; but if it were a boy, she would make it pertain more to a little boy's character. Tom looked it over and complimented her work, but nothing was said about who might reside there.

Then the night of the big event came. It was storming and the wind was howling. The branches of the trees were nearly touching the ground and were being blown back and forth. Cassie was terribly uncomfortable and unable to sleep for the past several hours. As she lay listening to the sleet and rain, a strong pain brought her out of her warm bed. She knew the time had come. She immediately got dressed and prepared for the trip to the hospital. When she was completely ready and fairly sure this was not a false alarm, she woke up Tom to give him the news. He quickly dressed and they were soon on their way. The doctor's instruction had been to come on the first indication that it was time, because Cassie was going to have a Caesarian and, at the same time, the proposed surgery.

The surgery took longer than anticipated. Cassie was not doing well at first. Her pulse was very irregular, and her breathing was sporadic. The doctor stayed by her side until all her vital signs were normal again.

They immediately took the baby away to examine and bathe the little one for the grand appearance. Tom didn't see Cassie until she came out of the recovery room and didn't know the danger she had been in. When she was taken to her room, he stood by her, holding her hand and telling her how much he loved her. Then the doctor came in and patted Cassie on the arm.

"Well, little lady, you did a superb job. You have a beautiful little 7 pound 2 ounce baby girl. She's going to wrap this big guy around her little finger." He shook Tom's hand and went out the door.

Cassie felt Tom stiffen and then he dropped her hand. He stood glaring down at her, as if he were accusing her of being in some kind of conspiracy with God against him. Finally he said, "Well, you won. You got what you wanted." He turned, walked across the room, and gazed out the window. After about ten minutes, he walked out the door and down the hallway.

Cassie cried until her eyes were red and swollen. When they brought the baby in to her, the nurses were shocked to find her in that state. She tried to gain her composure and reached for her little daughter. Cassie thought she was the most beautiful baby she had ever seen. She was even more beautiful than Little Gray Eagle. Oh, if only TC could see her through my eyes, she thought.

Tom came back about two hours later. He talked with her and ask her how she felt, but he didn't say if he'd seen the baby.

"TC, we need to decide on a name for our baby."

"Whatever you want to call her is fine with me," he said.

"What about Tessie Cassandra Marshall?" Cassie asked. "She'd be named Cassandra after me, but her initials would be TC."

He squeezed her hand and smiled. "That's fine," he said.

Cassie was very weak, but she was able to go home on the sixth day after little Tessie was born. Cassie's mother stayed with her until she was able to be up and about. She could tell something was wrong between Cassie and TC, but she didn't know what.

Finally, Cassie was strong enough to care for little Tessie and do minimal tasks around the house. So her mother went back to her own home, but she visited often to check on Cassie and see the baby.

One morning Cassie was preparing breakfast and Tom entered the kitchen. He poured a cup of coffee and sat down at the table. When Cassie sat his plate in front of him, he began to eat.

"Well, TC, aren't you going to give thanks to the Lord?"

"Why should I pray to the Lord? He's going to do things His way, no matter what I say," Tom growled.

"Thomas Colbert Marshall! I can't believe my ears! You have a precious little daughter that is perfect in every way. You have a lot for which to be thankful! I hope you have a change of heart, and very soon, for all our sakes. If you persist on carrying on this way, I'll take my little daughter and go home. This has certainly not been a home of late." Cassie turned and left the room. She didn't return until Tom was gone.

Tom left the ranch and was gone until 6 o'clock that evening. When he came in, he had his hand behind his back. He walked over to Cassie and leaned down and kissed her. Then he drew his hand out and presented her with a beautiful bouquet of roses and a tiny rose bud, which he explained was for his other girl.

"Oh, Cassie! I've been such a fool. And, yes, you were right. I was selfish. I know God knows best. What if He had not let us have little Tessie? I wanted a son. But you, in your thoughtfulness and wisdom, gave me a little TC Marshall. Oh, Cassie! Can you ever forgive me?"

She threw her arms around him and they both shed tears of joy. Cassie said, "Daddy's little girl is calling. Would you go get her?"

Tom held her most of the evening. He was silently thanking the Lord that he had gone into town and talked with his pastor—who firmly scolded him and made him wake up and realize all the blessings God had given him. He later told Cassie that he had had a spiritual kick in the pants.

Chapter 15

Irresistible Flower

Cassie was busy in the kitchen when she heard someone at the door. She dried her hands and hurried to find TC coming in with arms full of beautiful yellow roses.

"Where can I put these? They're full of thorns. Ouch! My, those are vicious little rascals. Do you have a jar I can put them in?"

"A jar?" laughed Cassie. "I'll get a lovely vase for those beauties. Where did you get them? They don't look like they came from a florist."

"They didn't. They came from my wife's beautiful flower garden," he said.

"What flower garden? I didn't know your wife had a flower garden with beautiful yellow roses in it," she said, as she helped arrange the roses in a big crystal vase.

"Come with me and I'll show you." He took her out to see the biggest display of roses she had ever seen in one place.

"Oh my!" she gasped. "They're gorgeous! They must have cost a fortune. Oh, thank you, TC! I love roses. Where did you get them?" She walked through the flowers, touching, smelling, and awing. "I'm overwhelmed. You're a prince of a husband."

"Well, of course I am," he said grinning. "But actually, these are from Tessie. You know tomorrow is Mother's Day, and you are the prettiest, sweetest little mother I know. Tessie said she wanted her mommy to have the best."

"Oh, this is my first Mother's Day," she exclaimed. "She didn't even tell me," Cassie said jokingly.

"By the way, where is my little flower?" he asked. "Daddy hasn't got to rock her all day. She was asleep when I left this morning."

"You know, you make ten times as many trips in the house since she came than you ever did before," she teased.

"I have to. Every time I leave, she grows an inch. If I stayed away too long, I wouldn't recognize her."

Cassie laughed. "I think she's awake. Go get her. You're going to have her spoiled rotten, you know."

Well, TC didn't need to have his arm twisted to follow those instructions. When he went into the nursery, Tessie was sucking on her little fist like she was starving. She had one little shoe and sock off and was kicking as fast as her little feet would go. She was just beginning to cry when TC scooped her up in his arms.

"Were you calling your daddy, Punkin?" TC held her up to his face and kissed her little cheek. "Mommy, she gets more beautiful every time I see her. She is my little irresistible flower. Do you think I could take her over to the cook shack and let the fellows over there see her?"

Cassie smiled. "She's hungry, TC. Let me feed her first. Then you can go show her off."

Cassie watched them out the window as TC took Tessie off on her debut. He was talking to her and kissing her on the cheek as they went. Cassie's heart was overjoyed as she realized that TC really loved his baby girl. Dr. Grayson had been right. Tessie did wrap that big guy around her little finger.

It seemed like they had been gone for hours. Cassie again looked out the window to see TC holding Tessie and riding around the corral on Daisy, a black spotted Appaloosa. Cassie grinned. "Looks like I've lost my little sewing and cooking partner. She's destined to be a cowgirl, I'm afraid."

When they came in, TC said, "Boy, Mommy, we worked so hard. We're ready for a nap. We're going to rock-a-bye and go to sleep."

From that day on, the horseback ride was part of the daily routine. Tessie seemed to enjoy just about everything. She loved her bath, playing with toys, eating, anything that came her way—but the horseback ride topped them all. It always brought squeals and claps.

One evening, Cassie invited Joe and Josie over for dinner. She reminded TC that morning to be sure and be on time because they had guests coming. She spent a lot of time preparing the dinner that day. She felt a little uneasy about it because Josie was known as being the town's best cook. She had put off inviting them for that very reason. When she realized how unfair that was to Josie, she decided to put forth her best effort and do it. Probably everyone felt inadequate cooking for Josie, but if anyone deserved to have a night away from the stove, it was her.

Cassie went through several cookbooks trying to come up with a really elaborate menu, but finally concluded that simple was the best. She put a pot-roast in the oven with potatoes and carrots and onions. She had homemade rolls, pineapple-cheese salad, and cherry pie. It was simple, but always brought raves from TC. Cassie told them to be there at 6 o'clock and they were right on time.

"My, my, Cassie! It smells wonderful in here," Josie said as she came through the door.

"Well, it won't be as good as your cooking, Josie, but at least you won't have to cook. You definitely need a break." Cassie had become a really good cook though. She liked cooking and enjoyed trying out various recipes.

"Where's my little girl?" Joe asked.

"She's in her room playing. You can bring her in here if you like."

"Well, I think I hear my little princess calling me." he said as he went to her room. "Hi there, Sweetie. How's Uncle Joe's baby?"

Tessie was sitting in her playpen, playing with some bright colored beads. When Joe came in, she looked up and squealed with delight. She loved Uncle Joe and Aunt Josie. She loved everyone for that matter, but they were among her favorites.

Tessie was now able to sit alone. She was trying her very best to crawl, but still wasn't able to get up on her knees and move . All she could accomplish was just rocking back and forth. When something she wanted was out of her reach, she would lie on her tummy and stretch. If that didn't work, she would yell. That usually brought help.

Cassie was busily putting everything on the table, which was set with a white linen table cloth and napkins and a beautiful arrangement of fresh flowers. Cassie pulled the high chair to the table for Tessie. Everything was going great until little Tessie reached out and grabbed TC's glass and dumped water all over the table.

"Oh no!" Cassie exclaimed. She felt like the entire dinner was spoiled.

"Well, Mommy, we didn't break anything," Josie said. "We're just thirsty."

TC immediately whisked Tessie out of the kitchen for dry clothes, and away from an upset mommy. When they returned, the high chair was pushed back a few inches.

Cassie was afraid that Joe and Josie, not being used to babies, would be upset by this little mishap, but it didn't seem to bother them in the least. The mess was quickly cleaned up with everyone's help. They all laughed, and Cassie began to feel a little bit better about the situation. Laughter is a great cure for many things. Cassie, apparently, was the only one who got upset.

Everyone enjoyed the dinner. Josie insisted on helping with the cleanup. Cassie told her that this was to be a night out for her with no work. Josie said she couldn't possibly enjoy the evening if she left Cassie with the mess. So they worked together and visited and laughed. Everything was cleaned up in no time at all. Josie said, "My philosophy is, What's work for one is fun for two."

Little Tessie was dressed for bed shortly after dinner and tucked in for the night. She had enjoyed a busy day and was very soon sound asleep.

Joe and Josie stayed for several hours after dinner. They talked, played a couple table games, and seemed to have a great time. All in all, Cassie felt like it was a very successful evening. In fact, she felt so good about it that she decided to invite them at least once a month. She had invited her parents and Rheanna and Cherokee over quite often in the past. She was very happy that she could now comfortably add Joe and Josie to that list.

After they left, Cassie got Tessie's baby book out of the desk drawer and wrote in the book about her little mishap at dinner—also about being the center of attention most of the evening. Someday the little water incident would be funny to mother and daughter, but not just yet.

The following months seemed to pass so quickly. Cassie was now adding things to the baby book such as Tessie's first steps, her first words, her first boots, falls, scares, and more. She wrote about Kent's dog coming up to Tessie and Tessie reaching for the dog. When she touched it, she started screaming, scaring the poor dog to death. All evening, every time she thought about it, she would say, "Doggie," and then cry again.

Cassie thought TC was going to cry, too. He could not stand to see Tessie cry. It broke his heart every time.

One night TC took her outside to see the moon, which was especially beautiful that night. When she saw it, she reached for it and said, "Ball." When he told her it was the moon, she started crying. She wanted the big ball. He went to town the next day and bought the biggest ball he could find for her. Cassie teased him about giving Tessie the moon.

Chapter 16

My Little Shadow

It was a beautiful Sunday morning. Cassie was getting dressed for church. She was sitting in front of her mirror in her bedroom brushing her hair. Cassie had already gotten Tessie dressed and ready to go, so Tessie was watching her mommy. "I wants to brush my hair," Tessie said.

Cassie handed her the brush. She stood in front of the mirror, and with the back side of the brush, she started stroking her hair. Cassie said, "Turn the brush over, sweetheart. That's the wrong side."

"No, Mommy. That hoots de bebe."

Cassie laughed and took the brush and brushed her hair. "Okay, Mommy will do it. We don't want to hurt the baby."

Tessie's hair was a light blonde, almost white. Her big blue eyes were shining. She looked so much like Cassie. Cassie's hair was a shade darker though (more golden, but still very blonde) and her eyes were a clear, sparkling blue.

"Oh, that's a poody bebe," Tessie said, as she looked in the mirror.

"Well, you're a conceited little girl, aren't you?" Cassie said as she tickled Tessie. "But, yes, that's a poody bebe. You're Mommy's little beauty. Come on, Sweetie. Your daddy is going to be waiting for us. We better hurry."

When Tessie went into the living room, she held her dress out to show her daddy. "Looky, Daddy. See my dwessy."

"Well, there's my two pretty girls. I was about to give up on you. Wow! You are gorgeous, Princess. Are you ready to go?" TC asked.

"I weady," Tessie said.

TC picked her up and swung her around, and then kissed her on the cheek. "Away we go, Little Princess."

"I don't wanna ride in the car. I wanna ride the horsey," Tessie said.

"No, Punkin, not to church. You'd get your pretty dress all dirty."

"Daisy's not dooty."

"Sorry, Honey, it's the car today," TC said. "Mommy wouldn't want to go to church on a horse. We'll ride Daisy later."

"Okay, Daddy. We don't want Mommy to cry," she said as she reached up to hold her mommy's hand.

The church service was very uplifting, as it nearly always was. Pastor Dan preached a message on the family. Cassie was thinking that they were so blessed to have a pastor who was in tune with God and always seemed to know just what people needed to hear. She felt God was speaking directly to her heart. And the music was always so fitting with the sermon. Probably the choir director knew what the pastor was preaching on before he made his selections; but if that were the case, she didn't want to know. It was better to think that God was speaking directly to each man, telling him what He wanted the people to hear. But regardless, God was definitely in charge.

Their church was not a large church. There were two other churches in their town. Usually, they had a class for the children Tessie's age, but Miss Madge was sick today. So Tessie had to go in the church service with Tom and Cassie. She got pretty restless before the service was over. She didn't understand why she couldn't talk—she could talk in her class. Finally she leaned on her daddy and went to sleep.

On their way home, Cassie sensed that something was bothering TC. "You're awfully quiet, TC," Cassie said. "You haven't said two words since we left the church. And you have such a frown on your face. What's the matter?"

"Oh, I was just thinking. Isn't it strange how much you grow to care about people who aren't even related to you and how it hurts to lose them. I guess, in a sense, we are related, if we know the Lord."

"TC, did somebody die? What are you talking about?"

He grinned as he looked at her. "No. I didn't mean to alarm you. It's just that Johnnie is leaving us, and I'm sure going to miss him."

"Cookie? You can't mean that Cookie is going away? Why? Where?" Cassie asked in shock.

"Whoa! One question at a time. Yes, Cookie is leaving. His brother in Oklahoma is starting a drain tile business and wants him to go in partnership with him. It's probably a great opportunity. I won't discourage him. I think they'll be very successful."

"Drain tile? How boring! How could he leave the ranch for drain tile? I thought he loved it here. Drain tile? I can't believe it. How could Johnny leave us? I really like him. I guess he is my favorite of all the hands," she said.

"Hey! I didn't know you cared so much for Johnny. Maybe I'd better be glad he's leaving," he teased.

"Oh, really, TC! Don't be silly! You knew I liked Johnny. He's a great guy, and a gentleman, I might add. Everyone liked him. I just can't understand how he could leave this beautiful place for drain tile."

"Well, Cassie, there's more to life than just beauty. I understand there's big money in drain tile. Besides, maybe Johnny wants to be close to his brother. Anyway, aren't you the one who thinks this place is a lonely place, not exciting like the city?"

"Oh, TC, don't rub that in. I've learned to love your silly old ranch, and I thought everyone else here did, too. What'll we do for a cook? Maybe we could talk Josie and Joe into moving here and Josie could cook for the crew."

Tom grinned. "You know, I had thought of that. I even asked her one time. But, realistically, can you imagine Josie going on a roundup or trail ride? They have to be fed on those trips, you know. I'm not sure who we'll get. We need to really pray about that one. We'll never find another Johnny."

Tessie began to stretch and open her eyes. "Daddy, can we ride the horsey? Can we?"

"Punkin, when we get home, we're going to eat, and then I have some work to do."

"Can I work wif you?" she pleaded with a longing look.

"Daddy will take you for a ride tomorrow afternoon, right after lunch. Okay?"

Cassie spoke up. "Oh, thanks a lot. We have an appointment to get pictures taken. Now I'll be an old meanie if I make her go."

Tom winced. "Whoops! Sorry! I forgot about the pictures. We'll go when you get back from getting your picture taken, if it isn't too late. Daddy wants a picture of his little princess. Will you smile pretty for your picture?"

"I don't wanna take a picture. I wanna ride Daisy. She misses me."

"Right now, let's go eat some lunch. I'm starving. How about you?" TC said, in hopes of changing the subject.

"Me too," Tessie said. "Can I have some ice cream?"

"Maybe after you eat your dinner" Cassie said.

Cassie had dinner in the oven. When they entered, they were overtaken by the delectable aroma that filled the house. The food was delicious. Any other day the meal would have been enjoyed, but not today. Not much was said throughout the meal. Cassie's thoughts were on Cookie leaving. It was like losing a brother. She never had a brother, but she was sure she couldn't care more for a one than she did for Johnny. She was pretty sure TC was thinking about Johnny, too.

After eating, Tom went out to the barn to repair the broken door, while Cassie cleaned up the kitchen. Then she put Tessie in bed for her nap. Tessie was usually very good about going right to sleep, but today (maybe because she had slept in church) she climbed out of her bed and went outside to find her daddy. She heard him hammering in the barn, so in she went. Like a little shadow, she was right behind him. He was making so much noise, he didn't even hear her. Then she spotted Daisy. She climbed through the rail that kept Daisy in her stall.

Then she said, "Hi, Daisy. Did you miss me?"

TC's heart jumped into his throat. "Tessie!" he yelled. "What are you doing out here?" He leaped over the rail and grabbed her. He was so scared he could hardly talk. He held her close to him and trembled with fright. His actions startled little Tessie and she started screaming.

"It's okay, Precious. You scared Daddy. You must never come out here by the horses, Baby. They might step on you."

"Daisy wouldn't step on me, Daddy. She loves me."

"I know Daisy loves you, but she might not see you. You mind Daddy, and never do that again. Okay?"

"Okay, Daddy."

Cassie and TC started being more watchful, since they learned that Tessie could now open doors. That was a new feat for her. It became more difficult every day to keep her inside. She wanted to follow her daddy everywhere. TC even started calling her my little shadow.

One night, after they had gone to bed, it started to storm. There was thunder and lightening. Tessie became frightened and started screaming. TC ran and picked her up in his arms.

"Don't cry, Precious. Daddy and Mommy are here. It's okay. That's just thunder. It won't hurt you. Jesus is watering the flowers and the grass. That's good. We need the rain. God says that the rain is a blessing. Don't cry."

"I don't want it to rain, Daddy. Tell God to turn it off," Tessie said.

"Well, Honey, we don't tell God what to do. He knows best," TC said.

"Yes, you do. You tell him to bless our food. You tell him lots of things. Tell him to turn it off, Daddy. Please."

"Honey, the rain is good. If we didn't have rain, the flowers would die, and the grass would die. Everything needs rain."

"We have our river, Daddy."

"Yes, but the rain keeps the river full. If God didn't send the rain, the river and the lakes would all dry up. The animals wouldn't even have anything to drink."

"Okay, Daddy, you can let it rain, but can I sleep wif you?"

"Sure. You can sleep with Mommy and Daddy tonight. I love you. Now you go to sleep."

Tessie remained Daddy's Little Shadow and went everywhere he went. She tried to do everything just like he did. When he took his boots off, she put them on. When he read the paper, she would peak at him beneath the paper and try to get his attention. One of her favorite times was riding on his back while he crawled on the floor. She also liked riding on his shoulders as he walked over the ranch. Cassie started reciting this little poem to them.

I have a little shadow
That goes in and out with me,
And what can be the use of him
Is more that I can see.

TC said, "Well, this little shadow is useful. I couldn't get along without her. She's is Daddy's helper and she keeps Daddy in line. Knowing I'm being watched so closely, and knowing that my steps are being followed every day is sure a big responsibility."

He was reminded of that fact the next morning when he started to put his boots on. Tessie's little boots were sitting right next to his at the foot of his bed. TC had Cassie get the camera and take a picture. This was a memory he would treasure.

Chapter 17

Wild Flowers for Tessie

"Hi, Mommy. What're you doing?" Tessie asked.

"I'm cooking dinner," Cassie replied.

"I want to help you," she said with pleading eyes.

"Okay, you can set the table, if you want to."

"I don't want to set the table. I want to cook. I could make the salad."

"Honey, you're too little to make the salad. I have everything else nearly finished. Won't you set the table for me?" her mommy said.

"Babies do that. I'm big. I could make the salad," Tessie said in a pouty voice.

"Okay, go wash your hands very, very clean. I'll let you tear the lettuce while I chop the tomatoes." Cassie wanted Tessie to work with her in the kitchen, but the things she wanted to do were not the things she could do.

Tessie washed her hands and returned. "Why can't I do the fun stuff?" Tessie asked.

Cassie frowned at her and said, "You can set the table or tear the lettuce. Which is it?"

"Okay, I'll tear the lettuce."

"I like it when you help me, Tessie, but I want you to be sweet so we can have fun together. Don't be a little grump."

Cassie stood there looking at her. Tessie knew she was waiting for a reply. "Okay, Mommy. I'll be sweet. Will you tell Daddy that I made the salad for him?"

"Yes, I'll tell him, or you can tell him yourself. He'll be so pleased. He loves salad and he'll really like this salad because you made it."

When TC came in, Tessie ran to meet him and her first words were, "Daddy, Daddy, I made the salad. I made it just for you."

"Oh, boy! I can hardly wait to eat it. I'll bet it's the best salad in the world. But aren't you going to let Mommy have any?" TC carried her into the dining room and put her in her chair.

"Sure, Mommy can have some if she wants."

They had just finished asking the Lord to bless the food when the door bell rang. TC went to the door. Sheriff Buckner and another man, not in uniform, were standing there.

"Come on in," Tom said. "Have a seat."

"Thanks, TC. We won't stay long. This is my nephew, Willis Buckner. He thinks he might want to get into law enforcement, so I'm taking him around with me for a few days just to get a taste of it."

Tom leaned over and shook his hand. "Glad to meet you, Willis. You're learning from the best."

"I just wanted to bring you up to date on the Hollis situation," the sheriff said. "We brought Mr. Hollis here to stand trial, but yesterday he collapsed and is in the hospital. To tell you the truth, I don't think he'll pull out of it. He sure doesn't look good to me."

"Will they let me see him?" Tom asked.

"Well, I suppose you could, but why would you want to? You wouldn't be wantin' to take the law into your own hands, now would you, TC?"

"Of course not, Sheriff. You know me better than that. I just don't want Mr. Hollis to go out of this world with bitterness in his heart and meeting his Maker in that condition. He needs to know he can be forgiven. Maybe he won't listen, but it's worth a try."

"Come on over tomorrow afternoon and I'll tell them to let you in. He sure needs somebody. None of his family has come yet. I don't know if they will or not. We can't locate Kenneth. If you decide to press charges, we'll try to run him down for you."

"I'll be there about 2 o'clock. I may bring my pastor with me. I'm not sure about that yet. He might be totally turned off by a preacher. Either way, I'll be there. I'll get back with you about Kenneth. Pressing charges may be the only way I'll get to talk to him."

"Whatever you say, TC. I know what I'd do, but I'm not as forgiving as you. We'll see you tomorrow."

Tom went back to his dinner, but his appetite was gone. He had little to say throughout the meal. Tessie did most of the talking. She was never without anything to say.

After dinner, Tom went to his desk and sat there with his head in his hands. He was thinking about what he should say to Mr. Hollis. He was afraid he would not be received well. He decided not to ask Pastor Dan to go with him. This was something he must do, and he needed to do it alone.

Tom had originally planned on spending tomorrow plowing the Winston field, which was a 120 acre tract that was purchased from Josiah Winston. He wanted to sow alfalfa for hay to feed the cattle next winter. It was nothing more than scrub brush, weeds, and wild flowers now. One more day wouldn't matter though. When he mentioned his intentions to Cassie, Tessie started screaming, "No, Daddy, no, Daddy. You can't chop down my flowers. Those are my flowers. That's my pretty garden."

"Honey, those are just weeds. You don't want those. We have pretty flowers in the yard. We need to raise food in that field to feed the cattle."

"No, Daddy, not in my garden. Please, Daddy. Don't cut down my garden," Tessie begged.

Tom looked up at Cassie with questioning eyes, hoping for help from her, but all he got was a grin and a shrug of the shoulders. Then she turned and left the room. Tom picked Tessie up and said, "Well, we'll work something out tomorrow."

Later, Cassie said, "You old softie. Looks like we're going to have a big plot of wild flowers for Tessie, never mind if the cattle starve." Then she laughed.

Tom frowned at her and said, "Well, you sure weren't any help."

"I was just enjoying the show," she said.

"Thanks heaps," he growled.

"You are most welcome, sir," she said as she blew him a kiss.

TC woke early the next morning and was outside before Cassie even knew morning had come. When Cassie got up, she went outside to see if TC was ready to eat breakfast, but she didn't see him. Cal was just coming out of the cook shack, so Cassie thought he might know his whereabouts.

"Hey, Cal! Have you seen TC?"

"Well, yes, as a matter of fact I have. What's he up to anyway? He's down at the Winston Field putting fertilizer on that patch of weeds. I thought he was going to plow that under today. He surely isn't planning on killing them all out with fertilizer. He didn't seem to want to talk about it though."

Cassie laughed and said, "I knew it! I guess you could say, he's just developed a new love for wild flowers, Cal. I'd be willing to bet that next year that will be the prettiest field of wild flowers you've ever seen."

"Well, to each his own, I guess. But I'm thinkin' old TC has slipped a cog."

Cassie giggled and said, "I'll relay that message to him for you."

"Maybe you better not do that. He didn't seem too happy with me this morning anyway."

It was nearly three hours later when TC came in the house. "TC, where have you been? You left without even eating breakfast this morning."

"Oh, I had some toast and coffee. I wasn't very hungry. I had some things I wanted to get done early this morning."

"Oh! You mean, some things you didn't want anyone else to know about."

"Now what do you mean by that?" he said, frowning.

"Well, I just thought you might have a difficult time explaining to the men why you were fertilizing weeds," she teased.

"Okay, Miss Smarty, if you knew where I was, why did you ask?" He was hoping he could get that little chore done early enough that no one would even know about it—but Cal had to get up early and spill the beans.

"If we're going to have wild flowers, we need to get the weeds out of them, don't we?" he said.

She smiled and put her arms around him and said, "Of course we do, and I think you are wonderful. And I know someone else who thinks you're wonderful, too."

"Well, just how is Mr. Wonderful going to explain to everyone that he is babying 120 acres of weeds so his little girl can have a garden of wild flowers without looking like a complete idiot?" he grumbled.

"I'm sure you'll get teased some for it, but you're a good sport. They'll respect and admire you for being a good daddy, even if that is a little extreme. Besides, it's your 120 acres. You can do with it as you please. You might consider just leaving an acre of wild flowers though, instead of the whole field."

"Guess I'll think on that later. I'm going to get cleaned up and go on into town to talk to Mr. Hollis. Say, why don't you go with me, Cassie? He might just listen better with a beauty like you there."

"I'd love to go with you, TC, but I don't think my being there would have any influence on Mr. Hollis. I'd have to see if my mom or Rheanna would keep Tessie for me. She couldn't go in the hospital, you know."

"Why don't you check on that. Then you and I can spend some time together, maybe dinner and whatever you would like to do."

Cassie called her mother. She was elated, as she felt she didn't get to see Tessie nearly enough. Cassie told her they might be late, since she wasn't sure what all they were going to do.

Cassie told Tessie she was going to Grandma's. She jumped up and down, squealed, and clapped. She always loved to go there because Grandma spoiled her so much. She began singing the song Cassie made up for her.

Away we go to Grandma's house,
Grandma's house, Grandma's house,
Away we go to Grandma's house,
To give her hugs and kisses.

Tessie always liked to dress in something really frilly when she went to see Grandma and Grandpa. They always fussed over her and told her how pretty she was. She got to wear her blue dotted swiss dress with all the ruffles. That was her favorite. She looked especially good in blue, because it highlighted her blue eyes.

Grandpa must have been watching for them, because the front door opened before they even had the motor turned off. Grandpa ran out with his arms outstretched, and Tessie flew into them.

After TC and Cassie left her parents' home, she said, "You know, it's strange. I lived most of my life in that house. I thought I would be homesick after I left it, but it doesn't seem like home anymore."

"Do you still long for the city, Cassie?" TC asked.

"I still love the city, but I don't long for it. There is a difference, you know. I enjoy shopping in the city. I love the lights, the excitement. I would like to vacation there, but I wouldn't want to live anywhere but where I am."

"I sure am glad. I didn't know how I was going to get all our cattle in our city home," he said with a grin.

She laughed and laid her head on his shoulder. "It seems strange sitting this close to you without having little Miss Jealousy squeezing in between. She sure doesn't like to be left out."

"It's nice to have an evening out occasionally, but I miss that little squirt when she's not with us, don't you?"

"Yes, I do. The crazy thing is, we talk about and look forward to having a night out, just the two of us, and then we spend the entire time talking about her, and all the cute things she does."

When they arrived at the hospital, the doctor and two nurses were in the room with Mr. Hollis. TC was concerned that perhaps he had taken a turn for the worse; but as it happened, it was just the daily routine visit. When the doctor came out, TC asked about him. The doctor told him he was weak, but holding his own.

TC and Cassie went into the room. "Hello, Mr. Hollis." TC offered his hand, but Mr. Hollis just grunted and turned his head. "We heard you were in the hospital and we were concerned."

"Afraid you wouldn't get to hear me fry?" Mr. Hollis growled.

"Mr. Hollis, I'm Cassie, TC's wife. My husband is not like that. Your being brought back here for trial was not his doing. Whether you intended to or not, you took my husband's father's life. According to the law, you must pay. That's why you're here. My husband has forgiven you. I don't think I could have been that forgiving, but my husband is like that. He's very concerned about you. You'd better listen to him."

"Well, I'm still alive and kickin', so you two can go on about your business," he said, as he motioned with his hand for them to leave.

"Mr. Hollis, I'd like to stay for just a minute and ask you a couple questions, if you don't mind."

"Well, you're gonna ask 'em whether I want ya to or not, so let's hear it," he said.

"I don't know what the reason might be for the grudge you had against my father. That really doesn't matter now. I loved my father. I always felt like he couldn't do any wrong. But I know he was just human, and humans are prone to make mistakes. I'm sure he made some. It wouldn't help anything for me to know about them, and I would prefer not to. I'm sure you can understand that. The reason I'm here today is that we both know that you've made mistakes, too. So have I. All mistakes or sins, I call them, have to be paid for. God's Son, Jesus, paid for all of our sins for us. Some of them, according to the law, we have to pay for ourselves on this earth. But we don't have to go to hell for them. God will forgive them. I've asked God to forgive my sins. I was just hoping you would do that, too. Mr. Hollis, don't leave this world carrying a grudge. God wants to forgive you."

There was a tear rolling out of the corner of Mr. Hollis' eye. "I think you two better go on home now. I'll give it some thought."

"I'd like to pray with you, but if you are uncomfortable with that, could I send my pastor over here to pray with you?" TC asked.

"Not now. I'll think about it. I can't see why your pastor would want to come."

"Please consider what I've said," TC pleaded. "I'll be back tomorrow. If you need me, have the nurse call me. I don't care what time it is. I'll come. It takes me an hour to drive here from the ranch, but I'll come as quickly as possible."

After they left, Tom asked Cassie if she minded if they stopped by Pastor Dan's to share the situation with him and have him pray for Mr. Hollis. She, too, felt they should do that. After they told him all the details, Pastor Dan suggested that he might just stop in that evening to see if Mr. Hollis had a change of heart. Tom felt a little relieved. His pastor said he would call him and let him know the outcome.

"You have sown a good seed," he said.

Tom and Cassie left. They drove on to Tulsa where they did some shopping, had a nice dinner, and drove back to her parents to get Tessie.

Little Tessie fell asleep in the car and didn't even wake up when Cassie put her in bed. She must have played very hard at Grandma's house. Tom and Cassie sat in the den talking for a long time and then had a snack before going to bed. Just as they were about to leave the kitchen, the phone rang. It was the hospital.

The caller said, "Mr. Marshall, this is Mrs. Coburn at Mercy Hospital. I'm calling about Mr. Hollis. He expired a short time ago. Before he died, he had asked us to give you a message. He said to tell you that everything was all right. He would see you in a few years. He said you'd understand. He seemed to be in much better spirits right before he died than he had anytime since he'd been here. I guess his pain left him. I'm sorry about your friend."

"Thank you, Mrs. Coburn. I do understand his message. I appreciate your concern," Tom said.

Tom relayed the message to Cassie and they thanked the Lord for it. The next day, Pastor Dan confirmed what Mrs. Coburn had told him. He said he had been at the hospital and had prayed with Mr. Hollis. He said that Mr. Hollis had been very receptive and had indeed trusted the Lord.

Death brings sadness, but with God, there can still be joy.

Chapter 18

Midnight at Noon

Cassie was sitting at the desk writing a letter, when Tom came into the house. Tessie heard him come in and ran to greet him.

"Daddy! Daddy! Did you know that tomorrow is my birthday? I'll be six years old."

"I know. You're going to be an old woman," he said.

"Daddy! You're silly. Are you gonna to get me a present?"

"As a matter of fact, I have a surprise for you, but you'll have to wait until tomorrow to find out about it. I'll give it to you at noon."

"I'm going to have a birthday party, and all my friends from church are coming, and Buddy is coming. We're best friends. Did you know that?" she asked.

"You mean Little Eagle?" TC questioned.

"Yes, Daddy, but he won't let anyone call him Little Eagle anymore. He wants to be called Buddy, cause that's what you call him. We're not just best friends. I'm going to marry him when I grow up. Then I'll be an Indian," she said.

TC grinned. "Is that what you want to be when you grow up?"

"Oh, yes, Daddy. More than anything. Maybe you can be one, too."

"Well, I think that would be just wonderful, but I guess we'll just have to wait and see," he said as he walked out the door.

"Mommy, Daddy has a birthday surprise for me. I know what it is."

"I know. I heard him tell you, but how do you know what it is?"

"Well, when he got you a surprise, it was a ring. I don't think Daddy would buy toys, and he doesn't know what size I wear, so I think it's a ring," Tessie said.

"I think you're a very smart little girl. You might just be right," she said as she bent down and kissed her on the cheek.

Cassie left Tessie at the kitchen table, coloring a picture while she went outside to water her flowers and talk to TC without little ears listening. TC was cinching the saddle on his horse when she walked up to him. Cassie reached over and patted Drake, a dark brown quarter horse.

"TC, don't you think you should have told Tessie that God didn't intend for her to be an Indian?"

"No. By the time she realizes that, she probably won't want to be an Indian anyway, or it won't make any difference. In the meantime, she's happy thinking that she will be one someday. Don't you think that's okay?"

Cassie raised her eyebrows and said, "Yes, I suppose you're right. She would really be disappointed to learn that it won't happen. What do you think about your prospective son-in-law?"

"Well, I couldn't pick a better one in that age bracket," he said with a laugh. "They sure are a fine family, but I don't think I'm going to let my daughter date until she's at least forty. Little Eagle may not choose to wait on her."

Cassie snickered. "I wonder how many fathers have made that statement. By the way, how's the new cook doing?"

"Oh, he's going to take some getting used to. Butch sure doesn't take any guff from anyone. He came out of a different mold than Johnny. But he's a pretty good cook, and that's what we hired him for. The men will break him in after awhile. Either that, or he will break their necks."

"Have you heard from Johnny since he left? I wonder how he's doing."

"No, not yet, but I expect him to write or call in a few days."

"Oh, what about Mr. Hollis? Have they made funeral arrangements yet. Will the funeral be in Illinois?"

"I haven't heard anything yet. Sheriff Buckner said he'd let me know as soon as the preparations were finalized."

"Well, I'm going to water my flowers. I'll see you in a little while." Tessie came out and began pestering her mom to let her take her shoes off and play in the water.

"This water is very, very cold, Tessie. But if you really want to, you may try it. Don't step on any of my flowers. What about your flowers? Don't they look pretty? Daddy got rid of most of the old ugly weeds. That was sweet of him to do that for you, wasn't it?" Cassie asked.

"Oh yes, Mommy. He's the best daddy in the whole world. I love my garden. He said next year I can only keep part of it, but he's going to let me have the whole garden this year. Look, Mommy. It looks like purple water. The wind is blowing the flowers and it looks like waves. They're beautiful, aren't they, Mommy?"

"Yes, Sweetheart, I have to admit, they are gorgeous. No one has a more beautiful garden than you."

Just about that time, they heard the door slam at the cook shack. Cal came out muttering something and wiping his clothes off with both hands. Then he shoved his hands down in his pockets and stomped out across the barn lot, kicking a can as he went.

"He and Kent must be feuding again, and looks like Kent got the best of him this time," Cassie said.

What actually happened didn't involve Kent at all. Cal had been giving Butch a rough time about how bad the coffee was. He said, "Do you expect us to drink this mud. I think this stuff came out of an old stump."

"No, I don't expect you to drink it. It would do you more good on the outside." Then he slung a mug full all over Cal. "There, you needed a bath, and that's probably as close as you'll get to one this week." Then he turned back to the kitchen and Cal stomped out the door.

The only one who got to witness this little session was Jack, and he wasn't usually one to get involved in all their scrapping. He would sit back, watch and grin, but he never participated. However, later that day he went up to Cal, put his arm around him and said, "If you don't know how to fight, Son, you better stay out of the ring."

Cal frowned and said, "Now what's that supposed to mean?"

"Well, one thing it means, Little Buddy Boy, is, that if you like to eat, you better not antagonize the cook. I just think you've met your match, my friend. And, if you're going to dish it out, you better sure learn to take it." Jack walked away, grinning and shaking his head.

Cassie finished watering her flowers when TC came riding his horse toward the house. When Tessie saw him, she yelled, "Daddy, Daddy, can I ride with you? We didn't ride today." She started to run toward him, but the grass was wet and her feet slipped. She slid into the flower bed and fell, face first into the mud. She started screaming.

Cassie couldn't help laughing. "It's all right Tessie. You aren't hurt. You'll be fine."

Tom jumped off the horse and ran to her. "Maybe we could use the hose and get some of this mud off."

"No, wait!" Cassie shouted. "I have a better idea." She turned to TC. "Why don't you go in the house and get the camera. Remember the picture of me in the cement. She will enjoy looking at it someday."

TC smiled and said, "That's how memories are made."

After they took her picture, Cassie took her out by the back door and brought a pan of warm water and washed most of the mud off before taking her in for a bath. Tessie was just worried about her clothes. But then she decided to look on the bright side. "Well, at least I didn't have on my boots." But then she remembered that she didn't get to ride today, and she was upset again.

"You and your daddy can go riding tomorrow. We have too much to do today. We have to get everything ready for your party tomorrow. I need you to help me."

Some little girls would love a surprise party, but Tessie enjoyed the planning as much as the party. She could hardly wait to get dressed and help with all the decorations.

After they had finished decorating, Tessie got to print everyone's name on a little placecard (with Cassie's help) and put them on the table. She was so excited about the party, Cassie knew she wouldn't be able to sleep that night.

After they finished and Tessie was in bed, Cassie asked TC what his big surprise was. He waved his forefinger back and forth and said, "No, no, no. You have to wait, too. This is a deep, dark secret. No one finds out until noon tomorrow."

"Won't you even give a little hint?" Cassie pleaded.

"My lips are sealed—not a word." Cassie knew TC well enough to know there was no use in pursuing the issue, so she decided to go on to bed.

TC had to go back out to the barn. Oscar, one of his favorite horses, was acting a little strange so he had Dale stay with it until he returned. He wanted to make sure the horse was all right. Dale had noticed it as he was riding in earlier that evening. Oscar was having difficulty standing up, and he was jerking his head and rolling his eyes. Tom thought perhaps he had gotten into some locoweed. If he had, and if he had eaten very much, it could be fatal. They took all the other horses out of that pasture just in case that was the problem. Tom decided if there was no change in the horse, or if he was worse, he would call the veterinarian tonight. He surely didn't want to lose a good horse.

When Tom opened the barn door, the horse whinnied and turned in his direction. "Well, that's an improvement," Tom said.

"Yeah," Dale replied. "I think he's going to be all right. He still refuses food or water, but he's standing up now without reeling or falling. His eyes are steady now, too. Maybe he'll be okay by morning."

"You can go on to the bunkhouse, Dale. I'll check on him early in the morning. I do think he got into some locoweed. I'm going to mow that field down in the morning and maybe fertilize it pretty heavily. I think I'll still call Doc Eber in the morning and see what he has to say about it.

Doc Eber was the town veterinarian. There was another vet in town, Sam Barlow, but he mostly treated just dogs and cats. Doc Eber was the only one for miles who treated farm animals. Tom looked Oscar over, then picked up a brush and gave him a good brushing and a few pats before leaving the barn. All of the animals on the ranch were always well cared for. Tom would never allow any animal on the ranch to be mistreated, even if it were not his own.

Old Gus was almost an exception to that rule though. Gus was a large white stallion that was very possessive of his stall. He would not permit anyone to be there with him. One night Tom dropped his pocket knife and it fell into Gus' stall. Tom climbed over the rail to retrieve it. Gus pinned him against the wall and tried to crush him. If Johnny hadn't come in, Tom might not be around to tell about it. Johnny threw a rope around Gus' neck and pulled him away from Tom. Tom picked up a board and started to club Gus with it, then slammed it down and went into the house. Old Gus didn't remain on the ranch very long. He was taken to an auction and sold to the highest bidder.

Tom took a last look around the barn and went back to the house, wondering if he was doing the right thing by not calling the vet tonight. He was thinking about the awesome responsibility it must be to be a doctor—having human lives in your hands, making life and death decisions. At that moment, he was thankful that was not his calling.

Sleep didn't come easily that night. In fact, Tom was restless throughout the entire night, tossing and turning. He had unpleasant dreams about horses dying, the Hollis family, someone getting stuck in quicksand, something burning, and someone calling for help, but he was not able to get to him. When he woke up, he felt like he'd been beaten. Cassie tried, unsuccessfully, to persuade him to go back to sleep, but he insisted that he needed to check on Oscar and call the veterinarian.

Dale was with Oscar when Tom went in the barn. Oscar was his old frisky self again. He had eaten and his water was nearly half gone. Tom told Dale to take him back out with the other horses. The vet said he couldn't be sure what the cause was. It could have been locoweed, something could have bitten him, or a number of other things. He suggested that they watch him and the other horses for a few days to make sure it didn't recur or that it wasn't something contagious being passed through the entire ranch.

While Tom was in the barn talking with Dale, the phone rang. Cassie answered and the caller replied, "This is Sheriff Buckner. Is TC in?"

"Oh, hello, Sheriff. TC is here, but not in the house. If you don't mind waiting, I'll go find him."

"That won't be necessary. I just wanted to let him know about the funeral arrangements for Mr. Hollis," Sheriff Buckner said. "You can just give him the message, if you will."

"Of course," Cassie said.

"They are burying him in Illinois in the same cemetery where Curly was buried. They're just having a graveside service. That was Mr. Hollis' request. It will be next Tuesday afternoon at 3 o'clock."

"I'll give TC this information right away."

"Thank you, Mrs. Marshall. Tell TC to give me a call about Kenneth. You have a good day now."

"Thank you, Sheriff. I'll be sure and tell him. Good bye."

Cassie relayed the message to TC. He frowned. He was still unsettled about his decision regarding Kenneth. He wasn't looking forward to the trip to Illinois, but that might be the best opportunity to talk with Kenneth. Maybe his father's death would give him a new perspective on life. On the other hand, he might be even more bitter as the Sheriff anticipated and be bad news. Either way, he guessed it was necessary for him to go.

Meanwhile, Tessie was excitedly getting ready for her big event. "Mommy, is it noon yet? Daddy said he would give me his present at noon."

"It's 11:30, Tessie. You have thirty minutes to wait."

"Why do I have to wait until noon? Do you think he would give it to me now?" Tessie asked.

"I'm sure I don't know, Sweetheart, but your daddy is coming toward the house right now. You can ask him when he comes in."

When TC opened the door he was greeted with "Daddy, Daddy, may I have my present now? Please, Please! Oh, Daddy, do I have to wait?"

"Yes, you do have to wait, Tessie. Your present isn't here yet. It is supposed to arrive at noon. Your mommy is getting a surprise, too. Is that all right with you for Mommy to get a surprise on your birthday?"

"Oh, yes. That would be very special." She jumped up and down and said, "We both get a surprise, Mommy." Then she frowned and said, "But Mommy doesn't need another ring, Daddy."

TC laughed and said, "You gals don't give me credit for having any imagination at all do you?"

"Those were not my sentiments, Mister. And tell me, sir, why do I get a surprise when it isn't even close to my birthday?"

His reply was just, "You'll see, you'll see."

Just then, Cassie heard someone driving down the lane. She went over to the window to see who was coming.

"It's Cherokee and Rheanna," she exclaimed. "I wonder why they are coming so early. The party isn't until 2 o'clock."

TC grinned and said, "Maybe they got confused." Then he walked out to the truck to meet them. Cassie and Tessie followed him to welcome their visitors.

"What'cha got in your truck, Cherokee? Those horses are beauties," Tom said.

"Oh look, Daddy! It's a baby. May I touch it? Please, Daddy!"

Cassie said, "Cherokee, they're gorgeous! I've never seen such beautiful horses. She's the shiniest black I've ever seen."

TC opened the truck and helped unload the horses. "Surprise, ladies. These are your two new rings. Actually, this is Mama and Baby."

"What!" Cassie gave a surprised shriek. "These are ours? I can't believe it. Oh, TC, you are wonderful."

"Daddy, Daddy, may I keep it? Is it really mine. Is it a little boy or a little girl?" Tessie was jumping, clapping, and screaming in between questions.

"Whoa!" TC said. "One question at a time. Your little girl horse is really yours. You may keep her and you'll have to give her a name. Cassie, yours already has a name. It's Ebony." He turned to Tessie. "What about yours, Sweetheart? Do you have a name for your little colt?"

"Oh yes, Daddy. Her name is Midnight."

Cassie smiled. "How ironic! Midnight at noon! Look, TC! She has a white heart on her chest. That's the only white on her. It's almost a perfect heart."

"I want to ride her, Daddy. May I ride her?" Tessie begged.

"No, Honey," TC told her. "Not yet. She isn't broken yet. We're going to let Cherokee work with her for awhile first. Also, she needs to get used to you and we have to get a saddle for her. It won't be long though—maybe in a couple weeks."

"Oh, Daddy, this is the very best day of my life."

Chapter 19

School is for Sissies

The summer seemed to fly. Tessie spent most of her time with her new friend, Midnight. For several weeks, she led him around the yard by his reins. After awhile TC left the reins off and Midnight followed Tessie around like a little puppy. It wasn't long until they had a saddle for Midnight and she was riding with TC by her side. Midnight never minded the saddle from the very first. He seemed to enjoy the rides as much as Tessie.

When August rolled around, Cassie announced that Tessie would be starting school in three weeks.

"Oh no, Mommy. I can't go to school. I have to work here on the ranch. Daddy needs me. I already know my ABC's, I can count to 100, and I can write my name. Besides, school is for sissies. I just can't go to school."

"I'm sorry, Honey. That is something we don't have a choice about. Everyone has to go to school. Someday you'll be very glad you went. When you get there, you will love it. There will be a lot of children to play with, and many, many things to learn," Cassie told her. "Buddy goes to school. You'll get to see him there. He went to school last year."

"Can Midnight go?" Tessie asked.

"No. They don't have a place for horses. Besides, he wouldn't like it there. He would rather stay in the pasture where he can run and eat all day," Cassie told her.

"Well, so would I. We are best friends and we can't be parted, Mommy. That isn't fair. She'll think I don't love her anymore. It will break her heart."

"She knows you love her. She'll look forward to you coming home every day. This will also give her time to spend with her mommy. Her mommy loves her, too, you know. You can ride her every evening when you get home."

That night when Tessie went to bed, TC went in to pray with her. She asked her daddy to pray that they would make a new law that people didn't have to go to school if they didn't want to. TC talked with her for a long time about the importance of school and how much he wanted her to go, so that she could be his partner on the ranch.

"Okay, Daddy. If you really want me to go, I will, but I will miss you and Midnight and Mommy. Will you miss me, too?" she asked.

"Of course. we'll miss you, Honey. But we want you to be the smartest girl in town, so we'll just have to deal with that, won't we?"

Tessie still wasn't at all happy about school, but she decided if her daddy wanted her to go so badly, she would make the most of it. She sure wanted to be his partner. She did, however, shed some tears after he went out and closed the door.

The next morning, Tessie was back to her happy little self again. She woke up singing "Somewhere Over the Rainbow." She dressed, danced around her room, and then started to run outside, but Cassie stopped her, insisting that she have a good breakfast first.

"After you finish eating, we're going to the city with Grandma to buy you some new school clothes and new crayons, pencils, and scissors. Won't that be fun?"

"I like buying new clothes, but let's not say that word all day today, okay?"

"What word, Tessie?" Cassie asked.

"You know. School! Let's pretend that we're all getting married, and weere going shopping to buy our wedding things. Won't that be fun?"

Cassie laughed and then agreed that would be great fun. She and Tessie and Grandma would pretend they were getting married.

"Are we going shopping for our trousseau?" Cassie asked.

"What is that, Mommy?"

"Why that's the clothes we take on our honeymoon after we get married."

"Oh, yes! We must buy our trousseau." Tessie used that word over and over. She liked the sound and it was new to her. When her daddy came in, she said, "Daddy, Grandma and Mommy and I are all going to the city to buy our trousseau."

"Your trousseau! Now, Cassie, don't you think this Little Gray Eagle thing has gone a bit far?"

Cassie said, "Well, we're pretending, so we don't have to use that big bad word. You know, S-C-H-O-O-L."

"Well, we sure don't want to cloud our day with wicked words like that. You gals have a good time, but be careful. You have my favorite women in your care, you know. I'm going to be quite busy today. We're going to round up 500 head of cattle to sell to the Brecher farm tomorrow. I probably won't be home tonight. They are way out past Rocky Canyon. We're taking provisions with us to camp there tonight," TC said.

"In that case, we might just stay in the city tonight and drive back in the morning," said Cassie.

"I think that's a good idea," he said. He leaned down and gave her a kiss, and then kissed Tessie. "Take good care of my girls," he instructed, and then he walked out the door.

Cassie called her mom and suggested the new arrangement for her approval. Her mom paused for a moment to think about tomorrow's schedule. Since nothing came to mind, she agreed that it was a great idea to spend the night in the city and return home the next day. She knew Cassie's dad wouldn't mind. She already had plenty of food prepared for him. Since he had retired, he always enjoyed concocting things in the kitchen anyway.

They had a wonderful time, and didn't say that horrible word one time. They bought all the things they needed and a few that were not on the list. Tessie could hardly wait to wear her trousseau.

They ate at a quaint little outdoor café that had a white wrought iron fence encompassing the area, which gave it a French flair. An elderly gentleman played the violin. He had a cup beside him for tips. It felt good just to sit and relax after shopping so long, and enjoy the music and visit. Tessie got a special delight out of putting money in the old man's cup and telling him she enjoyed his music. She decided that he could play in her wedding. When she delivered that news to him, he laughed and said he would be delighted to do that.

When they went to their hotel, Tessie insisted on trying on her new clothes again. She especially liked the little plaid dress with the red weskit and matching tam. Tessie went to sleep early. She was exhausted from her busy day.

Cassie and her mother enjoyed the opportunity to have a long, uninterrupted visit. They talked about many things, but one in particular was a lengthy conversation about the Bible. Cassie had discovered some things in the Bible that were confusing to her, and she wanted her mother's thoughts about them. They talked for several hours. Upon realizing the lateness of the hour, they reluctantly decided they had better join Tessie in dreamland.

It was a beautiful day for driving home. Tessie was busy in the back seat playing with a new doll, which was part of the unplanned purchases. Cassie and her mother continued their conversation from the night before. All in all, it was a very successful trip.

The following three weeks passed quickly. The new clothes helped Tessie's attitude about school. She was still unhappy about leaving Midnight. But she had reconciled herself to the fact that school must not be just for sissies, because her daddy had gone to school, and he definitely was not a sissy. In fact, he was the greatest, and the biggest, and the funnest person in the whole world.

When the big day arrived, Cassie took pictures of Tessie leaving for school. Tessie waved good-bye to everyone and gave Midnight an extra pat, telling her that she would miss her. Then she started to cry again. Cassie assured her that she would go into her school with her and stay until she felt comfortable with her leaving. That ended up being most of the morning. Her teacher was a sweet, compassionate lady in her early fifties. She recognized the problem and gave Tessie the project of feeding the goldfish. Then she told Tessie to tell her mommy goodbye. Tessie turned and smiled, waving to her mommy.

Cassie was relieved that she was content, but a little sad that her baby was growing up. As she drove back home alone, she dearly missed her little girl.

Chapter 20

Tessie Grows Up

Tessie made it through the first grade somehow, but she really never did want to be there. The first few weeks were difficult, but it got easier as time passed. She made friends easily and she didn't have any difficulty with learning, but she still missed Mommy, Daddy, and Midnight. Cassie attributed her difficult time with school to being an only child.

Each year her enthusiasm about school improved. She liked being involved with school activities. She was in choir, school plays, and she loved to play softball and basketball. She had many friends who came out to the ranch frequently. They all liked to ride horses and there was always a lot to do on the ranch. But Tessie still preferred being with her dad. She considered herself his partner. After all, that was the deal when she agreed to go to school in the first place.

The first time Tessie realized that her and her daddy's initials were the same, she was ecstatic. She was in the sixth grade and was doing her homework at the time. She started doodling on a piece of paper. Among other things, she wrote her initials and repeated them aloud. She screamed out, "That's my daddy!"

Cassie looked around the door of the kitchen to see what she was talking about. "What's your daddy?" she asked.

"My initials are the same as Daddy's."

"Of course, dear. That's why we chose your name. This ranch will always belong to TC Marshall." Cassie tilted her head and waited to see Tessie's reaction to that comment.

"This ranch will actually be mine someday?" Tessie asked.

"Well, you didn't think we'd leave it to a stranger, now did you?" Cassie asked with a grin.

Tessie went back to her homework, but it was difficult to concentrate on her work while thinking about being TC Marshall.

As Tessie grew, she became a very valuable worker on the ranch. She went with her father on round-ups, watered and fed the horses, brushed the horses, and cleaned tools. Tom dreaded school starting each year almost as much as Tessie did.

This year for Tessie's birthday, her mom and dad bought her a car. It was not a new one by any means, but one that would be reliable for her to drive to school. It was no longer practical for her to ride the bus because of all the activities she had after school. The agreement was that she had to take care of it, which meant paying for gas, oil, and any repairs that became necessary. She took care of the license and insurance, also. She received an allowance for working at the ranch. She worked hard and sometimes put in long hours. She put most of her money in the bank, but probably had spent one third on clothes and entertainment. She always tithed when she received her money. She had been taught that from the time she received her first pennies. She didn't have any problem with that. It was always a joy to be able to give something to the Lord. It gave her a good feeling.

TC was always fair with her. He gave her raises as she grew because she really did earn what she made. She could almost run the ranch without him. There were times when she felt like she was overworked. But most of the time she considered herself to be a very spoiled girl when she compared herself with her classmates. She wasn't about to admit that fact to her parents though.

Tessie had a real interest in art. In fact, her teacher talked with Cassie about her work. Because she had excelled so, she felt that Tessie should take special art classes. Tessie especially enjoyed making sketches of horses. Cassie had them hanging all over the house. It wasn't until Tessie's sophomore year in high school that she actually took up painting, but she still preferred it to be just a hobby.

One of her most beautiful works was a painting of Midnight and Ebony. It was a perfect picture of the love of a mare and her colt. Ebony had her head over Midnight's neck. The picture was done by memory, because Midnight was now as big as her mother.

Tessie was working on two life-size paintings of her mother and her father. She was using two snapshots and doing the work at school so that it would be a surprise for their anniversary. Her father's picture was in work clothes, boots, and cowboy hat. Her mother's was in a long, full, blue dress. Only the face and pose were from the snapshot. The clothes were her own creation. It took much longer to do the paintings than she had anticipated. She was afraid they weren't going to be completed in time. However, if they weren't, she was going to make the presentation anyway. She had already made arrangements with her art teacher to bring them to the school on their anniversary for the unveiling. They would be far enough along to get the full effect.

One afternoon when Tessie was working on her paintings, she was sitting back looking at her work and thinking what a perfect couple her parents were. Her art teacher came in and asked her, "Tessie, what are your plans for your future?"

"Oh, hi, Mrs. Archer. Well, that's easy. I'm going to work on the ranch."

"What? That's all! Tessie, you can't throw away your wonderful talent. Aren't you going to pursue a future in art?" she asked in shock.

"Mrs. Archer, I deeply appreciate all the time you've given me. I hope I haven't misled you, but I will never leave the ranch. I will always sketch and paint, but it will be just a hobby. My heart is there at the ranch."

"What are you going to do about college? You know you could easily get a scholarship in art," Mrs. Archer said.

"Oh, I will go to college, I suppose. My parents both have their hearts set on it. If it were up to me though, I would just stay at the ranch."

"You are a jewel, Tessie. I wish you every happiness. What will you do when that certain young man comes along and sweeps you off your feet, and his heart is not on the ranch?"

"That won't happen. I don't think there's a man who could measure up to my dad, and he would have to—to win my heart."

"Oh, Tessie, that scares me. I'm afraid you're in for a heartbreak someday. I hope I'm wrong, Honey. You pray about that, Child. God can bring you the right man, but don't expect him to be like your dad."

Tessie gave her a sweet, appreciative smile and said, "Thank you, Mrs. Archer, for your sincere concern. You are special."

Tessie had many invitations for dates, but she kept most of her social life with groups of friends and not just one person. Occasionally, she would let a young man take her home from a church function, but she never permitted it to progress to a serious nature. Her church had frequent youth activities that she always attended, but she mingled with all her friends. Her friends often questioned her about dating. They thought perhaps her parents were against it, but it was of her own choosing.

There was one young man who was pursuing Tessie. In fact, he had his heart set on winning her. His name was Robbie Moreland. He was a handsome young man who could have dated nearly any girl in the high school. He tried to get a date with her for two years, but every attempt failed. He called her a number of times, but always she was busy or, for one reason or another, could not go out with him. One day in the lunch room at school, he sat down next to her and asked her, in an almost demanding tone, "Tessie, why are you avoiding me? I don't have a horrible reputation or anything. I make good grades. I don't have any wicked habits. I take baths. I wear deodorant. I go to church. Why won't you go out with me?"

Tessie threw her head back in laughter. "Oh, Robbie, I think you're a great guy, but I'm not looking to date anyone right now. I suppose, if I were going to date, I would sooner date you than anyone, but I don't want to get involved with one person. Can you understand that?" she asked.

"What about the prom, Tessie? You can't go with a group to the prom. Will you go with me?" he pleaded.

"Can you give me a week to give you an answer?" she asked.

"To see if you get a better offer?" he asked with searching eyes.

"Of course not, silly. If I decide to go, I'll go with you. Okay? But either way, Robbie, I'll just be your friend."

"Tessie, I promise you. I'll show you a wonderful time. It's a deal. I won't say anymore. One week, then I'll come back for your answer." He squeezed her hand, and left the lunch room to go to his next class.

Tessie sat at the table for several minutes thinking about the conversation with Robbie. Was she dopey, as her friends called her? A lot of the girls would have given their right arm to go to the prom with Robbie Moreland. All of her friends were dating. A couple of them were even engaged. That was sure scary. Maybe that was the problem. Maybe she was afraid she would fall in love. She needed to talk to her mother about it and get her thoughts. Her mother certainly had a lot of wisdom and would know what she should do.

Sharon Bishop was her best friend, except for Buddy. She couldn't talk to her about it. She's the one who started calling her dopey in the first place because she had been avoiding Robbie. And Buddy, well, he thought she should date him. They had always been such good friends. Why did he have to ruin it by thinking they should date. He even tried to kiss her the last time they went horseback riding—which made it the last time they rode together. She smiled as she thought about how she used to think she would someday marry Buddy. He sure was a sweet boy, but she certainly did not want to get married to Buddy or anyone else. Why did life have to be so complicated anyway?

Tessie went to the rest of her classes in body only, for her mind was in another world. She had to stay after school that night for cheerleading try-outs. What was she doing there anyway? That was something she let her friends talk her into. She would much rather be back at the ranch. Oh well, it wouldn't hurt to give it a shot. After all, she did enjoy her friends and didn't want to lose touch with them. It wouldn't break her heart, though, if she didn't make it. She, Jo Ellen, Bonnie, Sharon, and Carla all went in together. They were all friends and did most things with each other. They were hoping they would all make the cheerleading squad. That is, except for Tessie. She was having second thoughts. Sixteen girls tried out and they were choosing only ten. Tessie thought they were all good. She was thankful that she was not a judge. The girls wouldn't know who was selected until the next day.

She went home that night, barely said hi to her mother, and went straight to her room. She threw herself down on her bed, which was not normal for Tessie. She usually came in all bubbly and full of chatter. Her mother followed her into her room.

"Tessie, are you all right? What's wrong?" her mother asked.

"I'm fine Mom. I'm just confused. I think I want to be a hermit."

Cassie laughed. "Boy, that's a switch. You, who always have a pack around you, wanting to be a hermit."

"That's the problem, Mom. I just want to be alone sometimes, and they're always there. Is that bad? Is there something wrong with me to feel that way? I love my friends, but should I have to do everything with them? And not only that, should I want to date? Mom, Robbie Moreland has asked me to the prom. I don't know what to tell him. He's a very nice boy, but I already know he has a crush on me. He's told everyone. I don't want to be anyone's steady girlfriend. Would I be making a mistake to go with him?"

"Well, Honey, those are tough questions. You are a Junior. The prom is a big event. If you don't go, will you regret it later? That's a question no one else can answer for you. If you do go with him and don't want to date him again, you'll have to be firm but tactful in telling him so. It may hurt him, but you can't let yourself get involved in a relationship with which you are uncomfortable. If you don't go at all, you may always regret it. I know these are not the answers you were wanting, but only you can decide what's best for you. You could talk to your daddy about it, but you and I both know what he would say. He'll never be ready for you to date."

Tessie grinned. "Yes, I know that Mom. I'm still his baby until it comes to driving cattle. Then he thinks I'm a man."

"Tessie, as for your question about being alone, sometimes it's very good to spend time alone, just meditating on things and sorting out matters in your life that you can't do with a lot of people around. Don't feel guilty about wanting time to yourself. That's the artist in you, Honey. I can feel that when you're playing the piano. I've noticed that when you have thinking to do, you either paint or play the piano. I think that's a very good thing. Your friends have different talents and different personalities. They may not react to situations in that manner. That's all right. Don't expect them to. But you, you need that time alone. You must take it, Tessie. Don't let anyone rob you of it. Tessie, why don't you talk to the Lord about it? You know He cares about every facet of your life."

"I know He does, Mom, but sometimes I sure wish I could audibly hear His answers. I'm not always sure I'm doing His will. Do you ever feel that way?"

"Of course, I do. I think probably everyone does. But He will give you direction or lead you to someone who will have the right answers for you. Just always be sure you have peace about something before you act on it. If you don't have peace in your heart, you can be sure it's not God's will for you to do it."

Tessie did pray that night about her problems and was able to go to sleep, leaving it in the Lord's hands. But the next morning, she still didn't have any answers.

She didn't discuss the prom with any of her friends at school that day, and again avoided Robbie. After school, she called her mother and told her she would be late coming home from school. She had some things to take care of and would be home as soon as she was finished. She went into town and drove over to her church. Pastor Dan was there finishing some work in his study. She actually had gone in to talk with the youth pastor, Pastor Ken Rich, but he wasn't in, so she asked if Pastor Dan could talk with her.

He said, "Why sure, Tessie. I always have time for you. What can I do for you?" She poured her whole story out to him, and he listened intently. "Well, Tessie, here's what I think. First of all, I know Robbie Moreland. He's a fine young man. He has fine Christian parents. You couldn't go wrong having a date with him, I feel sure. But, I don't think that's the problem here. I think you're afraid of displeasing your father. I know TC. You're his only daughter, his only child, in fact. He'll have a hard time ever letting you go; but someday, he will have to. In the meantime, dating is a part of preparing for marriage. I'm not too sure the world has presented the best plan for it. I think your choice of group activities is far better than couple dating. However, your school has put its stamp of approval on this prom. If you decide you want to go, Robbie Moreland would be my choice for your escort. Now that is probably not the answer you were looking for, but it is the best I can do. You must make that final decision."

Tessie thanked Pastor Dan and told him how much she appreciated him taking the time to talk with her, then she left to go to the ranch. All the way home she thought about what her pastor had said. Robbie Moreland was a fine young man. Her mother had said she might regret it if she didn't go. Her friends all thought she should go. So why did she still feel this way. She would go! There was no reason to refuse to go. She wouldn't make Robbie wait a week. She would tell him tomorrow. Then she could put it behind her and get on with things and get it out of her mind. Would it be that simple? She hoped so. Anyway, she had made up her mind. She smiled as she thought, Yes, I do have peace about it.

The next day when she arrived at school, she immediately started looking for Robbie. He was usually in the library every morning before school started, reading or finishing homework. She looked inside and glanced around the room, but he wasn't there. As she turned, she nearly ran into him as he came around the corner.

"Robbie!" she screamed. "I was looking for you."

"Well, you found me, and nearly scared me to death, I might add. Should I be happy or disappointed?"

"Well, I'm not sure about that, but I have decided to go to the prom with you."

He grabbed her hands and smiled. "I want to shout. Thanks, Tessie! Thanks! I don't know who or what caused you to decide in my favor, but I'm grateful."

"Well, there were a lot of deciding factors, but we won't go into that now." She smiled and waved as she walked down the corridor.

She felt good about her decision. After the prom, she would insist on keeping their time together going to church activities or school functions with the group and not single dating. She knew in her heart, that was the best way.

Chapter 21
Remember the Land

Tessie bounded in from school doing her latest cheer. "Hi Mom. Where's Daddy?"

"He took Sunshine out. I think he rode down to the river."

Sunshine was one of the newest horses on the ranch. She was a beautiful Palomino. Her coat shone like gold in the sun. Her beauty was exceeded only by her stubbornness. If she decided not to move, you might as well decide that where you are is the spot you wanted to be, because no one was going anywhere.

"I'm going to ride, Mom. I'll be back in a little while."

"Okay, Honey. Don't forget your piano lesson," her mother reminded.

Tessie quickly saddled her horse and rode down to see her dad. He was sitting on his big rock spinning rocks into the river.

"Hey!" she hailed. "You can't catch any fish that way."

"I can probably catch just as many this way as I could with a pole over here. I have never had any luck fishing here. Ole Davey sure used to catch some nice ones here though, so I can't say it can't be done. What are you up to, Sugar?"

"Oh, I just wanted to tell you about my date," she said.

"Date? What date?" he asked.

"Robbie Moreland invited me to the prom. I told him I would go."

"Is that Roger and Clara's son?"

"Yes, Daddy, he's the one."

"I thought you said you weren't ready to date."

"Well, I didn't think I wanted to miss the prom, so when Robbie asked me to go with him I did some checking on him, and decided to go. You don't mind, do you?"

"Well, since you already accepted, would it make any difference?" he growled.

"If you're not happy about it, Daddy, I can cancel."

"Did your mother approve of this date?"

"She said since Robbie was a nice boy from a good family, I should make my own decision. That's why I accepted. I never dreamed you would mind."

"Oh, I guess it's okay. I just don't like the idea of my little girl out with some old, grubby boy," he said, and then he reached over and hugged her.

"He's really a nice guy, Daddy. You'll like him. He's your kind of person."

"No he's not! Not if he's taking my little girl out." TC grinned. "There's not a boy in this world good enough for my little girl."

"Daddy, I'm not a little girl anymore, you know. You don't want me to be an old maid now, do you?"

"Well, it wins hands down over any other alternative I can think of. Do you think you could be serious about this Robbie guy?"

"No, of course not, Daddy. But someday, if the right one comes along, I want to get married. He'll have to be just like you. Do they still have your mold, Daddy ?" she asked with a grin.

They laughed and Tessie stood up. He reached his hand up to her and said, "Here, pull your old dad up. I think these bones have grown down into that rock." He groaned as she pulled him up. She put her arm around his waist and he put his arm around her shoulder and they walked back to the horses.

"We'd better get up to the house if we want any supper tonight," she said. "If we're any later, Mom won't let us in." Then she threw her hands up to her face and her mouth popped open as she gasped, "Late! Oh no! Mom's going to kill me! I forgot my piano lesson."

"Well, you'd better go call Mrs. Brian and apologize pronto."

Tessie ran to the house expecting a good scolding from her mother only to find her singing in the kitchen. Tessie stuck her head around the corner and said, "Mom, guess what I forgot."

"You forgot your piano lesson, of course."

"And you're not upset?" Tessie asked in surprise.

Her mother smiled and asked, "Would it help?"

Tessie just stood there with a puzzled frown. This was not at all the mom she knew.

"Mrs. Brian called shortly after you went out to ride. She said something had come up and she had to cancel tonight. I told her that would be fine. Feel better now?"

"Oh, Mom, you are ornery. You're worse than Daddy." Then she kissed her mother's cheek and ran upstairs.

Cassie called after her, "Wash your hands and come to dinner."

Tessie enjoyed the time she spent with her dad that afternoon. She enjoyed talking with him more than almost anything she did. She was glad he wasn't too unhappy about the prom. She knew he wouldn't say no, but she also knew he wouldn't be overjoyed about it.

The prom had come and gone. Robbie Moreland kept his promise. He did show her a wonderful time and was a perfect gentleman. He was not that *Mr. Right,* who comes along once in a lifetime though. He already had his plans charted and Tessie couldn't envision herself anywhere in them He certainly wouldn't ever become a rancher, but he was a swell friend.

Tessie completed her junior year and was enjoying every moment at the ranch. She never tired of the work or lacked for things to do. She didn't have much time to paint since school was out, but she did make some sketches one afternoon when she went riding. She always took her sketch book with her everywhere she went.

She was in contact with the university she planned to attend after high school. She applied for an art scholarship with the assistance of Mrs. Archer, but wouldn't have an answer on that for some time. She decided she would go to the university where her mother had attended. She and her parents were going to tour the university a couple weeks before school started this year. Tessie, strangely enough, was looking forward to college life. She looked at it as an adventure. If she focused on the fact that she was leaving the ranch, she probably would change her mind and not go.

Tessie spent her summer working, riding, roping, and learning everything she could about the ranch. Her father taught her about the buying and selling, financing, everything she could possibly ever need to know. She developed the same love for the land that her father had. He could sense that. For that reason, he was eager to teach her all he could. He could not have been prouder of a son or loved a son any more than he loved Tessie. When he thought how childish and selfish he had once been, he felt ashamed and foolish . He thought that when he found out he would never have a son, his dreams were gone. It was as if his world ended. But here was his sweet little Tessie, doing everything that he could do, himself, and loving it just as he did. God always knows best.

When Tessie's high school years were over and she left that first time for college, it was a very difficult time for Tom. He had an unexplainable fear that gripped his heart. He knew she would be back, but this feeling was so strong that he almost asked her not to go. There was no foundation to warrant his fears, so he tried to hide his feelings. This was something he must give to the Lord. He must have faith and trust the Lord to take care of his precious little Tessie. He knew Cassie loved Tessie just as much as he did, but she seemed to handle her leaving much better than he did.

After Tessie left, he threw himself into his work. He put in many long hours, doing many of the jobs himself which he normally assigned to his men. He felt it was better to work than to think. Tessie was a good girl, and wise. He knew she was in good hands, and that he had no cause to worry. But he somehow could not put his fears behind him. He should have discussed his feelings with Cassie so they could have prayed together; but he felt foolish in his fears, so he kept his feelings to himself. Cassie sensed his aloofness and thought it was because she had encouraged Tessie to go to the same university where she had gone. When she tried to talk to TC about it, he always had something else that required his time.

Things went on this way for some time. One day Cherokee came by with three new horses for TC to look over. Cassie came out to give TC a message. Not too much was said, but enough that Cherokee was aware of the problem.

"TC," Cherokee said. "You are a very stubborn man. And sometimes you are very foolish. This is not my business, but you are my friend. I must tell you. It would be an awful thing if you lose her love. Don't be blind to her needs and her feelings. I see the hurt in her eyes when you distance yourself from her. Think about it, TC. We all make mistakes, but we can all turn from those mistakes and make amends. I say this because I don't want to see you make this big mistake. I have said enough." He gave TC a pat on the back and walked off.

Tom stood there with his mouth open watching Cherokee walk away. He felt stunned. He couldn't believe what he had heard. Was he stubborn? Was he foolish? Had he been blind to Cassie's feelings? He knew that he had poured all his time and effort into the ranch, but it was not his intent to withdraw from Cassie. Had he been so selfish as to not recognize that she was hurting? Cherokee said we could turn from our mistakes and make amends. What could he do to make amends? He looked toward the house and saw Cassie looking out the window. Yes, Cherokee had been right. He had been a very foolish man. TC recognized at that moment what a wise and valuable friend Cherokee was.

TC walked up to the house. When he went in, he turned around and bent over. "Cassie, kick me," he said.

"What! What are you talking about, TC?" she asked.

"I need a good swift kick in the seat of the pants." He walked over to her shaking his head and smiling. "Oh, Cassie, why do you put up with me? I didn't realize what I was doing to you. I'm sorry, Cassie. Will you forgive me?"

"Well, I don't know what or who shook you out of your trance, but welcome home, Sweetheart. It's good to have you back." She put her hands on his shoulders and kissed him on the cheek.

He threw his arms around her and said, "Oh no! Not a little peck like that." He then gave her a long, meaningful kiss and said, "It's good to be home. I love you."

They spent the evening pouring out their hearts and sharing their hurts and fears. Things always look brighter and there's always hope when shared with someone you love.

That night, Tom sat down at his desk and wrote Tessie a letter. He wanted her to know that he missed her, but that he was trusting God to take care of her. He wrote:

Dear Tessie,

We miss you so very much. I hope you are having a wonderful time, but not so much that you won't want to come home. We are managing to keep everything going around here, but it will run a lot smoother when you get home.

Honey, I hope you meet a lot of good friends and have some sweet, meaningful relationships, but Remember the Land. It will always be here for you. Except for the Lord, it is the only thing you can count on to never change. Cherish it, Honey. Let it become a part of you, and you become a part of it. It will always be here. Don't forget it. I'm counting on you.

Your mother and I love you with all our hearts. Take care of yourself, and write when you can.

Love, Dad

Chapter 22

The Handsome Stranger

Now in her second year in college, it was only two weeks before Tessie would be coming home for Christmas vacation. Cassie was baking and decorating. She wanted the house to look its very best for Tessie. She wouldn't put the tree up until Tessie came home though. Tessie always loved decorating the tree. Putting up the tree was the only part of decorating with which TC became involved, but he enjoyed that event almost as much as Tessie and Cassie.

They always did special things on that night—things they reserved for that night only, to make it an extraordinary occasion. For instance, Cassie always made wassail, Tessie made popcorn balls, and TC either roasted chestnuts or cracked pecans. Cassie always made special, festive sandwiches for this night. She used white bread and dyed the filling red and green, or on some of them she dyed the bread dough. Then she layered the bread and filling ten layers deep and sliced the bread and filling into small triangles. TC always made fun of them, but he enjoyed the fancies as much as the ladies did.

This year Grandma and Grandpa Layne were going to join them. Grandma made something special for the decorating party, but she was keeping it a secret until the big event. Cassie didn't know if it was to eat or to use for decorating. Cassie make an ornament every year and put a date on it. She started this practice their first year together. When Tessie was three, she began helping. Then when she was eight, she started making her own decoration. This made the tree more meaningful. One year when Johnny was still at the ranch, he brought a decoration that he made for their tree. It was a cookie, baked until it was as hard as a rock, then decorated with paint. He wrote on it, "Merry Christmas, Cookie." Cassie treasured it and used it every year. Surprisingly enough, it held up well over the years.

They were hoping for snow while Tessie was home. TC purchased an old sleigh and spent a lot of time refurbishing it. Cassie planned on inviting several of Tessie's friends over for a sleigh ride. The ranch would be the perfect place for this. It was so beautiful in the winter. The rolling hills and all the evergreens were so picturesque when they were covered with snow. The place looked like the perfect setting for a Christmas card.

TC and Cassie always did something special for the ranch hands before Christmas. One year TC cleaned out the barn and invited everyone in town to come over. He hired a group of musicians and they had a barn dance. He dug a hole in the corral and roasted a pig. It wasn't very cold that year, so they had outdoor games. Some of the men played horse shoes, others had roping contests—about ten different events in all. TC was thinking about doing it again this year, and perhaps making it a yearly event, because it went over so well.

It was the night before Tessie was to leave Tulsa to come home. She was planning on driving home with a friend from Rolla. Cassie noticed there were snowflakes falling when she went out to shake a rug. Her first thought was about Tessie driving home in bad weather. Maybe it wouldn't amount to much, but she was going to pray about it.

TC hadn't said anything to Cassie about it, but she knew he was concerned, too, because he kept going to the window and looking at the sky. Once he went into the den and closed the door. She could hear the sound of the radio filtering through as he located a station giving the weather forecast. When he came out, he was frowning and pacing the floor. Finally he said, "Cassie, I think perhaps I should go to Tulsa and pick up Tessie. I don't want her to drive in this weather. I'm going to call her and let her know, so she won't be worried about driving."

TC got out the little book in which they kept telephone numbers and looked up her number. Cassie had drawn little hearts all around her name. He smiled when he saw it. He gave the number to the operator and listened while the phone rang. Several rings passed and still no answer. Finally the operator said, "I'm sorry, your party does not answer. You'll need to place your call later."

TC's frown deepened. He took Cassie's hand and said, "Come on, Cassie. We need to pray for her. God will get her home." They knelt down by the sofa and were just beginning to pray when the door flew open and the cold wind rushed in. Startled, they both jumped to their feet. Tessie ran in with suitcase in hand and yelled, "Surprise!"

"Oh, Tessie, you're home! We were just praying you'd get home safely."

"No, Cassie, we were just about to pray that she would get home safely. The Lord answered before we even asked. Isn't God good?"

"I heard the weather report this morning, so I left a day early," Tessie said.

They hugged and talked and talked and hugged and thanked the Lord again and again. By morning, the ground was covered with the most beautiful snowfall they recalled ever having.

When they went out that morning to bring in Tessie's things, they were surprised to see a small trailer behind Tessie's car. "Did you need a trailer to haul all your stuff?" her dad asked.

"You'll see," she said. "You know how I've made an ornament every year, Mom? Well, this year I've made a special decoration for you and Daddy. It's your Christmas present from me." They opened the trailer to view a set of beautifully sculpted Nativity figures. The tallest one was of Joseph. He was about three feet tall.

"Oh, Tessie, they're beautiful. I didn't know you could do that. You didn't tell me you could do that. When did you learn? When did you have time? Oh, they're gorgeous," her mother said.

"Sweetheart, that's the most beautiful creation I've ever seen," her father said.

"I've been doing this in art class all last year and this semester. I still don't have a couple of the pieces finished, so I guess you'll get them next year. They've had them on display at the school all year. I didn't tell you, because I wanted to surprise you. They were too big to get in the car, so I had to borrow this trailer to bring them home. I thought, after Christmas maybe you could store them in the barn loft."

"In the barn loft! I think not!" Cassie said in a startled voice.

"Well now, you just think about that, sweet little Mama. Where in the world do you think you will store something that big after Christmas is over?"

"Well. I will just have to think about that, but definitely not in the barn."

TC said, "I'll unload them for you."

"Oh, wait, Daddy. They're very heavy. Decide exactly where you want them and then pull the trailer to that spot and have one of the men help you. I'm serious. They are very, very heavy."

Cassie spent nearly an hour examining the beautiful pieces of art. She could hardly believe her own eyes. She was amazed at her daughter's talent. Her eyes filled with tears as she walked around them, touching them, and marveling over their beauty.

On the night of the tree trimming, Grandma presented them with a large scrap book of things she had been collecting for many years—including pictures taken of Tessie every Christmas since she was born. They were pictures she had stored away for this purpose and had never shown to Cassie. It was a beautiful book and a real treasure. It was evident that much thought and love went into its making.

Everything about Tessie's time at home was perfect—the decorating, the sleigh ride, even the weather for the return trip to Tulsa. The parting was difficult for everyone though. Tessie had a lump in her throat, but she held back the tears. TC hugged her, and then quickly walked back to the house. Cassie said, "Oh, Baby, I will miss you so much," as a big tear rolled down her cheek. She quickly wiped it away, hoping Tessie hadn't seen it.

Tessie drove into town to pick up her friend, Paula, who was going to return to school with her. As she drove, she thought about how very special her family was. She felt so loved and privileged to have such caring parents. Not everyone was so fortunate, as she had learned this year. She had encountered some very sad situations. But they had given her opportunities to minister and discover some possibilities the Lord might have in store for her. She had been giving some thought to starting a student support group. She hadn't discussed this with anyone yet. Her grandfather had a saying he used sometimes that fit this situation perfectly. He would say, "I think I'll just have to chew on that awhile." Well, that's what she needed to do, chew and pray.

Tessie and Paula chattered all the way back to school. Paula was one of the girls for whom Tessie had a real concern. This past week was an example of the reason for her concern. Paula just arrived home from school when her parents announced that they were leaving on a trip the next day and would be gone for a week. They informed Paula that she could stay with her aunt if she chose. As it turned out, they returned home the day before she had to leave. They weren't home to spend Christmas with her and were both napping when Paula left. Tessie could see the sadness in her face. She wished she had invited her to spend this time at the ranch. Money, apparently, was not a real problem in her family. Her parents just never had any time for her.

When they arrived at the dorm, Tessie was thankful that she had a another day before classes started. She wasn't quite sure why, but she felt totally exhausted. Now she could rest, unpack, and prepare her mind for classes.

While she was unpacking, she started thinking about her parents and the love and care they always lavished on her. All of a sudden, she began to cry uncontrollably. At last, when her tears disappeared, she went to her small desk, turned on the table lamp, and began composing a love letter to her parents.

> *Dear Mom and Dad,*
>
> *I have so much in my heart. I can't begin to put it all down on paper nor express to you how very much you mean to me. God has been so good to me to allow me to have such wonderful parents. There are so many students here who are hurting because they don't have caring parents like I do. I would even venture to say that my parents are more wonderful than any parents in the world. I love you so much, I could never explain it. Not only that, but I admire you, and I'm so very proud of you for the high standards you have set for yourselves. You are so steady and dependable. I appreciate the way you have always encouraged me and given me faith in the Lord and in myself. There are so many things I have accomplished that I would never have attempted without knowing you were behind me to give me assurance and love, even if I failed.*
>
> *I am grateful to you for giving me faith in God and directing me to His Son. It would be very difficult to face the unknown without Him. It is good to know that. Even*

though you are not here with me, and being the baby that I am, and that was difficult for me at first, I still know that I am not alone. You taught me that Jesus said "I will never leave thee nor forsake thee."

> *Mom and Dad, I had such a wonderful time while I was at home. I was trying to think what was the very best memory. I enjoyed the sleigh ride and the special shindig you had for the ranch hands. But the very best memory was both of you and Grandma and Grandpa sitting around the fire looking at Grandma's scrapbook. That was a very special time.*

> *I had better close and finish unpacking. Give Grandma and Grandpa my love. They are such sweeties.*
> *All my love,*
> *Your rotten little girl, Tessie*

Tessie finished putting all her things away, and then picked up her mail and began to look through it to see if anything needed immediate attention. The first one to grab her attention was from a classmate named Charles Ammert. Tessie had gone to the Sweet Shop with him for a Coke, shortly before she went home for Christmas. He was having a lot of difficulty keeping his grades up. He was working long hours to put himself through college and he didn't have enough time to get his homework done. His parents weren't giving him any financial support. His note read:

> *Tessie,*

> *Thanks for being such a good friend and for listening to all my woes. I won't be coming back to school. I lost my job, and I doubt if I can find anything that will pay enough to cover all my expenses. But don't fret. I will probably come back in a couple years, after I have earned and saved enough to finish. I probably would have just given up entirely, if it hadn't been for you. Some of the things you said to me have given me a new encouragement. I won't quit, Tessie. I promise.*

> *Love, Chuck*

As Tessie read the note, tears filled her eyes. She was more determined now than ever to get involved in a student support group. There were so many hurting kids who didn't know which way to turn. Sometimes just a little encouragement is all they need to keep on keeping on. She wasn't sure just who she needed to talk with, but she would do something tomorrow.

Tessie pulled out her pen and paper and replied to his note, telling him that she was proud of him for his determination to complete school. She told him she was sure he would finish, because he had the character and qualities to be successful. She said that she would be praying for him.

After she finished her letter to him, she glanced through the rest of her mail. There were a couple cards from friends and the rest was just junk mail which she discarded. The cards didn't require a reply, so she straightened her desk and pulled down her bed. A good night's sleep and a fresh new morning can sometimes open your mind to solutions you couldn't see before.

Tessie woke up early the next morning by the sound of screeching brakes. She jumped up and looked out the window to see a little squirrel standing erect in the middle of the street, as if he had turned to stone by fright. The driver in the car honked and he scurried on across.

Tessie stretched and groaned, glancing at the clock. It was still 45 minutes before her alarm would ring. She could get a little more sleep, but instead, she splashed water on her face and quickly dressed. She had been thinking about turning over a new leaf and jogging every morning—but every day it was easier to say, "I'll start tomorrow." Well, today would be a good time to begin, so she dashed out to get this day off to a good start.

She had decided not to share this with her friends because she wanted to jog alone. She wanted to jog and pray. The fresh, crisp air would give her a clear mind. Being alone would allow her to focus on the things she wanted to give to the Lord.

She chose the little park down the street as her spot for jogging. She started out slowly, increasing her speed as she went, then slowing down about one hundred yards from the dorm. When she got back in the room, she was panting. "Yes, I really need this," she said aloud. "Old girl, you are completely out of shape."

She showered, ate, and headed to her first class. The exercise and fresh air had invigorated her body and her mind. She was glad she forced herself to start her jogging program, even though it was an effort. She would have to set her alarm that early every morning because she hadn't had even a minute to waste.

Tessie breezed through her classes, but as she expected, she was loaded down with homework. She still felt an urgency to start the student support program, so she stopped in at her counselor's office to discuss it with her. She thought it was an excellent idea, but suggested it would be better to make it an off-campus program. She had some pretty sound reasons for that advice, so now Tessie had to come up with a place to hold the group meetings. She would have to ask around to see what might be available.   She went over to the Sweet Shop, as was her usual practice, to have a Coke and study. Some of her friends came in and she told them what she was planning. As they were discussing it, Sam, the proprietor, overheard their conversation. He said," So you are looking for a place for a meeting, are you?"

Tessie explained in detail what she was looking for. "You wouldn't happen to know of a place, would you, Sam?"

"Well, maybe yes, maybe no," he replied. "If you and your friends would want to come up with a little elbow grease, I might have just the place for you. There is a vacant room behind my place, but it's in pretty bad shape. It would need cleaning, some paint, and a little bit of repair. You can look it over if you want."

"Boy, would we! Could we see it now?" she asked enthusiastically.

"Come on. Just follow me." He led them to the back of his shop. When he opened the door, he switched on the light to display a room full of junk. The walls were dark and dingy and the floor was missing some boards. Tessie looked around and drew a long breath.

"Well, it would take a lot of work. What would you charge?" she asked.

"Well, I figure it this way. The clean-up and the work you do could only help the value of my place. It might draw some business and I think your plan of helping these kids is a worthwhile project. So if you want to do the work, there's no charge."

Tessie squealed with delight. "Oh Sam, you are an angel! I'll get my work crew together, and we'll get on it right away." She looked around at all the kids that were present and said with a mischievous grin, "I guess you know you are recruited."

They all seemed as excited about the quest as Tessie. The clean-up started that night. It took several weeks before the place was ready for the first meeting, but it was a work to behold. There was such a transition, Sam couldn't believe his eyes. The students had posted requests for donations and had procured a fantastic response. They had donations of paint, paintings, furniture, cleaning supplies, and a store down the street had donated some floor covering. Some of the professors even donated their time to work. All of the students were proud of their new project.

The night the work was completed, they had their first meeting. Tessie, being the originator of the group, was the first speaker. She began by opening the meeting with prayer and dedicating the room, their efforts, and the results to the Lord. She asked for His blessings on their group and for wisdom to accomplish their goals.

Tessie started by encouraging all students to come. "Everyone needs encouragement. By our coming, the ones who have insurmountable problems will be more apt to come," she said. " Please be on the lookout for those who need support and invite visitors to every meeting just to see the work. We want to make this a real ministry for our school, to help every student who is in need—any kind of need."

Tessie was so excited, she could hardly sleep. She could hardly wait to tell her parents about it. It was so much easier than she had anticipated. Her next task was to acquire speakers for the meetings. She wanted to try to have a diverse selection, perhaps counselors, preachers, professors, other students, and sometimes just discussions among themselves. The important thing was that the students knew someone cared and that there was help when they needed it.

They wanted a name for their group. Everyone was to submit a suggestion. They came up with the name COIN Club, which stood for Caring for Others In Need. It proved to be very successful. Many students were helped. It brought about an awareness in the community of the great need, so many people, besides students, got involved. Many people donated money and started projects to raise money for students. Some even offered free housing for those proving worthy.

The local newspaper wrote an article on the spectacular success of the COIN Club and the outstanding efforts of the students with special recognition for Tessie. It wasn't long before the group was packing out the room at the Sweet Shop. Tessie made the announcement that she thought the time had come for them to start paying rent for the facility. Sam's contribution of the room had been a blessing to them. It was now their turn to be a blessing to him. He was not a man of means, so there was no doubt he could use the extra money. He was very appreciative of their concern for him. He had a special pride for the students and their club. He called them *My Kids.*

After the club was well on its way, they elected officers (which would be done yearly) and Tessie bowed out as the leader. She still participated when she was at school though.

The school year passed so quickly. Tessie's time was so full that she didn't have time for much socializing, so dating was still not an issue, and definitely not a priority.   She finished the Nativity pieces for her mother and was thankful that project was finally done. This was a real concern for her because she was giving serious thought about not coming back to school next year. So she worked extra hours in order to get them finished. Tessie's desire was to stay at the ranch and devote her time to learning all she could about running it. She wanted to be a real help to her dad. He deserved to be relieved of some of the responsibility. After all, if the ranch was to be hers, she should take some of that responsibility. She knew it would take some concentrated effort to convince her parents that her decision was sound, but she was going to try. She saw no value in her returning to school.

When she arrived home, her mother ran out to meet her. They hugged each other for several minutes before saying anything. Her dad was in the driveway, leaning on a new shiny red convertible, talking to a very handsome stranger. Tessie's heart skipped a beat when she saw him. "Who is talking with Daddy?"

"I couldn't tell you, Honey. He just drove in. I don't know if your daddy knows him or not," her mother replied. "Come on in the house. We'll get your things later. I want to hear all about you."

Cassie had so much to tell her mother, she hardly knew where to begin. She was pouring out the news when her daddy came in. He reached his arms out and she threw her arms around his neck.

"Oh, Punkin, I've missed you so much. This place is dead without you."

"Well, we'll see about getting some life back in these hills," she said jokingly. "What's new around here. You haven't told me much in your letters. I feel like I'm out of touch with all that's going on.""

Well now, let's see," he began. "We've lost several men since you were home and we've hired some replacements. Jack retired. I think you met Bert when you were home for Christmas. Kent and Cal both left to take jobs in Canada. That was pretty hard on everybody. We purchased 500 new head of cattle. We're experimenting with a new breed. Supposedly they are stronger with more endurance and have more tender meat. Oh, and another thing, they're putting in a new highway over past Emery's Creek. The state wants to buy that south 50 acres on the other side of the creek. We've never used it for anything, but I wanted to wait until you got home to make that decision. It would make a beautiful building site, but it isn't very practical to run cattle. Since this place is going to be yours someday, I thought I'd let you make that decision. You can think that over. I guess that's about all the news."

"Who were you talking to when I drove up?" she asked.

"Oh, he's some lawyer from Tulsa driving to Minnesota to visit his mother. He was inquiring about bringing some friends here to vacation. They'd like to ride horses and work on the ranch just for kicks. I told him we could probably work something out." Then he grinned and said, "Maybe we'll start a dude ranch."

"Daddy! You don't mean it."

"No. I think we pretty much have all we can cope with. But, I don't mind some city dudes just once. It might be an experience for all of us."

After dinner that evening, Tessie and her parents sat in the library and talked for hours. Tessie told them all about the COIN club, about her friends, about her new art projects, and most of all, about how glad she was to be home. Finally, Tessie said she thought she would turn in. She was getting sleepy and wanted to get an early start in the morning.

"No need for that," her dad said. "You can sleep as long as you want to. We can hit it hard the next day."

She laughed. "What happened to you? I never thought I'd hear you tell me to sleep as long as I wanted to. Am I hearing things, or am I delirious or something?"

"You make me sound like a mean old ogre or worse. I just thought you might like to have a day to relax and visit with your mother."

"Oh, we'll do plenty of that, but I like to ride early. Everything is so much fresher and more beautiful. That's okay with you, isn't it, Mama?"

"Sure, Honey. Whatever you want to do is fine with me."

After Tessie went to bed, Cassie turned to TC with a frown and a sharp tone and asked, "TC, whatever made you tell Tessie you were thinking about selling that 50 acres? You told me you wouldn't even consider it."

"Well, I wanted to get Tessie's reaction. I wanted to see if the land was as important to her as it is to me. She didn't have much to say about it. I'm not sure what that means, but she'll bring it up in a few days."

Tessie was in riding clothes bright and early the next morning. She was ready to get back in the groove and go to work. She rode out past Emery Creek to look over the 50 acres the state wanted to buy. She got off her horse and took her hat off. She threw her head back as she turned toward the wind. Her hair was blowing freely and the breeze felt so good on her face. Her hair looked like gold with the sun shining on it. It had not darkened any since she was a little girl.

She turned around several times looking in all directions. This was a beautiful place. The view was breathtaking. Her dad was right about it being a beautiful building site. How could he even think about selling any part of the ranch? Was she being selfish when they had so much land? She didn't want to stand in the way of progress, but she didn't want to sell, not even an acre. If he wanted to buy more, she could understand that. But sell! She thought her dad felt the same way she did about the land. She stood looking at the layout of the land. It was rolling with many beautiful trees and a gorgeous view. It would be a place she might build her home someday, or perhaps a home for her children. "Oh well now, that's not likely to ever happen," she said aloud.

She stomped her feet and kicked a rock that went rolling over the hill. A tear came trickling down her cheek. She quickly wiped it away as if in fear someone would see it. She grabbed her horse's reins and jumped on, turning the horse back toward home. She rode hard back to the ranch.

When she got back, she went to the cook shack to ask where she might find her father. Ben Meyers, one of the new men, whistled as she walked through the door. She ignored him and turned toward Bart, directing her question to him. He told her that her father was going into town. He thought she had missed him, but he might still be out by the barn. He was taking the truck and that was where he had it parked. She quickly thanked him and ran out the door. After she was gone, Bart said, "Oh, did you ever make a mistake! That's the quickest way in the world to lose your job, and maybe your head. Keep your distance from TC's daughter."

As Tessie ran out toward the barn, her dad's truck was just pulling out. She waved her arms and yelled. He stuck his head out the window and said, "Good morning, Sugar. What's up?"

"I want to go with you if you don't mind."

"Hop in," he said. "I have to go pick up a part for my tractor. I'd love to have your company. Been riding?"

"Yes, I've been out for awhile."

"Did you go over by the creek?"

"How did you know?"

"I thought you might. What do you think?" he said.

She turned toward him, and in an angry tone she almost yelled, "Daddy, I just can't believe you would sell our land." Then she burst out in tears.

TC pulled the truck over and stopped. He put his arm around her and pulled her over to him. "Honey, you make me feel like a monster. I really have no intentions of selling the land. I just wanted to see what your reaction would be. I'm sorry that I upset you. You don't have to worry. Our ranch is going to remain intact."

"Thank you Daddy. I'm glad to hear you say that." She dried her tears and their conversation changed to the new men on the ranch. TC told her as much as he could about them, which wasn't much. They were all hard workers, and for the most part, got along well. They weren't like his first bunch though. The first ones were special. They seemed almost like family.

"Oh, by the way, did your mother tell you that Jed and his family are coming to visit us next month. He and Shirley have two boys, eleven and thirteen. We haven't seen them since their oldest was a baby. I still miss him. He's a doctor now, living in Colorado Springs. His mother lives with them, but Tillie died last winter. Jed had built his mother and Tillie a little home close to them. After Tillie died, they persuaded her to move in with them. I sure am proud of Jed. That was his goal before he ever came to work for me. He's a great guy."

"I didn't know Jed very well. I was pretty small when he left, but I can still see his big smile."

It was so good to spend time with her dad again. She had missed that so very much. She worked with him everyday. Nearly three weeks had passed and she still hadn't mentioned wanting to drop out of school. The time had to be just right and she hoped that such a time would come soon.

One morning, as she was leaving the house, a truck came through the big gate. It was a bright blue Chevrolet, new and shiny. When it stopped, she saw that the driver was the same man who had been in the red convertible. He had two men with him. He waved at her and smiled, displaying beautiful white teeth and a deep dimple. He was the best looking man she had ever seen. He had dark hair, almost black, sort of wavy. His eyes were a sparkling black. She said to herself, *Tessie, I don't think your heart can take two weeks of his presence.* They all got out of the truck, but her eyes were still focused on him.

"Hi. I'm Jeffery Randall. This is Ron Stuber and Larry Meyers. We came to work. Well, not all work. We're going to do some fishing and riding, too."

"Hi, I'm Tessie, Mr. Marshall's daughter. I'll go find my father for you. He'll show you around. Glad to have you at the ranch."

After she left, Jeffery said, "Wow! I think I could learn to love ranch life. Maybe I'll give up law and become a cowboy."

Chapter 23
Torn Between Loves

The next two weeks found Jeff and his friends working harder than they had ever worked in their lives. The ornery ranch hands taunted them. "Work! They can't work. They'll just get in the way. You city slickers couldn't keep up with me if I had one hand tied behind my back." Well, that was all it took for them to nearly kill themselves proving they could work just as hard and accomplish just as much as any man on the ranch. In the meantime, the ranch hands were rolling in the floor laughing. Jeff, Ron, and Larry, not used to riding, were so sore they could hardly walk. They tried not to walk in a peculiar fashion, but their pain could not be disguised. They didn't utter one complaint though and were good sports when the men teased them.

There were only two days left before they were to leave the ranch. They had saddled up their horses and were about to ride out to the herd as the foreman had directed, when TC came around the corner and called out to them.

"Hey, fellows, hold up a minute. I thought this was supposed to be a vacation. You haven't fished or just ridden for the enjoyment of riding since you've been here. All you've done is work, and very hard, I might add. I'm going to have to put you on the payroll if you keep this up. No more work! That's an order. Grab your poles and go fishing, or just ride for the fun of it."

"Thanks, Mr. Marshall, but your foreman said we had to cut 100 head of cattle out of the herd before the end of the day," Jeff said.

TC grinned and shook his head. "Well, you just remind him who he works for if he gives you any trouble. Go fishing. I'll deal with him."

"Thanks, Mr. Marshall," Jeff said. "I think we'll be fishing. Horseback riding has ceased to be an enjoyment. I don't think I'll even be able to walk tomorrow."

Jake Reimer had taken over as foreman when Clay left. He was tough on the men, especially when they were new. His bark was a lot worse than his bite though. After the men got to know him, they realized he wasn't as mean as he first appeared and could be a lot of fun. The truth was, he and all the ranch hands were just having a lot of fun right now, at the newcomers' expense. TC walked out to the barn where they were congregating and called everyone to him.

"Okay, now let's lay off the city boys. They're our guests. You've just about worked them into the ground. They're good kids and need to have some fun. Enough is enough. I know they said they wanted a taste of ranch work, but you've gone beyond the limit. Give them a break, and help show them a good time for the next couple days."

TC heard some snickers and saw the grin on Jake's face. He wondered just how hard they had really been on them.

After he left, Jake said, "Okay, boys. The boss says show 'em a good time. I guess they've had enough and deserve some fun. They have been good sports, so let's go all out and show 'em how much fun a ranch can be. I'll talk to Butch and see about havin' a fish cookout tonight, and maybe a hoedown or a rodeo. We pretty much have our work all caught up anyway." With that last statement they all hollered with laughter. "Go grab your poles, boys, and catch us some fish. Give them guys a hand, if they don't know what they're doing. They need to catch some big ones.

Jeff and his friends just got their poles in the water when Ron saw Jake coming toward them. "Look out, Jeff. Here comes trouble."

Jeff looked up and said, "Hi Jake. I guess you've lost three workers. We're going to try our luck with the fish. Maybe we'll be better fishermen than we were ranch hands."

Jake smiled at him and said, "You boys are good sports and good workers. Hope you don't hold no grudges. We were just havin' fun. Anytime you boys want a job, you got one here at the ranch. You're all right."

"Thanks! We might just take you up on that. Who knows?" Jeff said.

They fished for nearly an hour with no luck. Tessie took her horse out of the barn and was cinching up the saddle. Jeff said, "You guys go ahead and fish. I think I'll go help the little lady saddle her horse. It looks like she's having trouble."

Ron and Larry let out a hardy laugh. "That little lady could probably saddle three horses before you could decide which way to turn the saddle," Larry said.

Jeff turned to him with a big smile, "In that case, maybe she can teach me. I'm a willing learner."

They grinned, shook their heads, and went back to fishing.

Ron said, "Man, he's wasting his time there. Mr. Marshall will slaughter him."

"Boy, you got that right!" Larry replied. "I value my neck too much to even look in her direction in Mr. Marshall's presence."

Tessie saw Jeff coming and waved. "Good morning. How are you liking ranch life?"

"Well, I'm still alive. That's something to be thankful for around here."

Tessie looked at him and smiled. "I've heard what they put you through. They're an ornery bunch. I hope they haven't given you a bad impression of us here at the ranch."

"No way! We've had a good time. We learned a lot and found out what ranch life is all about. Your dad is sure a swell guy. Are you riding?"

"Yes. I was going down by Rocky Canyon to do some sketching. Want to come along? It's beautiful over there."

"I'd love to. It's beautiful everywhere on this ranch. It's like another world here."

Tessie brought out another horse for Jeff. As he mounted the horse, he groaned in a low tone. Tessie smiled a sympathetic smile. "The soreness will go away in about another week."

Butch watched with a frown on his face as they rode off together. TC was out working on his tractor. Butch decided he should be informed about Tessie's possible danger. He approached TC and volunteered the information. TC didn't seem at all concerned. He said, "Thanks, Butch. I'm not too worried about Jeff though. I think Tessie will be all right with him." Butch shrugged his shoulders and walked back to the cook shack.

Tessie and Jeff rode and talked and enjoyed the beautiful view. She found him easy to talk to. He was a good listener and interesting as well. He told her all about his future law practice, his school, his family, and about some of his goals. She learned that his full name was Jefferson Dereck Randall. He was a young man with high aspirations. His father and grandfather had a law firm, Randall & Randall. His grandfather had retired, moved to Minnesota, and had purchased several lots on Pequot Lakes and built a cabin there. It was a lovely, serene place with fish in abundance. His grandfather had learned the lakes and knew just where to find the fish. One of Jeff's favorite memories was the loons on the lake at sunset. He described to her their mournful call, and how they would dive under the water and stay under for long periods of time catching their dinner. He truly loved it there. He went on to tell her that when he finished law school (which was one year away), he would become a partner with his dad. The law firm would remain Randall & Randall. He asked her about her art and music and what her plans were for her future. When they reached the canyon, they dismounted and sat on a big rock and talked for nearly two hours. Tessie told him all about the tragedy that took place here at the canyon years before. It happened before she was born, but she knew the story well.

All the while they were talking, Tessie was sketching Jeff's picture. She quickly flipped to a different sketch when he asked to see it. It was one she had done another time when she had come up here alone.

Tessie glanced at her watch and suggested that they head back toward the ranch as it was nearing the noon hour and lunch would be served soon. "I'm sure you are getting hungry. I'd hate to be the cause of you missing lunch."

"Well, I am getting a little hungry, but then, I'm always hungry. I've thoroughly enjoyed our ride and the beautiful canyon. This would be well worth the prospect of missing a meal."

"Well, I'm glad you like our canyon. I don't want all of your memories here at the ranch to be unpleasant and painful," she said with a grin.

"No, Ma'am. I will have no unpleasant memories. In fact, I probably won't think of much else but you."

The subject was changed, but Tessie's heart was pounding. She would probably dream about his gorgeous eyes and crooked smile tonight. He was unlike anyone she had ever met. She truly enjoyed being with him. No one had ever made her feel this way before.

When they rode back to the ranch, Jeff's buddies were walking toward the barn holding up a string of nice-sized fish. Jeff joined them and Tessie went up to the house.

"Wow, which one of you went to the fish market to get those?" Jeff asked.

"You'd like to think that. The truth is, we just had to get you out of there. You were jinxing us. Actually, it was either catch fish or go hungry. This is our dinner tonight, they tell us. It seems they're having a fish fry in our honor. Imagine that?" Ron said.

Jeff raised his eyebrows and said, "Hey, all right! I'm all for that."

"Oh, not only that," Larry said, "They have some musicians coming and they're clearing out the barn for some kind of dance. The ranch hands are bringing their girlfriends and wives in. And Tessie is inviting some of her friends. Jake said they're doing this for us. That blows my mind. He nearly kills us and then has a party for us."

"Yeah, ride us until we're so sore we can't walk, then have a dance for us. I think that's some kind of unique new torture," Ron said jokingly.

Jeff spoke up, "Come on guys. They're trying to make amends. I think they're an all right bunch."

"Well looks like you're warming up to everyone around here, Old Buddy," Ron said. Jeff just raised his eye brows and grinned.

When Tessie went in the house, her mother looked around the corner to see who was coming in. "Hi Honey, I was getting a little concerned about you."

"Hi, Mama. Why, I told you where I was going. Was it because I was with Jeff?"

"Well, yes, I suppose. After all, we don't know him."

"He's really nice, Mama. He and Daddy really hit it off."

"They must have. Your daddy is having a get-together tonight for him and his friends. It's a fish fry and hoedown. He had me call some of your friends this morning and invite them to come. You weren't available to make the calls. The hands are each to bring someone, and invite another couple if they want. I wrote down the names of those I invited and their response. If there's anyone else you want to come, you'd better call them as soon as you finish eating."

"Daddy's having a shindig tonight? Whatever possessed him to do that?"

"Well, actually, I think it was Jake's idea. I think he got to feeling guilty because they worked those boys so hard. Anyway, I think it's a nice gesture. I'm glad they're doing it. But back to Jeff."

"Oh, you would like him, Mama. You need to get better acquainted with him."

"I do? Why is that?" She asked in a teasing tone.

"I just told you, Mama. Because he's nice, and I think you'd like him. You can get that suspicious tone out of your voice. If you must know, yes, I think he's handsome. Anyone who doesn't, needs glasses. And yes, if he asks me out, I'll go. And no, we aren't getting married tomorrow, so don't start counting your grandchildren yet. Oh, Mama! Just when I think I have my life all figured out, he has to come along. I'm not ready for him—but I sure wouldn't want someone else to get him."

"My goodness! That was quick. I do believe my baby girl has fallen in love." Her mother stood there with her hands on her hips frowning at Tessie. "Now what?"

Tessie stomped her foot. "I don't know! I don't want to fall in love. I just want everything to be uncomplicated and normal."

"Well, Honey, it is normal to fall in love," her mother said.

"I know, Mama, but not with someone who doesn't fit into your plans."

"And what are your plans, dear?"

"You know what my plans are. I want someone who wants to be a rancher. He's a lawyer. He already has his own law firm. He wouldn't give that up. Besides, he probably has a girlfriend back in Tulsa. I'm going to go wash for lunch. I'll be down shortly." She stomped up the stairs.

Her mother just stood there watching Tessie. As she started toward the kitchen, she said to herself, "Oh, my poor baby. Growing up can be so painful sometimes."

TC came in and gave a shout, "Hey, where is everyone?"

"In here, Honey. Tessie is upstairs. She'll be down in a minute."

"Are you two girls ready to get your dancing slippers on. I'm ready to swing the prettiest girl in town."

"Well, I have my slippers handy, but I don't know about Tessie?"

"What's the matter with Tessie?" he asked with a concerned frown.

"Well, I think Cupid hit her, and she doesn't like it very well."

"Tessie? No! You don't mean Jeff? When did all this take place? She was only with him for a couple hours. I can't believe it."

"Just take one look at her and you'll know."

"Well, maybe we just ought to cancel this thing," he said as he grabbed his chair and set it down with a bang.

"Don't be silly," Cassie said. "This will be good for everyone. Don't look so upset. You knew this would happen sooner or later."

"Well it would've been okay with me if it had been much later," he snapped.

"I knew this was coming the minute she saw him the other night. It was as if a magical spark zapped her. But anyway, TC, we've prayed about this very situation. If God wants it to be, it will be."

When Tessie came down, she had regained her spirit and was in a better mood. The same could not be said for her dad, however. He sat at the table, not saying a word, just frowning as he stared at Tessie.

"Well, what's the matter with you, Smiley?" Tessie asked. "Did someone steal your sunshine?"

"Something like that," he replied.

"Daddy, is something wrong?"

"No, Punkin, nothing's wrong. Sometimes things just don't go exactly the way you plan."

"I can surely attest to that," Tessie said. Nothing more was said about Jeff during lunch.

Tessie said, "Oh, Mama, did you invite Grandma and Grandpa? They would simply adore one of these shindigs."

"I think you're right. But no, I didn't invite them. Why don't you give them a call."

That evening as the people arrived, Tessie ran out to greet them and show them where to go. Carla, Paula, and Jo Ellen (three of Tessie's friends) all rode together. They all lived in Rolla, so it made more sense to ride in one car. Sharon, another friend, lived about ten miles past

Rolla. Her dad was going to drop her off at the ranch. Tessie hoped she could get Bonnie to come, but she never could get an answer on the phone. She thought Bonnie would be the perfect match for Ron.

Tessie looked so beautiful in her blue full skirt with a matching blue bow at the neck of her white piquet blouse and one in her hair. She had pulled her hair back in a pony tail. It was so long, it got in the way when she danced.

Tessie motioned to her friends. "Come with me," she said. "I'll introduce you to everyone." She started with some of the ranch hands that had their wives there. That might be a more comfortable situation for starters. Then she introduced them to Butch. Butch had lost his wife several years ago. He was sort of grumpy, but he had a heart of gold and everyone had grown to like him. Next she led them over to Jeff, Ron, and Larry and made the introductions.

Tessie's mother sent word to her that she was wanted on the phone, so she excused herself and left her friends talking with the three city boys.

Her phone call was from her grandmother. She was letting Tessie know that they were still coming but had been delayed.

"I'm so glad you're coming, Grandma. Don't let anything stop you. We haven't started eating yet. I'll make sure they don't eat it all." Tessie hadn't spent much time with her grandparents since she came home. She was looking forward to seeing them.

She started back down to the barn, but wasn't sure just which way to go. Her friends were sort of paired off with Jeff, Ron, and Larry. It might be a little awkward to be with them. Her mother was visiting with Jake's wife and most everyone else was with either a date or a spouse. She spotted her dad and started in his direction, but Bert Willis spotted her first and grabbed this opportunity to talk to her.

"Hi. Care if I join you? I wanted to apologize for the whistle the other day. I didn't mean to offend you. It was meant as a compliment, but I could tell you didn't take it that way. Am I forgiven?"

"Forgiven," Tessie said with a smile. "Actually, I didn't think too much about it. I had too much else on my mind at the time. I had some important things I had to talk over with my dad and I was afraid he was going to get away before I caught him."

"Mind if I join you for dinner?" he asked.

"No, I don't mind, but there will probably be several of us eating together. I have friends here from town and I want to show them a good time."

"Looks like they're doing all right."

"Well, I don't want them to think I've deserted them."

"Sure that's who you're concerned about?" he asked.

"What do you mean?" she snapped.

"Sorry! Pretend I didn't ask that."

"Okay, it's forgotten. Let's go eat. Looks like Butch is ready for us."

She waved to her friends and motioned them to come. Her dad had some of the men bring up some long picnic tables and cover them with white paper. Butch brought out plates and stainless steel tableware for everyone. He wouldn't permit the use of paper plates or plastic forks, not for any occasion. When anyone suggested using paper plates, he would say,"Plates aren't that hard to wash, and I have plenty of help. My boys all love to wash dishes."

She remembered one occasion when Calvin was still here, he said, "Oh sure, we're wild about it." Butch overheard him and gave him the honor of the entire job that night.

Butch had a large iron stove set up with long frying pans for the fish and potatoes. There was a huge pot of baked beans that had been cooking for several hours. Tessie wasn't sure what he put in his baked beans. They were different and better than any she had ever eaten, even Cookie's. There was corn on the cob wrapped in foil and heaped up in a large pan, big bowls of coleslaw, corn bread, and pans of cobbler. No one would ever go hungry at one of Butch's cookouts.

They all filled their plates and began to find seats. Bert put his hand on Tessie's elbow to direct her to a table. Jeff came by and said in a rather loud tone,"Don't forget, you promised me the first dance, Tessie." Tessie whirled around and looked at him in total surprise. He just stood looking into her eyes, waiting for her reply.

"Oh, I won't forget," she said.

Bert sat on Tessie's left and Jeff sat on the right. Sharon sat next to him on his right. Jo Ellen sat across from Bert and Ron next to her. Paula and Larry were next to them.

Everyone enjoyed the food. Before they were through eating, the musicians began to play softly. As soon as everyone was finished, Jessie

Brennan picked up the microphone and called out, "Grab your partner for a good old square dance." Jessie had been calling square dances for many years and he was the best one anywhere around.

Tessie looked over at Jeff and said, "Well, looks like this is our dance."

He looked at her and gulped, "I don't know how to square dance."

"Well, looks like you learn tonight," she said with a grin. "You can't renege on a dance that easy."

They walked out to the floor. Tessie said, "Take it slow, Jess. We have a newcomer here." Jessie picked an easy call, and the music began. Tessie explained as they went what to do, but before it was over he was totally lost. They were laughing so hard, their sides ached.

"Well, I made a complete fool of myself, but I had a great time. I hope I didn't embarrass you too much. I need to learn how to do that. Maybe you could teach me."

She laughed and said, "Well now, that's a challenge, but I'll try."

On their way back to the table, Jeff asked her, "Am I interrupting something special here? Who is this guy?"

"He's just a ranch hand here. Actually, this is the first time I've even talked with him. I don't know any more about him than you do. He seems like a nice guy, but that's all I know."

"Well, that's a relief. I would sure hate to break up you and a beau, but you gotta do what you gotta do," he said with a mischievous grin. Then he turned her toward him and erased the grin. His hands were on her shoulders as he looked intently into her eyes and asked her in a low, serious tone, "Tessie, is there someone special in your life? I don't want to let my heart get totally out of control here, if I don't even have a chance."

"No, Jeff, there's no one special, but..." He put his hand over her mouth.

"No buts. That's all I need to know," he said.

"You can sure tell you're a lawyer. A lawyer will never let the witness finish a statement."

"Not if they're going to say something he doesn't want to hear." He squeezed her hand and they sat down.

Bert and Sharon were gone when they returned. "Looks like we lost our dates," he said."Guess we'll have to console each other."

Someone came up behind her and put their hands over her eyes. Then she heard her dad say as he tried to disguise his voice, "I think this is my dance."

"Oh, Daddy! Excuse me, I mean Humphrey Bogart."

"Humphrey Bogart? That was John Wayne!" he said.

"Oh, excuse me, Duke. Of course I'll dance with you."

She and her dad walked toward the floor, but they didn't dance. Her dad simply said, "Tessie, be careful. Don't jump into something you'll regret. He may be charming, and he may have big dreams, but are they your dreams? Are you willing to leave the land? Remember what you said to me in the truck? You're a grown young lady, Tessie. I can't rule your life, but I don't want you to make any mistakes. Just be sure you think it through and know what you are doing. Jeff seems like a fine young man, but I hesitate to think that he is right for you. I love you and want you to be happy. That's all. Now do you still want to dance with your old dad?"

They gave one whirl and the song ended. He bowed to her and she grinned. "Thank you kindly, Ma'am," he said in a John Wayne tone.

"Daddy, you're impossible. Thanks for the advice. I won't make any hasty decisions. Don't worry. I will talk it over with you before I ever do anything." He returned her to her seat.

Jeff looked at her with searching eyes. "Is everything all right?"

"Oh, sure. Just a concerned father."

"He doesn't like me, does he?"

"Yes, he does. In fact, he just said he thinks you're a fine young man. But Jeff, we live in different worlds. He doesn't want me to make any mistakes."

"So he thinks I'm a mistake?"

"Jeff! I didn't say that. But my father knows what my dreams are, and they're quite different from yours."

"Why couldn't your dreams and my dreams be combined?"

"I don't see how that could be possible. But aren't we a little out of line talking about such things. This is a little premature."

"Okay. We'll drop it for now. Let's just have a good time tonight and continue this another time," he said.

They walked around the yard talking about many things, but avoiding the very thing that Jeff wanted to discuss. The time seemed to pass so quickly. The musicians had begun putting their instruments away, and everyone had started to leave. Tessie's mom and dad were sitting in lawn chairs by the house. Tessie said, "Let's go join my parents. You haven't met my mother yet, have you?"

She started toward the house. This wasn't really what he wanted, but he followed. He wanted to pursue their earlier conversation in hopes of persuading her to see his point of view. But Tessie definitely wanted to avoid that conversation tonight.

They sat in the yard for a long time talking with her parents. They talked about the dinner, his home, his grandfather's place in Minnesota, and then started talking about the cattle. The mosquitoes were starting to bite, so Tessie said she was going in and would see everyone tomorrow.

Jeff jumped up and said, "I'll walk you to the door." When they reached the porch, he said, "You know I'm leaving for Tulsa tomorrow, don't you?"

"Yes. My dad told me. What time will you be leaving?"

"We wanted to get an early start, but I hate to leave you when we just got acquainted. May I call you?"

"Sure. You may call me. It will have to be in the evening though. I'm never here during the day. I'm a working girl, you know."

"No, I didn't know. What do you do?"

"I work here on the ranch. If you think working for Jake is hard, you should work for my dad. He's a hard taskmaster."

"Yeah, I'll bet he works his little baby girl to death."

"Go ahead and laugh. I work hard." She showed him her hands. "I didn't get these calluses drawing pictures."

He frowned. "How did you get those?"

"Mending fences. I told you, I work. I'm kidding about Daddy, though. I work because I want to. This ranch is my life. I love it, and I love the work."

"You're quite a gal, you know that?"

They parted that night, but Tessie was out to see him off bright and early the next morning. She didn't let Jeff leaving spoil her day though. She had her day planned and it was a full one. They were moving the herd to a different location and it would be an all day job. When she came in that night, she was exhausted. She was looking forward to a good long soaking in the tub. After her bath, she decided to curl up with a good book and relax; but she was so tired, she couldn't keep her eyes open. She had just decided to give in and go to bed when the phone rang. Her mother announced that the call was for her.

Tessie sprang to her feet and excitedly asked, "Is it Jeff?"

Her mother grinned and shook her head. "Yes, it's Jeff."

"Hi, Jeff. How was your trip home?"

"Hi, Tessie. Trip was all right I guess. I sure hated to leave you. I wish we could have talked some more about your plans."

"Are you rested up from your bout with ranch life?"

"Well, I'm still feeling the effects, if that's what you mean. I didn't wake you up, did I?"

"No. I hadn't gone to bed yet. I was thinking about it though."

Their conversation continued for twenty minutes. Tessie refused to let it get on a serious note. She knew there would be some difficult decisions ahead. She wasn't prepared to think about that yet.

Tessie had already put on her pajamas. After their talk ended, she climbed in her bed, but didn't turn the light out. She sat in the middle of her bed with her legs crossed and her arms around her knees for a long time, just thinking about the possibilities. It was either leave her wonderful ranch or lose Jeff. There didn't seem to be any other solution. Then there was a knock on her door.

"Come in," she said.

"I saw your light still on. I just wanted to tell you good night. Did you have a good talk with Jeff?" her mother asked.

"Oh, Mama, why did he have to come here? I'm so confused, I don't know what to do. I've heard Daddy say that there are no accidents in a Christian's life. Do you think God planned Jeff's coming to the ranch? Is there some purpose to this? I sure wish He would give me some answers."

"Sweetheart, we'll all pray about it. God does have the answer. I'm sure He will give you direction. I don't have the answer to all your questions and answers don't always come immediately. Sometimes answers come in the form of either having or not having peace about a thing. Just pray and have patience, Honey. Your answer will come."

"There's something else I want to discuss with you, Mama. I've decided not to go back to school this year. I know how badly you want me to finish, but I truly believe I should stay here at the ranch. This is where I need to be. If ever I decide to finish, I can always do that. But for now, I want to stay here."

Her mother looked stunned. "I don't understand, Tessie. I thought you liked school. Have you prayed about this decision?"

"Yes, I have. I do like school, Mama," Tessie said. "That isn't why I don't want to return. I just feel the need to be here."

"Well, that has to be your decision, Honey. But I can't help thinking you're making a mistake. Have you told your Daddy yet?"

"No, I haven't had a chance. I don't know what he'll think, but I was hoping you would help me convince him that I shouldn't go back."

Her mother kissed her on the forehead and left her room. The next morning TC met Tessie as she was coming down the stairs.

"Hey Beautiful, come talk to your old dad." She followed him into the breakfast room. "What's this about not returning to school? What brought this about? What makes you think you need to be here instead of going back to school? I love having you home, Honey, but I want you to get your education. That's more important right now."

"Why, Daddy? Why is that so important. I will never need or use anything I learned this year at school. You are paying heaps of money just for me to have a good time. This is where I belong. I don't need to go to college for that."

"Is this where you belong? I know that I've tried to convince you that you should cherish this land as I always have, but I know I spoke out of turn night before last. What you do with your life must be your decision. I can't dictate to you what you choose to do with your life. If you choose to marry Jeff and be a lawyer's wife, you might need that education. A good education never hurt anyone, no matter what they choose to do with their life. Your mother and I had a long talk about you the other night. She thinks I might be forcing my way of life on you, causing you to make a mistake that you would always regret. I'd never want that to happen. If Jeff is the right one for you, don't choose the ranch over him or you'll wind up hating it. I was ready to give it up for your mother, if she hadn't chosen to come here. I'm very thankful she chose the ranch over the city, but she was far more important to me than a bunch of cows."

"I haven't made a decision about Jeff yet. But I do know, that for right now, I'm supposed to be here. You're not forcing your way of life on me, Daddy. I love the ranch. I always have."

"Your happiness is what matters to me. Whatever you decide to do will be okay with me." He kissed her on the cheek and walked into the kitchen to pour a cup of coffee.

The following weekend Jeff came back to the ranch. Jeff and Tessie rode and talked and walked while Jeff tried his best to convince her that being a lawyer's wife was the best life any woman could have. "It might be a little tough at first," he said. "but it's already an established law practice. It isn't as if we're starting out from scratch. My dad will funnel business to me. I will do well. I'm sure of it."

"I know you will, Jeff. That isn't my concern. And I don't care about the money. I could handle hard times if it came to that. But I don't know if I could handle leaving the ranch. Don't push me for a decision, Jeff, please."

This went on for months. Jeff came to the ranch nearly every weekend. Every weekend he tried to persuade her that being a lawyer's wife would make her happier than any other kind of life she could choose. Sometimes she would refuse to discuss it. Other times their discussion would end in an argument. One visit ended on a sour note—he jumped in his car and sped out without even saying goodbye. He called her as soon as he reached Tulsa, though, and apologized. During these months, Tessie shed many tears. She was torn between loves and her answer didn't seem to be coming.

One weekend Jeff persuaded her to go home with him to visit his parents. She was reluctant at first, but finally relented. She had a nice time, even though she was a little uncomfortable. Conversation with his parents was fairly easy, but she felt like she was being drilled to see if she measured up to their expectations of a mate for their son. His mother wasn't what you would call pretty; but she was a slender, attractive woman, and very friendly. She had a gruff voice, probably from too much smoking over the years. There was no visual evidence that she smoked anywhere in the house. It was almost as if she were trying to hide the fact, but the smell of smoke on her clothing and in the house exposed her obvious secret.

Her impression of Jeff's father was that he was a very demanding person. Oh, he was nice enough to her, but every request made to his wife or Jeff was more in the nature of an order, and in a stern, harsh tone. Maybe that came from being a lawyer. She couldn't imagine Jeff ever being that way though. Mr. Randall was balding on top, and his general appearance reminded her of the poem, The Night Before Christmas, that says,"He had a droll little mouth and a round little belly, that shook when he laughed like a bowl full of jelly." She wished she hadn't thought of that because now it was difficult for her not to laugh when she looked at him. They had requested that she call them Gerald and Emily, but she was not comfortable with that. She could almost hear her mother scolding her every time she addressed them.

Jeff took her to his future office where he would someday spend many hours. She thought it was a most depressing place. She couldn't imagine anyone choosing this over the beauty of her wonderful ranch. Jeff was certain that when she met his family and learned more about his future plans, she would like the idea of being a lawyer's wife. But if he could read her mind, he would know that his plan had failed. Oh, his parents did have a large impressive home and many luxuries unaffordable to the average family, but that didn't entice her.

That evening, Jeff took Tessie to a dinner theater. She enjoyed being with him. He had an adorable sense of humor. She knew her heart would ache without him. On the other hand, would she always be miserable with him? She hated living in indecision. She was one who decided to do a thing and did it, or decided not to do something and put it out of her mind; but with Jeff, it wasn't that simple.

The weekend finally came to an end. She was more than ready to return home. She was unable to tell Jeff the words he wanted so badly to hear. Little was said on the way home, but finally he asked, "What do you think of my parents, Tessie?"

"I think your parents are very sweet, Jeff. I think your home is beautiful. And I had a wonderful time with you, but please don't ask me any more questions."

"I love you, Tessie. I would make you happy. You know we're good for each other. You always avoid the real issue. I need some answers. Are we ever going to be able to discuss it?"

"Jeff, we'd be able to make just as much money on the ranch, or at least enough to be very comfortable. You said you loved the ranch. Could you not consider ranch life?"

"I have considered it, Tessie. I've given it hours of consideration. But I don't think you realize what I'm faced with. My parents have put a lot of money into my education with the intent of my joining my father's firm. He would be devastated if I backed out on him now. Besides, I love law. That's all I've heard since I was a small boy. I've planned on it all my life."

"Well, Jeff, I am sorry. As much as you want an immediate answer, I just can't give you one now. If you require an answer now, it would have to be no, because I don't have peace about leaving the ranch. I do love you Jeff, but for now that's all I can say."

They drove on in silence until they reached the ranch.

The next morning, after Jeff returned to Tulsa, Tessie went down to the river and sat staring at the water with her chin on her knee. She didn't want to ride or work today. Her heart wasn't in it. She pulled out her sketch pad and started flipping through the pages, looking at some of the sketches she had done. She came across the unfinished sketch of Jeff. She pulled her pencil out and started working on it. "He is so handsome," she said aloud."He's the only man I've ever seen that's as good looking as Daddy."

"Well now, I'm jealous," came a voice from behind her. She jumped and whirled around in shock, thinking she was alone.

"A girl can't keep a secret around here, can she? What're you up to, Daddy?"

"I came to check on you and find out why you are playing hooky today. How's my little girl?"

"Oh, I'm fine. I'm just lazy today, I guess. I really didn't want to work down there with Bert today anyway. He sure is a persistent character. I think I'll have to use a ball bat to make him understand that I'm not going to date him."

TC grinned and said, "That's the price you have to pay for being so irresistible." He sat down next to her and put his arm around her. "Well, let's have a look at that handsome dude." He looked at her sketch and said, "Honey, where in the world did you get all that talent. That is excellent. You absolutely amaze me. Honey, what are you thinking about? You look like you're in another world."

"Oh, I was just thinking about all the men that have worked at the ranch over the years. You seem to get so close to all of them. Do you miss them when they leave?"

"Sure I do, Honey, some of them more than others. We've had some really great men work for us."

"What about Davey? What was he like?"

"Davey! Davey was very unique. Everybody missed Davey. Of course he's been gone a long time, but I still think about him. He was like you, Tessie. Oh, I don't suppose he could sketch and paint, but, my, what he could do with music. He could sing and play just about any instrument, although he preferred the harmonica, and he could compose beautiful songs. Did I ever tell you, he wrote the music for our wedding when your mother and I got married?"

"No, and Mama didn't tell me that either. All I heard about was Davey's Song, something about a river. Do you have the music for those songs?"

"You'll have to ask your mother about them. I don't know if we have music or just words. One thing I know for sure, if she ever did have the music, she still has it. She keeps everything."

Tessie smiled because she knew it was true. Her mother kept everything in case they might need it someday. And on many occasions it proved to be a very valuable trait, which she was always quick to point out to them.

"Well, Honey, I think I'm going up to the house. I'll see you after while." When he pulled himself up, he groaned and held his chest.

"What's wrong, Daddy? Are you all right?" Tessie asked.

"I'm fine, Honey. Just gettin' old. These bones aren't as young as they used to be."

Tessie rubbed his back and gave him a pat. "Tell Mama I'll be up in a little bit. Tell her that I'm fixing lunch today."

She finished her sketch, gathered her belongings, and headed toward the house. There were two little squirrels scampering across the lawn. They were busily gathering nuts and hiding them in their secret places, preparing for winter. School had started this week. A feeling of sadness came over her as she thought about the COIN club. She wondered how it was going, and if everyone was still participating to make it successful. She longed to see some of her friends, but she was still sure her decision to stay at the ranch and not return to school was the right one.

When she went in the house, her dad was sleeping in the recliner in the library. He must not have slept well last night, she thought. That was not at all like him. He never napped in the daytime. She quietly tiptoed through the house so as not to waken him, motioning to her mother to follow her into the kitchen.

"Mama, what's wrong with Daddy? Is he not feeling well? I noticed he was holding his chest when he was down at the river. Has he said anything to you?"

"No, Honey. I think he's just been working too hard. I'm sure he'll be all right."

Tessie prepared lunch for the three of them. She was thankful to be home and for the wonderful parents she had. At this moment, nothing else seemed to matter.

Chapter 24

Losing My First Love

It was a cold windy morning, unusually cold for November. The fine mist seemed to cut into the skin. Tessie was out helping cut the calves out of the herd for branding when Toby Jackson came riding up carrying a newborn calf.

"Where are you taking that little fellow," Tessie asked.

"As a matter of fact, I was bringing him to you. His mama abandoned him, and somebody needs to feed this little guy. I'm going to take him to the barn."

"I'll be right up, as soon as I tell Jake I'm leaving."

Toby pitched some new straw in a warm corner of the barn and placed the little calf in the middle. Tessie came in shortly and prepared some formula in a bucket with a nipple on it that they kept on hand for that very purpose. The calf didn't take to it right away. Tessie had to work with him, but soon he was nursing and getting his nourishment.

"You sure have a sweet little face. I can't imagine why your mama didn't want you," Tessie said. He was all black with white on his forehead and big sad eyes. After he ate, Tessie pushed the straw up around him and sat by him, rubbing his head for awhile.

When Tessie left the barn, she saw Jake and the others riding up. She met them by the fence. "Are you quitting?" she asked.

"Yeah," Jake said. "We need a better day for this job. This is miserable. We're goin' over to the cook shack and get some coffee. You better go in and warm up by the fire."

Tessie was thankful they weren't staying out there. The bitter cold and rain was hard to take, but she was determined to endure it if they

did. She didn't think they should be required to work longer or in worse conditions than she was willing to do.

When she went into the house, her dad was on the phone. She heard him say, "I'll be there at 10:00 in the morning."

Tessie was rubbing her hands from the cold. She walked over to the fire and held her hands out to warm them. "Where are you going in the morning," she asked. "If you're going into town, I'll go with you. I need to get some things."

"Sorry, Punkin. You can't go with me in the morning. I'm not sure how long I'll be tied up. I have an appointment that may take me the biggest part of the day. Maybe you and your mother could go do some shopping."

"Good idea. I'll ask her," Tessie said.

Cassie was in the kitchen, mixing some pumpkin bread when Tessie came in to ask her about going shopping. Tessie stuck her finger in the batter and her mother gave her hand a whack.

"How about going shopping with me tomorrow? There are several things I need from town. Are you busy tomorrow?" Tessie asked.

"I have someone coming at 10 o'clock to deliver some draperies I ordered. After she leaves, I could go with you."

"That would be good. I need to feed my baby before I leave anyway. I haven't told you, but we have a new addition to the ranch. A little abandoned calf was born yesterday. He's adorable. I think I'll keep this one for a pet. I need to come up with a fitting name for him. He has the most beautiful, sad eyes I've ever seen. Oh, speaking of 10 o'clock , what's the appointment that Daddy has in the morning?"

"I'm sure I don't know. He didn't mention it to me," her mother said. "Probably nothing important or he would have told me."

"Well, he said it might take most of the day. That sounded pretty important to me; but he didn't volunteer any information, so I didn't pry."

"Well, just leave it to your nosey mom. I'll see what I can find out," she replied with a wink and a grin.

Cassie scraped her batter into two bread pans and stuck them in the oven, and then went in search of TC. He was in the library by the fire looking at the newspaper. "Honey, could you get loose tomorrow to have lunch with two gals who love you?"

"Well, that sure is an enticing offer, especially since I know that both of those gals are beautiful blondes with gorgeous blue eyes, but I can't tomorrow. I have a full day and won't be able to get free."

"What have you got cooking tomorrow that takes precedence over such an enticing invitation?"

"I have an appointment, and I'm not sure how long it will take."

"What's the appointment? Anything important? You hadn't mentioned it," she said.

"Nah, nothing important. I'm going in to see Dr. Wilcox just for a routine yearly appointment. He said to plan on being there several hours. I thought I'd go ahead and get it out of the way while everything is slow around here."

"When did you ever go in before for a routine yearly appointment? Are you keeping something from me?" Cassie asked with a frown.

"Of course not. I just think, at my age, it's a good idea to have a check-up once in awhile. Don't you? It would be a good idea for you to consider that, too."

She just raised her eye brows at him and returned to the kitchen.

It was a beautiful day for their shopping trip, not at all like the day before. The sun was bright, the sky clear, and the wind was calm. As they were driving to Rolla, Tessie asked her mother, "Well, did you retain your title as number one snoop? Did you find out what is Daddy's secret appointment?"

"Yes, and I'm a little concerned about it. Your daddy has an appointment with Dr. Wilcox. He said it was a routine appointment, but it's always been like pulling teeth to get your father to a doctor, even for something serious. I can't believe he would go on his own, just for a routine appointment. Remember when he cut that big gash in his arm and needed stitches. We tried our best to get him to the doctor, but he insisted on soaking it in Epsom salts and bandaging it himself. Does that sound like someone who would go in for a routine check-up with no encouragement from anyone?"

"No, it certainly doesn't. Why do you suppose he's going?"

"I can't imagine. I guess we'll just have to wait until he's ready to tell us."

They went about their shopping and then had lunch at Josie's. Josie no longer worked in the restaurant. The food wasn't nearly as good as it had been when she was there. Joe had not been well, and Josie was getting too old to handle being on her feet for such a long time. She was even considering the possibility of selling the restaurant.

After finishing their lunch, they started back to the ranch. It was an enjoyable day for both mother and daughter. Tessie made her necessary purchases and they both bought a new pair of shoes. They had enjoyed just spending time together.

When they arrived at the ranch, Tessie opened the door just in time to hear the phone ring. She ran to pick it up, but she was too late. Her mother said, "I wonder who that was."

"It was probably Jeff," Tessie replied.

"Well, you didn't sound very excited about that," her mother said.

"Oh, I'm just tired of the hassle. I don't know what to do about him. He wants an answer and I don't have one for him. I can't blame him. He deserves an answer now. He has waited a long time, but I don't know what to do."

"Well, Honey, it's better to wait until you know you're doing the right thing. No one else can make that decision for you."

Tessie gave a sigh. "Yes, I know that Mama. I just wish I didn't love him and he didn't love me. It's gotten to the point where I almost dread talking to him, because he's pressuring me for a decision."

Tessie jumped as the phone rang again. She reached out and picked up the receiver. "Hello. Yes. Yes she is. Just a minute, please." She handed the phone to her mom. "It's the nurse at Dr. Wilcox's office."

Cassie was frowning as she took the phone. "Hello. Yes, this is Cassie. He what? Why was he sedated? Okay. We will be there shortly."

When she hung up the phone, she turned to Tessie with a worried look on her face. "We need to go pick up your daddy. He was sedated for the tests and can't drive home. I wonder what kind of tests he had that sedation was required?"

"Mama, do you think something's wrong with Daddy that he isn't telling us about?"

"That's what I'm thinking, Honey. But I don't know what it could be."

Tessie and her mother jumped in the car and drove to the doctor's office. When they arrived, Cassie ran in while Tessie parked the car. She found the nurse and asked where she would find her husband. The nurse directed her to a small room where TC was lying. He was awake, but not alert. When he saw Cassie, he said, "Cassie! What are you doing here?"

"Well, you aren't in any condition to drive now, are you?" she asked.

Cassie turned to the nurse. "Could I please speak with Dr. Wilcox?"

"He's with a patient right now, but he'll be in momentarily," she said.

Tessie came through the doorway and rushed over to her father. "Daddy, are you okay?" she asked.

"Wait, Tessie," her mother said. "He really isn't completely awake. I'm going to talk to the doctor in a minute." Tessie sat down and held her father's hand. She had a look of fear on her face. Cassie looked at her and realized how worried she was.

"Tessie, it's okay. Don't be scared." Cassie reached out and put her hand on Tessie's arm.

Dr. Wilcox opened the door and said, "Well, there are two of my favorite girls. He's going to be a little groggy for awhile, but he'll be awake in a little bit. He keeps going back to sleep on us. That sedative usually isn't that powerful, but it had an unusual effect on him."

"What were the tests for, Dr. Wilcox?" Cassie asked.

"Well, we just drew some fluid out of that lump on his chest to determine whether or not it's cancerous. We'll have an answer in a few days. I'll call you as soon as the results come in. If it is cancer, and I suspect that it might be, we'll need to get started on the treatments right away. The lump has been growing at a pretty rapid pace. It's already giving him some difficulty in breathing. I'm sure you have noticed that."

Cassie just sat there with her mouth open, not replying to him. Finally, still stunned by what she had just heard, she said, "May we take him home now?"

"Sure, Cassie. He'll probably be awake by the time you get him home. I'll be in touch."

Cassie drove TC's car around to the front of the building. The nurse brought TC up to the car in a wheelchair and helped Cassie get him into the car. Tessie followed them home in her car. Cassie prayed all the way home. She couldn't believe what she had just heard. Why hadn't she noticed a lump on her husband's chest? She knew why. He had been trying to keep it a secret from her until he knew what it was. What happened to sharing everything with each other? Had he forgotten that?

TC lifted his head up and looked around. "Where are we?" he asked.

"We're on our way home. Just rest until we get there," she said. She really didn't want to talk right now. She was stunned, she was angry, and she was very scared. When they stopped at the house, Tessie and Cassie walked him into the house and seated him in the recliner. After Cassie made sure he was comfortable, she ran in the kitchen and started crying. She was so confused, and so afraid.

In the days that followed, TC tried to go about his work as usual, but Cassie could tell that it was a real effort. She could tell that his breathing was labored. Why hadn't she noticed this before? She tried to keep him from working. There were plenty of hands to do the work, but he was a stubborn man. He insisted on being involved in everything that went on. This was a very difficult time for Tessie. She tried to carry on her work, but at the same time she wanted to spend every minute with her dad.

Jeff called on a Thursday night to tell her he was coming to the ranch Friday evening. Tessie shared the news about her father. "Jeff," she said, "We have to put us on hold for awhile, at least until I know what happens with my dad. I wish you wouldn't come this weekend. I just need time with him. I hope you understand."

"Sure, Tessie. I understand. But if you change your mind, call me. I want to be there for you."

"Thanks, Jeff."

They talked briefly for a few more minutes and then said their goodbyes.

Several days passed, and then the call came. It was Dr. Wilcox. Yes, TC had cancer.

The treatments started the following day. They started him on chemotherapy which made him very sick. He grew weaker and weaker.

The following months were a nightmare. One circumstance in particular was especially horrible. TC went in for a bone marrow test. He was not a person to ever complain, but he said it was the most painful thing he had ever experienced and he would not ever do that again.

His next words horrified Cassie. He said, "Just let me die in peace." Cassie locked herself in her room and cried until her eyes were swollen shut.

Some days, TC felt really good and worked around the ranch doing small jobs. But most of the time he was not able to carry out even minimal tasks.

Jeff never asked Tessie for permission to come to the ranch anymore, because her answer was always no. He just popped in from time to time. He spent a lot of time with TC. Jeff had a very compassionate heart. He wanted so desperately to comfort Tessie, but nothing he could say was any consolation. During these trying months, Cassie grew very fond of Jeff and learned why Tessie cared so much for him. He was really a fine, sweet young man. She dreaded the day when Tessie made her final decision, because it would mean broken hearts or Tessie leaving her precious ranch.

It was now August. TC wanted to walk around the yard and look at the flowers. He started having trouble breathing. Cassie had him sit in a lawn chair hoping his breathing would improve, but instead, he started gasping for air. She immediately called an ambulance. By the time the ambulance arrived, he was unconscious. They put an oxygen mask on him and rushed him to the hospital. Tessie had gone into town to pick up a few groceries for her mother. Cassie called the store from the hospital in hopes of catching Tessie before she left, but she had already left.

Cassie kept calling the house until Tessie came in. Jake brought Tessie back to the hospital. All of the men at the ranch came and stayed most of the night. TC remained in a coma throughout the night.

The next morning, TC opened his eyes and smiled at Cassie. He mouthed the words, "I love you." Then he shut his eyes again. Cassie stayed by his side all day and refused to leave even to get anything to eat. Finally Tessie brought her a sandwich, which she ate, only because Tessie nearly forced it down her. TC seemed to be breathing pretty well with the aid of the oxygen. They were also giving him something in an IV to help him relax . He never moaned or gasped for air throughout the day or the next night. But on the third morning, he opened his eyes, frowned, and reached his hands up to his chest. He gasped and slumped back on the bed. Cassie let out a scream and the nurses came running.

They listened for his pulse, but he was gone. Tessie grabbed her mother and they cried together. Jeff put his arms around them both, holding them until they took TC out of the room. Then Jeff drove them back to the ranch.

There were so many people at the funeral, they could not all get inside the church. Tessie had never seen so many flowers in her life. Everyone was so kind, wanting to be of help in some way. Cassie's mom and dad took her home with them, but Tessie would not go. She wanted to be alone. She wouldn't let Jeff stay. She insisted that he leave soon after they left the cemetery.

Tessie went back to the ranch, got her sketch book, and went down to the river. She started sketching pictures of her dad, not the way he looked these past few months, but the way he looked before the cancer. The sketches just seemed to flow from her pencil. She sketched pictures of him in every pose. Then she started to throw them in the river, but a hand reached over her shoulder and grabbed the sketch book. It was Josie.

"I thought I might find you down here. Come on, Child. You're going home with me. I won't take no for an answer. Let's go up and pack you a few things. I need you to keep me company tonight. He was like a son to me you know."

Tessie looked up at Josie, and saw that she had been crying, and knew that there was truth in what she had said. Tessie stood up and put her arm around Josie. They walked up to the house together.

Chapter 25

My Heart is Like the River

Tessie stayed with Josie for two days. Josie had a way of helping people through a bad situation. Tessie remembered her daddy telling her how much Josie had helped him when his father died. She was truly a wonderful lady, even if she was a very controlling person sometimes. She always wanted to give everyone advice and she wanted to be sure that advice was followed to the tee.

Tessie went to her grandparents' home that morning to be with her mother. She was doing better than Tessie had expected. Her grandmother was preparing breakfast. The coffee was perking in the little percolator, and it sounded almost like a song. Tessie didn't drink coffee, but it sure did smell good. In fact, it smelled so good, she decided to try a little. But when she took a sip, she made a face and said, "How on earth can anyone drink this stuff? It does smell good, but it tastes absolutely wicked."

Her mother smiled and said, "You'll probably like it when you grow up."

"Well, if I need to grow up, where does that leave you and Grandma. I'm at least two inches taller than either one of you."

"Grab a plate, Tessie, and have some breakfast. There's plenty here," her grandmother said.

"Thanks, Grandma, but I ate breakfast a couple hours ago. Can you imagine Josie letting anyone out of her house without feeding them. If I hang around there very much longer, I will be like the song, Mr. Five by Five."

Tessie stayed for a little over an hour, visiting with her grandparents and her mother, then she told them she needed to be on her way.

She kissed her mother and walked toward the door. She motioned to her grandmother to follow her. At the door, she said, "Grandma, I'm going back to the ranch today, but don't tell Mama. Thanks so much for helping her. Keep her here as long as you can. You and Grandpa are good for her. I love you. See ya later."

Her grandmother kissed her on the cheek. "I sure wish you would stay here too, Baby."

Tessie smiled. I guess I'll always be her baby, she thought. But she said to her grandmother, "I would love to spend the time with you, but I need to check on things at the ranch."

As she drove back home, she began thinking to herself, *How can I possibly do this without Daddy? What's the point? Jeff doesn't want me to. Mama might be better off with Grandma. Maybe it would be better if I talked to Mama about selling the ranch and just quitting.*

When she drove in at the ranch, there was a station wagon there that she didn't recognize. It was parked up by the house. She got out of the car and called out to Jake, "Whose wagon?"

"Come on out here, and I'll show you." He took her into the cook shack where Jed was having a cup of coffee. He turned and smiled at her. She remembered the smile, even though she was quite small when she last saw him. He stood and offered her his hand.

"I'm Jed Coulter. The last time I was here, you were in Tulsa, I believe. I just wanted to come over and talk with you before we headed back home. I knew your daddy pretty well. He was one fine person. He helped shape my life. No tellin' what I'd be if it weren't for him. Could we walk down to the river?"

"Sure, I'd like that."

They walked down to the river. Tessie was a little puzzled, because when they reached the river, he went straight to the place that her daddy called, "My rock."

"This is the spot where your daddy taught me to be consistent about reading the Bible and taught me to pray. Oh, not by telling me to or anything like that, but by example. He never missed a day reading his Bible and praying. He probably directed many lives to God just by his example. I think many of his prayers were about me. It was very difficult for him after his dad died. There were times that he wanted to quit, but he used a Scripture from the Bible, and it kept him going. He said, *I must press toward the mark.* That's what you must do, Tessie. Press toward the mark. I don't know what your mark is, but don't ever give up. Make sure you are in God's perfect will, and don't let anything or anybody discourage you. Don't let circumstances dampen your spirits and cause you to turn away from those things you know you should do. Tessie, I've never seen a father as proud of a child as your daddy was of you. You were his pride and joy."

"Jed, my daddy sure did think a lot of you. He called you his number one boy. He said he loved you like a son. I'm not sure why you came here today, but I'm sure glad you did. I really appreciate it. I'm sure going to miss him. I was even thinking of quitting before you came. I didn't know how I could go on without him, but you're right. I must *press toward the mark.* I've heard my daddy say those very words, too."

"Tessie, you don't look like your daddy. You look just like your mama, but you're like your daddy, I can tell. You're gonna be all right. If you ever need anything, or if I can ever be of any help to you, here's my address and telephone number. Just call me, and I'll come runnin'." He put his arm around her and gave her a hug. Then he said, "Bye, Tessie. I'm glad I got to meet you."

"Bye, Jed. I know now, why my dad thought so much of you. I hope we'll see each other again." She waved as he got in his station wagon and drove away.

"My goodness, my daddy was special. He loved this land. I can't sell it. It's my heritage. I think my mama loves this land. too. It would break her heart. I will press toward the mark. This is my calling."

Little Sad Eyes, her little pet calf, had just come out of the barn. He pretty much had the run of the place. He saw her and came running. She rubbed his head and said, "Well, hi, Sad Eyes. Did you miss me? You're getting so big. We're going to have to put you in the pasture." She patted him and led him out to the gate. When he went in, he kicked up his feet as if to show his approval of his new home. She stood and watched him for awhile, and then walked toward the house.

Tessie wasn't too anxious to go into the house, but she knew she must sooner or later. She took a deep breath and opened the door. She just stood there looking around for several minutes. Then she walked over to the piano. She sat down and thumbed through her music. Then she dusted the piano keys with her fingers, but never played anything.

She turned from the piano and walked into her dad's study. She walked all around the room, touching different things that belonged to him. Then she took a deep breath, put her hands on her hips and said, "TC, you have some big boots to fill, so get to work."

In the days ahead, she worked harder than she had ever worked in her life. She wasn't sure whether her daddy could see her or not; but if he could, she wanted him to be proud of her and proud of the ranch. This was TC Marshall land, and it would always be just that.

Her mother came back to the ranch. Tessie knew it was going to be very hard for her. She tried to keep everything cheerful, and not leave her alone very much, but sometimes her mother wanted to be alone. It seemed that she needed that time to herself. Maybe it was part of the healing process. Everyone is different. Some choose to have other people around them all of the time after the loss of a loved one, and others just want time alone. Tessie realized it was important to be there for her mother when she wanted her, but to let her have those special times alone.

Jeff came over the following weekend, as Tessie was sure he would. Tessie was down by the river with her horse. He drove his car down close to the river and they sat and talked for hours. He tried, with everything he had, to persuade her to come back to Tulsa with him. "Tessie, you can't run this ranch by yourself, and I can't help you. This is not my calling. Please don't be foolish. Come with me, Tessie. Let's get married. I know we would be happy. I'd do anything to make you happy."

"Jeff, I know you would, but I just can't leave the ranch. I'm truly sorry. I don't want to hurt you. This has been the hardest decision of my life, but I know this is what I must do. You said this is not your calling and I know you're right. But please understand, it is my calling and I must stay here. You've been wonderful. I wish there was a way that our plans could have been combined, but you and I both know that isn't possible. I know you'll be the greatest lawyer there ever was and I hope you'll be very happy. But I wouldn't make a good lawyer's wife. My heart is here. This is where I belong. It's my life."

"Tessie, I beg you to change your mind. I'm going back to Tulsa with you or without you, and I'm not coming back. I've poured my life into becoming a lawyer. It's important to me. I could never be a rancher. I don't know how I'll live without you, Tessie, but I must go."

Tessie gave him a hug and said, "Goodbye, sweet Jeff. I'll miss you so."

When he drove away, she stood watching him as his car drove around the bend and over the hill. She threw herself down in the grass and sobbed. How could she have let him go. Her heart ached. But then she stood up straight and threw her head back and said, "You're TC Marshall. You must *press toward the mark.*" She jumped on her horse and rode hard back to the ranch.

The next few weeks were difficult, but she was certain she had made the right decision. There was plenty of work to help her, and she had that peace that her mother told her she would have when she made the right decision. Oh, her heart still ached, and there were many tears at night. But her mother was very supportive, and Tessie dug into her work and did an excellent job of running the ranch. She really felt she had passed the test when she purchased a new herd without anyone's approval. As time passed, decision making became easier.

It had been nearly a year since her father died. She still missed him, but the pain wasn't as unbearable as it once was. She strived to be the kind of person he would be proud of.

And Jeff, she thought of him so often. She wondered how he was doing in his law practice. Of course, he was doing well. He would be an excellent lawyer. She wondered if he had found someone else, but did she really want to know? She hoped with all her heart that he was happy. It was important for them both to get on with their lives. She tried to do that, although she hadn't dated anyone else since he left. She did keep very busy with friends, church activities, and the ranch though.

One morning, Tessie was saddling her horse when a truck came through the gate. She looked up as it came down the lane. A young man got out and walked toward her. He was nice looking, not really what you would call handsome, but charming in a rugged sort of way. His eyes were blue or green, she couldn't tell for sure. One thing that was for certain, he had a big friendly smile. She would never forget that marvelous, crooked smile, which made her heart do a crazy flutter.

" Hi. I'm Tory Howell. I sure like your sign."

"Hi, Tory. I'm Tessie Marshall, and why do you like my sign?"

"My name is Torrence Clayton, but most people call me TC. I wonder if you would mind if I walk the river on your property and look it over. I build dams. We've been called here to survey the river with the possibility of putting in a dam. We aren't sure of the location just yet, or even for certain that it will happen. They want my opinion."

"Sure, that's fine. Be my guest," she said.

As he walked away, she realized her heart was skipping some beats. "My goodness, I wish he wouldn't smile at me that way," she thought. "This old heart can't take it."

She got on her horse and rode in the direction of the canyon, but all the way she kept saying, "Tory Howell, TC Howell." Then she found herself saying, "Tessie Howell. Oh, good grief! Have you lost your senses?" Then she gave her horse a whack and they sped on toward the canyon.

When she returned, Tessie and her mother sat eating their lunch and talking. During the conversation, her mother asked who the man was walking by the river this morning. Tessie felt her face flush and hoped her mother didn't notice. She explained to her mother why he was here. "He probably won't be back. He isn't even sure they'll put in a dam around here." Tessie changed the subject as quickly as she could, but she couldn't get him out of her mind.

Several days passed. Then one afternoon the same truck came through the gate. Tessie was in the house when he drove up. She saw him through the window. Again her heart started pounding. She felt like she couldn't breathe. She hurried to the door, opening it before he had time to come upon the porch.

"Well, hello Mr. TC Howell. What brings you back?"

"Several things, actually. I wanted to let you know what was going on with your river. I looked it over and submitted some ideas and some figures to the authorities. I'm not sure what their decision will be. Then next, I wanted to talk to you about your ranch. This is the most beautiful place I've ever seen. I have a little acreage in Montana, but nothing like this. I have 50 head of cattle, but someday I hope to have a whole lot more. How many head do you run here?"

"We have around 5,000, mostly Black Angus. We have a few hundred Herfords, out of loyalty to my grandfather."

"The other thing that brought me back was your beautiful blue eyes. I had to see if they were real, or if I dreamed them. Yep! They're real."

She turned and started back into the house. He reached out and held her arm and said, "I'm sorry if that was out of line. Don't leave. Could we just talk for awhile."

"I really do have to go now," she said. "I have a lot of work to do. Maybe another time."

"That's a date. I'll be here tomorrow night at 7. See ya then." He didn't wait for an answer. He just jumped in his truck and sped away.

She stood watching him as he drove off. When he was out of sight, she slowly went inside. She didn't know whether to be mad or happy or what. She was stunned by his strange farewell. Would he really be back? What should she do. She walked over to the piano and started fingering a song. She didn't want to feel like this about anyone, not ever again. She wished she could talk to her dad. Oh, how she missed him. He could give her some good advice

Her mother came in while she was playing. "That's Davey's song," she said.

"Do you still have the music, Mama?"

"Oh, yes, I'm sure I do. It's in that cabinet. I'll get it for you."

Tessie smiled as she recalled what her father had said. "If she ever had it, she still has it. She keeps everything."

"Here it is, Honey. Play it for me." Tessie started playing the music and singing the words as she played.

My heart is like the river
Can't be bound, it must be free.
No one can hold the river.
No one has a hold on me.

No one can chain the river.
No one can chain my heart.
My heart is free forever,
Like the river I'll be
For the river runs free.

No one can tame the river.
No one can tame my heart.
No one can bind the river.

No one can bind my heart.
No one can change the river.
No one can change my heart.
My heart is free forever
Like the river I'll be
For the river runs free.

"I wish I had known Davey. It's almost as if he had written this song for me. My heart is like the river. My heart is free." But as soon as she said those words, her heart nearly jumped out her mouth as she thought of Tory. She knew at that moment that her heart wasn't free. She had fallen in love with the man with the crooked smile and laughing eyes.

She sang the music again, but halfway through she stopped playing abruptly and slammed her fist down on the piano. "He builds dams!" she shrieked. "He can hold the river." Her mother turned to look at her with a most puzzled look on her face.

Yes, Tessie realized that TC Howell could hold the river and he definitely held her heart. She was convinced that her father would have approved of Tory and her mother certainly did. They dated for sixteen months and had a beautiful wedding on the ranch with all their friends and family in attendance.

Tessie had the Bible verses, Proverbs 3:5-6, printed on their wedding announcements. She knew with all her heart that it was through trusting in the Lord to guide her that He had brought Tory into her life and had given her the peace and the happiness she had longed for.

The sign on the gate which read *The T C Ranch* now represented Torrence Clay and Tessie Cassandra. Together, they would *press toward the mark* on this precious land.

There are women of the world and then there is God's woman. Having known Mrs. Ruth Nimmo since 1993, I can say truthfully say that King Solomon was writing about her in Proverbs 31. The only thing he left out was her name! Not only is this remarkable woman devoted to Jesus her Lord, but with her being their example, her whole family followed to serve Christ.

Ruth has many gifts and talents in life that she takes no credit for. One of them is that if someone is around her for any time at all, she makes them feel like they are very special to her and to God. Hospitality is a divine gift and she has it in abundance! When visiting the Nimmo's, you are not just a guest. She has the amazing ability to make you feel immediately at home and like family. Some people would give their eye teeth to have been raised in that home in part because of the love there and in part because of her superb cooking. I can tell you her pumpkin pie or peach cobbler is to die for!

A talent that she has kept secret for too many years is that she is a marvelous author who is able to communicate spiritual truths in the most fascinating and adventurous writing style. I personally endorse Ruth Nimmo and recommend her to you totally without reservation.

The Most Rev. Terry Lowe, MSSJ, ThD

Terry Lowe is the Archbishop of the Anglican Province of Saint Jude, President of the Missionary Society of Saint Jude, also President and Chancellor of St. Jude's Seminary. Archbishop Lowe has been in the ministry for almost 40 years and as a missionary has helped to plant hundreds of churches and schools in Oceania and Southeast Asia, particularly in Mindanao, Philippines.

LaVergne, TN USA
21 September 2009
158494LV00003B/2/P